THE GOLD FEDORA

DETECTIVE CARLA MCBRIDE CHRONICLES
BOOK 1

NICK LEWIS

ROUGH
EDGES
PRESS

The Gold Fedora
Paperback Edition

Rough Edges Press
An Imprint of Wolfpack Publishing
9850 S. Maryland Parkway, Suite A-5 #323
Las Vegas, Nevada 89183

roughedgespress.com

Paperback ISBN 978-1-68549-207-6
eBook ISBN 978-1-68549-206-9

THE GOLD FEDORA

PROLOGUE

United States Ambassador to Grenada, Leigh Taylor, sat bound, gagged, and blindfolded, wondering whether she would live to see another day. Tired and weak from being abused by the five guerrilla rebels holding her captive, she stood fast in honoring her homeland. A small compound in the jungle near Point Salinas had been her prison for the past several weeks. Her faith had kept her alive in hopes that the president would send the cavalry to her rescue before Operation Urgent Fury, to secure the island nation, began in less than twenty-four hours.

Alpha Tango, an elite Special Forces unit, was positioned in the jungle, waiting for the order to extract her from an agonizing death. Frog, Peanuts, Rocky, Spike, and Tater waited patiently with Casanova, captain of Alpha Tango, for the order. Alpha Tango had never failed to complete their missions successfully; they were one of the best teams, and safely rescuing the ambassador would be no different. Like blood brothers, they always had each other's back. The moment had arrived. Casanova nodded, their digital timers were activated, and each moved to their respective positions, ready to strike. Except for Peanuts, when their digital timers reached double-zero, everyone would strike simultaneously.

Double-zero glared from their watches; time to move. Rocky and Frog quickly neutralized the guard outside the front door without resistance, while the guard outside the rear door was no match for Spike and Tater, going down silently without a whimper. In position outside the rear window of the room where the guerilla held the ambassador, Peanuts focused on his digital watch. Anxious but cool. Double-zero finally stared back at him. A tap on the vertical window startled the rebel; a bewildered face appeared in the window. *Pfft.* The rebel crumbled to the dirt floor. The single-pane glass window shattered onto the dirt floor, and Peanuts entered the room, securing the ambassador.

After hearing the glass break, Alpha Tango crashed the compound from the front and rear doors simultaneously. A fierce firefight ensued; the two remaining rebels were no match for the experience and firepower of Alpha Tango. Another successful mission was in the books. Casanova, exuding great confidence and leadership, yelled out, "Peanuts, we all good back there?"

"Roger that, boss."

"Great. Spike, Tater…all good back there?"

Spike responded, "Roger that, captain."

Casanova gave out a big sigh. "Great job, bros. Let's get the ambassador to safety before all hell breaks loose."

A mile away, a Blackhawk helicopter sat ready to transport Alpha Tango and the ambassador to Barbados. From there, they would reach the United States mainland via military transport. Their mission was a huge success, and as it turned out, it was their last mission as none of them would re-up for another stint in the Army Special Forces. Each was ready to begin the next chapter of their lives.

Dressed in their fatigues, Casanova, Frog, Peanuts, Rocky, Spike, and Tater posed for a final photo-op. Picman, the base photojournalist, counted to three, and a serious but funny pose was captured. Flaunting their Alpha Tango tattoos, this memory would live on in infamy. No one knew what the future held for them; however, fate would eventually test their Alpha Tango brotherhood loyalty.

CHAPTER 1

TWENTY-EIGHT YEARS LATER

An annoying intermittent buzz filled the room. "Ugh." Fumbling around for the alarm clock, he quickly found the snooze button. Silence. Mark Alison turned toward his gorgeous wife, admiring her beauty. The alternating buzz had no effect on her peaceful sleep. Her stillness under the sheets excited him. As he closed his eyes, his subconscious took over, and an erotic smile crossed his lips.

Buzz-buzz-buzz interrupted an erotic fantasy playing out in his lustful subconscious world. Silently, he disdained its timing, turning it off. Tossing the sheets off his naked body, he yawned and stretched as the final episode of his sexual adventure lingered in his mind.

Joanne, oblivious to the annoying buzz, laid quietly. Fixated on her arousing curves caressing the sheets, he knew she was the envy of every man she met, married or not; she still turned heads. Movie star quality, her sexiness was undeniable, her personality infectious; Joanne, the perfect woman every man wanted, and every woman wanted to be, was all his, forever.

Twirling her hair, he nibbled on her earlobe whispering naughty suggestions in her ear. She continued to ignore his playful taunting. Her perfect body stirred under the sheets; her aroused features tantalized his raging desires. It was a flirtatious game of foreplay they enjoyed. After she removed her sleeping mask; the sheets slid off her enticing body. She turned toward him; her innocent gestures teased his uncontrollable quest for her. He moistened his lips as the fire in his groin burned out of control. Her delicate and firm breasts gently kissed his chest, while her nipples craved more of his soft, but arousing touch.

With her silky body next to him, his hunger exploded. A deep exploring kiss primed her engines as they begged for the ultimate pleasure and gratification. Whispers of naughtiness finally ignited the raw passion smoldering in their souls. As their bodies collided, they moved in rhythm toward a euphoric explosion of fulfillment and gratification.

Breathless, her head rested on his chest, her soul enjoyed the tingling remnants of pure ecstasy that lingered throughout her heart and soul. As his heart pulsated against her sensuality, he counted his many blessings. Not only married to her but as publisher of the *Daily Reporter*, he was a rising, shining star in the company, and his future looked brighter than ever.

After showering, they retreated to the second-floor balcony. Bright sunlight and warm breezes touched their souls as they enjoyed the serenity of the countryside. In a white wicker loveseat, they indulged themselves with fresh fruit, scones, and coffee.

Hilo and Kona, their fur babies, purred while they moved about their legs expressing their love. Treats placed on the floor attracted their attention. After eating them, they sauntered off to the other end of the veranda for an early morning siesta.

After another bite of Danish and a sip of coffee, Mark focused on his wife's perfect face, her flawless beauty. A taunting kiss floated his way, he nodded and returned the kiss. As she rolled her eyes, she nibbled on her lower lip taunting him. Flipping her hair away from her eyes, she scanned the countryside for a moment enjoying its tranquil beauty, its peacefulness. As she returned her gaze to him, a tempting sultry grin pleased her eyes.

"What?"

"Oh, nothing, just admiring you, uh, thinking how lucky I am, how fortunate we are, you know, that's all." Nodding, she smiled, another sensual air kiss touched him, he acknowledged her.

"Are you coming to the office this morning so we can plan our trip to The Greenbrier Resort? I'm excited about our first trip there together and meeting our friends, how about you?"

"Yeah, can't wait, and I'll be there at my usual time. Hm, you'll have coffee ready for me on the deck, right?"

Nodding, he leaned over, kissing her goodbye. Even though the coffee and Danish still lingered on his palate, her sweetness and sexiness left him gasping. Seizing the moment; a deep exploring kiss ignited his lust for her all over again. Gazing into her eyes; her playfulness and taunting foreplay revved-upped his hormones. Although he was the boss, and up to another round of hot sex, he reluctantly pulled away. "Honey, I'd love to take you to new sexual heights, but I must get to work. May I have a raincheck?"

Laughing under her breath, she replied, "A raincheck…it's not golf, honey." She winked; another flirtatious gesture pleased his eyes. "Of course, a rain check it is. I'll be there at my usual time. I love you!"

"Love you, too, babe."

While sipping on her coffee, she watched him drive up their long driveway. Leaning on the balcony railing, she waved as he came to a stop. He turned left onto the county highway toward Oakmont. Enjoying the scenery on this lovely spring morning, he was oblivious to the black Toyota Camry following him. Although it had pulled out from a side road shortly after he left his home, the best sex he had in a long time still lingered in his mind. In the rearview mirror, the black Camry carefully kept up with him. Remembering seeing it last Friday, and the previous Friday, the car was not anything to worry about.

Two blocks before the *Daily Reporter*, the car behind him inched-up closer but remaining a safe distance from him. He thought nothing of it again; he was used to people tailgating him. As he turned into the parking lot and into his spot, the black Camry cruised past the entrance and disappeared. Exiting his car, he entered the newspaper excited that it was going to be a great day.

Visiting Todd Hailey, editor of the *Daily Reporter*, was an everyday occurrence before going to his office. A knock on his partially open door, Todd's usual good-morning-boss grumbling greeted him.

"Good morning, Todd. What do you think of my column for the Sunday edition?"

"You will likely piss-off people as always, so prepare

for some angry backlash or something much worse; you know what could happen." A warming sensation spread throughout Mark's head; his forehead glistened under the fluorescent lights. With concern in Mark's eyes, a quirky grin covered Todd's face. "April Fool's Day, boss!"

"Hm, that's not funny at all." His worried expression morphed into one pissed-off wryly smile. "Nothing like that happens around here, right?" Still grinning, Todd nodded and continued editing his column. "Just what I thought. Better head to my office, take care of a few things before Joanne arrives."

Todd grumbled something indiscernible as Mark walked to his office. Entering his office, Mark fired up the Keurig before booting up his laptop. Keurig ready, he inserted a Starbucks Caffe Verona K-cup and hit the brew button. Walking back to the pressroom where the presses were already rolling; he grabbed one of the first proof copies coming off the conveyer belt.

Back in his office, steam floated from his coffee. After fixing Joanne's coffee, he tucked the newspaper under his arm and proceeded to the deck outside with both cups of coffee. Placing both cups of coffee on the table, he sat in a lounge chair and quickly reviewed the front page.

From the corner of his eye, movement in the thick grass a few feet from the deck caught his carefree eyes. "Is anyone there?" A familiar loud meow filled the air. "Oh, it's you Inky, you been hunting again?" Meowing loudly, Inky sauntered towards the woods. "Don't leave, Joanne is coming soon. She would love to see you." Meowing again, Inky double-winked shooting him a mysterious scowl before disappearing into the woods.

A thundering steel-on-steel roar emanated from the

plant, he smiled. The hum of the presses running at full speed was music to his ears. After finishing a quick review of the front page, he turned to the horoscopes which he found entertaining and insightful. Surprised at the weird and questionable horoscope for his sign, he laughed silently about its meaning. A slight glance at his watch, and he realized that Joanne would arrive any minute now. While he waited for her, he quickly reviewed the rest of the paper, making mental notes of the encouraging ad count in today's edition.

8:15 AM.

Like each Friday, Joanne entered the *Daily Reporter* with a smile on her face greeting the employees with great respect. Before going to Mark's office, she enjoyed talking with Mary Sturm, her husband's administrative assistant. Having been with the newspaper for over forty years, Mary thought she had seen it all, and nothing fazed her anymore. As Joanne approached her, a caring and attentive smile brought Joanne much joy.

"How are you doing today, Mary?"

"Great, how about you?"

"Fantastic, you have any big plans for this weekend?"

"Plans, well, John and I lead a simple life. We need to get started on our garden, you know, the lettuce, onions, all the cole crops, so that will take up most of the weekend. However, in the evenings, we'll likely take a walk around the lake, and enjoy the scenery."

"Hey, I say whatever rocks your world, go for it. As you know, Mark and I are in store for a long weekend at The Greenbrier Resort in West Virginia, pampering for me and golf for him. It's about living life to the fullest every single day regardless of your problems. You never know when it might just be your last day on earth."

"I hear you, Joanne. Life is short, enjoy your weekend."

"Thank you, Mary, and you do the same."

Before heading to Mark's office, Joanne stopped to chat with Todd Hailey. As usual, his door was partially open; a gentle tap on the door got his attention. "Hi Joanne, come in and sit while I finish editing Mark's column. It will shake things up as usual."

"Hm, I'm not surprised. After the last one, I thought we might need our Kevlar vests."

"Bulletproof vests?"

"I'm just kidding. Nothing like that happens here, right?"

He returned his gaze to his monitor. "Right, whatever you say."

"Well, thanks for your words of assurance, Todd. I'm sure he's waiting for me, have a great weekend."

"Yeah, you, too."

As Joanne walked down the long hallway to his office, she beamed with pride as the many awards the newspaper had won under his leadership hung proudly on the walls. With his office door open, an empty chair sat behind his massive desk. The back door was already open to the deck which meant her husband waited outside for her with a cup of coffee. After she walked through the office, she opened the storm door and stepped out on to the deck breathing the freshness of the morning.

She looked to her left expecting her husband's enticing and sexy smile; however, slumped back in a lounge chair Mark stared aimlessly at the bright morning sky. With his hands against his chest, a jagged crimson-red stain saturated the *Daily Reporter* logo on his white Nike golf shirt. She yelled for help; however, the roar of the presses swallowed up her desperate pleas.

Rushing to him; that day's newspaper blotted with his blood, laid at his feet. As she stood over him, she grabbed his hands and pressed them firmly against his chest hoping to prevent death from taking him away from her, stealing his soul forever. With his pupils widening, the last glimpse of her flawless beauty faded away into a world of eternal darkness.

CHAPTER 2

Mark Alison's death shook Oakmont, a sleepy quiet community in the Bluegrass Region of Kentucky, to its core. Well-liked and respected, his death circulated among the citizens and at local hangouts such as McGruder's Irish Pub. The heinous and senseless death of Mark Alison brought the community to its knees like never before. This April Fool's Day event was no joke.

In many ways, he was a public figure no different from the mayor or any other high-profile individual in a leadership role. Extremely popular and well respected by his peers and colleagues in the community, he was a fearless leader. Through his leadership and the newspaper team, he reshaped the political landscape of the city and county in many ways that even he never realized the impact he had on it. A powerful voice in the community, he spoke his conscience and was possibly murdered by doing so.

Through his hard-hitting commentary, he stepped on the toes of many in the community. For those on the receiving end, it was a love-hate relationship. From the city mayor to the county judge-executive to politicians to school superintendents, he pushed the envelope, hoping to evoke emotion in citizens and be a catalyst of positive change. Through of all of this, his killer could be anyone in the community.

McGruder's was the in-place in the city where all the movers and shakers congregated. Irish all the way, coat of arms flags hung from the ceiling, while every law enforcement badge imaginable proudly donned the walls. Accented in a hunter green motif, one side of the pub had wooden partitions separating seating areas with windows to give it the classic pub feel, while the other side of the pub had high-top tables and stools. Tucked in the left-hand corner at the front of the pub was a stage where bands played, where Mark and Joanne Alison once danced. They were a staple there most Friday nights.

However, since his death, the atmosphere was somber and subdued. Muted chatter on this particular day was eerily reverent as the community mourned his shocking death. In many ways, it was how the clientele showed their respect for him. On the pub's wall of fame, a framed picture of Mark and Joanne hung proudly alongside various other community members, recognizing them and the contributions they made to the community. His loss was devastating to Oakmont.

Virtually deserted after the lunch crowd had returned to their hectic work-life; an eerie silence greeted Spike as he entered the pub. Looking around, he noticed his friend right away. Seated at the far end of the bar like always, Rocky sipped on his beer. Spike, in his classic gold-colored straw fedora with a black puggaree, approached Rocky and sat in the stool beside him. For a moment they just stared at each other. A grin painted Spike's face. Rocky returned the smile and took another sip of his beer. Spike broke the silence between them. "Good to see you again, bro. What are you drinking?"

With a smirky grin across his face, Rocky replied, "Smithwick's Irish Ale, what else would you drink in an Irish Pub?"

Spike quickly replied, "Don't be such a smart-ass, bro." The bartender arrived asking him what he wanted to drink. "You know, hm, I'll have a Smithwick's Irish Ale, what else would you drink in an Irish Pub?"

The bartender gave Spike a quirky little smile and the thumbs-up gesture and left. Rocky laughed and shook his head back and forth. "You know, Spike, you can be a real asshole sometimes."

Spike patted his friend on the back and replied, "Touché, bro, Touché."

They shared a laugh as Samantha, known as Sam to just about everyone in the pub, brought Spike his beer and sat it in front of him. Picking it up, Spike raised his glass toward Rocky. Glasses clinked as a hearty Alpha Tango cheer rang out. Silence surrounded them; the nuances of the Smithwick's Irish Ale lingered on their palates.

Breaking the pleasant and reverent mood between them, Rocky said, "Nice job on Mark Alison, my friend. It's the talk of the town. Everyone has their own opinion whom the killer is. Makes for a great conversation, maybe even a novel one day, wouldn't you say?"

"Yeah, I'm sure it does, and maybe it will be a novel someday. However, you know, one part didn't go as we planned. The gold fedora golf ball marker slid off his body to the ground under the deck. You know I'm good at what I do, but that part couldn't have been rehearsed as you well know."

"Yeah, I understand, no problem. I have another job for you, but we need to let things cool down for a while. Don't know how long it will be, but I'll be in touch when we're ready to pull the trigger. It's important to get back to living our normal lives until then, okay?"

Casually shooting him the thumbs-up, they continued nursing their celebratory beers. Well into their second beer, Spike who was antsy abruptly changed the direction of their pointless conversation and asked, "Who's next bro?"

"Patience, bro, patience. Another ball marker and the name of your next target is in the envelope I'm sitting on. Make sure ball marker is found right away. Don't screw this one up, if you know what I mean."

After an electrified fist pump, Spike grinned. Acknowledging him, Rocky savored his last sip and left. Lying on the stool was a brown envelope, Spike picked it up and placed it in the pocket of his blazer. As he nursed the last few ounces of beer in his glass, two locals entered and sat near him. They quickly began a conversation about the death of Mark Alison. As he listened, the temptation was building inside him; however, he knew it was none of his business and the last ounces of Smithwick's quenched his thirst. Passing by them on the way out, he overheard one individual say to the other, "You know, Mark Alison got what he deserved." Before exiting the pub, Spike turned around and tipped his gold-colored fedora at them.

Back at his office near the city hall, curiosity was eating at him. Like a young child on Christmas morning, anticipation danced inside his head. The contents of the envelope fell onto his desk creating a happy demonized-gleam in his eyes. Another blue ball marker with an embossed gold fedora stared up at him. A blank business card grabbed his attention. Picking it up, he turned it over. Recognizing the name immediately, an ear-to-ear grin grew on his face. Pumped and aroused, using his right hand as a symbolic gun, he fired two kill-shots into an imaginary body. Visualizing the smoke emanating from the silencer, he blew it away and sighed. Walking over to a large window overlooking Main Street, people scurried about without a care in the world. As he watched them move about, one individual entering Parsons' Coffee Emporium caught his eye immediately. Bitter-sweet memories of what could have been flashed in his mind.

CHAPTER 3

As the summer solstice grew near, Mark Alison's death investigation, for the most part, had stalled. The lead detective, Dean Stephens, had unexpectedly been placed on administrative leave pending an Internal Affairs investigation for allegedly receiving sexual favors from a prostitute facing her third arrest.

Oakmont Police Chief Brock Evans assigned Detective Carla McBride as lead detective on the case. An excellent detective in her own right, she was small in stature but tough as nails on the exterior. However, emotionally, she was a very fragile person on the inside. Her personality was best described as a 'shoot and ask questions later' kind of gal. Working by herself mainly, she wanted it that way. It was her way or no way, and everyone knew that. Partners didn't last long with her, and that suited her just fine like everyone else.

A beautiful and voluptuous woman, she had fiery-red hair with curves in all the right places. Even though she was the desire of many men, she was single with no serious relationship to speak of. In fact, marriage was not her cup of tea. Many in the police force thought she was a lesbian because of the way she carried herself, but she was far from it. Creating that persona helped keep the wolves at bay while she waited for her knight in shining armor to sweep her off her feet.

Even though Carla had reviewed all the previous evidence and interview notes, her investigation would begin with Joanne Alison, wife of Mark Alison. Spouses were always at the top of the list of suspects until otherwise eliminated. Even though Mark and Joanne were known to have the perfect marriage, Carla wandered whether that was even possible in this day and age. Every relationship had its difficulties, and she was hoping to find out if there were skeletons hidden in their past.

Arriving a few minutes early for her meeting with Detective Carla McBride, Joanne Alison chose a table in the rear of Parsons' Coffee Emporium, providing the privacy needed for such an emotional interview. Several minutes later, Carla arrived in grand style. Dressed in slim-fitting designer jeans, a form-fitting designer top, leather jacket, and sneakers, she was not the typical police detective, nor did she look like one. Approaching the table, Carla flashed her badge and sat across from her. Making direct eye contact, she began, "Mrs. Alison, thank you for meeting with me. I'm very sorry for your loss. How are you doing?"

"Detective McBride, thanks for asking, I'm doing much better and putting my life back in order the best I can. Hm, you know it is still hard adjusting not having him around. He was my rock. They say time will eventually heal everything, uh, but for me, I'm not so sure I will ever get over losing him. You ever lose a loved one?"

"Yeah, my parents, so I fully understand what you are going through. I just have a few questions to ask you. And please call me Carla. I'm all about first names, it just seems more personable, okay?"

"Um, that's fine with me. Please call me Joanne. Being a real estate agent and all, uh, I like to keep the process casual and personable as well. I feel it works much better."

"Works for me, too. Shall we begin?"

At this point, a server stopped by and took their order and returned shortly with their coffee. Joanne took a sip, nodded, and said, "Okay, we can begin now."

"Tell me about your day leading up to when you found your husband? I want to find your husband's killer, so the more open you are, the better."

"I'll do my best. That day started like any other for us. Up around 6:00, started the coffee. Then back to the bedroom for a quickie. You know hot passionate sex in the morning gets your blood pumping, ready to take on whatever the day may throw at you."

Not expecting such an intimate response right from the start, a warm sensation filled Carla's face. "Hm, I see. Please continue."

"Well, we showered together. Then got dressed and headed up to the veranda for coffee and a light breakfast. We love the fresh air and scenery surrounding our home. It is secluded from everything, and we like it that way. Provides us a serene environment for relaxing and doing whatever we want, whenever we want, if you know what I mean?"

Glancing toward a man that just entered the café,

Carla returned her gaze to Joanne. "Did Mark seem any different that morning?"

"Not really, he was looking forward to his regular afternoon golf game with the guys, then a long weekend for us at The Greenbrier Resort in West Virginia. You know the newspaper business takes its toll on people. It's 24/7–365 days a year. He needed, well, *we* needed some time away to forget the pressure of his job even though it was short-lived."

"I'm sure it does. Do you know whether he ever received any threatening emails, letters, calls, things of that nature?"

"Nothing I'm aware of. At least nothing so bad that Mark ever feared for his life. He'd been told that he was full of it or didn't know what he was talking about in his columns, you know those types of comments. But you should already know that since copies of all his emails, business, and private were collected in the initial investigation."

Carla nodded and continued, "What about you, did you ever receive any strange or unusual emails, calls, anything out of the ordinary?"

"Hm, no. I'm a real estate agent. I don't piss-off people as far as I know. I help them find their dream home. That's a strange question. Why do you ask?"

"I'm just covering all the bases. I understand you were there each Friday morning, and someone probably knew that, maybe even saw you there before. And as strange as it may seem, maybe you were the target instead of Mark."

She laughed out loud and replied, "You're kidding, right?"

"I never kid. I'm dead serious when it comes to solving homicides."

As she gave a big sigh, Joanne wondered where this line of questioning was going. "My apologies, please continue."

"Is there anything from either of your pasts that I should know about such as an affair or something else more private that would cause someone to want to kill him or even you?"

While waiting for her to respond, Carla stared deep into her eyes and knew by the stoic expression spreading across her face, Joanne appeared reluctant to answer the question. Taking a deep breath, Joanne let out a cleansing sigh. Finally, she responded to such an intimate question. "Okay, I might as well get this out in the open. I doubt it was the reason someone wanted him or me dead. Over ten years ago, when we lived in Florida, we were going through a rough time in our marriage."

Emotions crept up in her throat, and she swallowed hard, letting out a big sigh. Carla continued to focus on the ever-changing expressions emanating from her face. "Um, Mark wanted to start a family, and I didn't. We fought a lot about that, which ultimately caused us to drift apart, and he got an apartment for a while. We didn't talk much and stayed away from each other. We both needed space to sort things out. We both ended up dating other people. Both flings meant nothing, and eventually we reconciled our differences and moved on. After that, we fell in love all over again, even renewed our wedding vows at a private ceremony among friends. We've been happy ever since. I just don't think someone wanted him dead over that."

"Who were the people involved?"

"You know, it's not important since it occurred well over ten years ago. Besides, I didn't know who Mark was seeing and didn't care. Likewise, he didn't care. When we got back together, we decided it was easier to reunite under those terms. And in hindsight, that was the best decision for us. We never talked about it again, and as I said, uh, we've been happily married since we reunited."

"Let me decide whether it's important or not. You never know how past relationships can surface and wreck your life."

"Sorry, detective, that's the best I can do. Uh, I've got an appointment soon. My sister, Kathy Wilcox, and I are showing my home to Nicole and Keith Edwards in an hour, so let's move on if you don't mind."

"Sure, but I may eventually want to talk to you more about that, okay?" Joanne nodded and broke eye contact. "Now, is there anything else from your past I should know about, like financial problems, business deals gone wrong, those kinds of things?"

"Nothing. That is the only skeleton in the closet. Is there anything else?"

Up to now, Joanne had managed to keep her emotions at bay; however, the personal digging question clearly affected her as tears welled up in her eyes. Seeing that the meeting was upsetting her, Carla knew it was time to end the interview and thanked Joanne for her open and honest comments. Carla got up to leave and started to walk away, but abruptly turned around to ask one more probing question trying to catch her off-guard.

"One more thing, Joanne, do you own a gun?"

"You're full of strange questions, aren't you?" Frowning at her, Carla waited for an answer. "Yeah, I do. I also have concealed carry permit. You know, that should already be in the previous notes from the first time I was interviewed by Detective Stephens. Is there anything else I may help you with?"

"Nah, that's it for now. If I do and I will, I'll be in contact with you. Thanks again, and I'm truly sorry for your loss."

CHAPTER 4

Chad Atley, the publisher of the *Daily Chronicle* in Altmont, Kentucky, had the responsibility for overseeing the day-to-day operations at the *Daily Reporter* until he could appoint a permanent publisher. In his absence, Walter Blevins, General Manager and Vice President of Audience Development, would be in charge at the *Daily Chronicle* in Altmont.

Because Walt had worked with Mark Alison on marketing projects in the past and developed a close relationship with him, he was saddened by his death. Walt had a genuine concern for the employees of the newspaper in Oakmont and understood what they must be going through. He believed he was the right person to take over when the time was right; however, convincing Chad would be a whole different story.

Frustration was eating away at Chad's usually patient demeanor, his search for a new publisher had not found the ideal person to lead and heal the *Daily Reporter*. He had interviewed several candidates, from inside and outside the company; however, the right fit hadn't surfaced. Traveling back and forth from Altmont for two months now, hotel life and fast food was taking its toll on his diet and personal life. Choosing the wrong individual could be a career-ending move, and he was not ready to retire or look for another job. Late Friday afternoon, after meeting with Oakmont's business manager, Chad's phone rang. Recognizing the caller ID, he immediately grabbed the receiver. "Hey, Walt, everything okay?"

"Of course, how is it going there?"

"How the hell do you think it is going? No publisher yet, and I'm getting tired as hell. Don't know if I can eat another Steak and Shake burger and fries. How did the month finish?"

"We had a great month, exceeded both budget and last year."

"Super. What else is going on?"

"I just wanted to call and suggest a solution for your dilemma in Oakmont."

"Yeah, I'm listening."

"Why not appoint me the interim publisher and see how I do? What have you got to lose? You know I can handle it. You always told me that the best way to get promoted was to work hard and have someone prepared to take your place, and I've done both."

Chad wasn't surprised because he knew Walt's career aspirations. After a bit of silence, he responded. "I'll give it some thought, and we can discuss it on Monday. How's that sound?"

With a big smile on his face, Walt replied, "Great, I look forward to it. Have a safe trip home."

The call ended. Walt couldn't get his mind off being the publisher in Oakmont and couldn't wait to discuss it with Chad on Monday. After a long quiet weekend, his meeting with Chad was just minutes away. Walt arrived a few minutes early and made himself a cup of coffee and took a seat on the sofa.

Chad finished writing an email and took a seat opposite him. Walt was very anxious about what Chad had decided, and like a child on Christmas morning, anticipation raced throughout his body. Getting right to the point as he always did, Chad asked, "So, you want to be a publisher. Why?"

"I've always wanted to be one ever since I got in the newspaper business, and I believe I would be good at it."

"Why Oakmont, with all their issues? They are still healing, and it won't be easy to get things back to normal."

"Oakmont has their issues as all papers do in some form or fashion. However, their situation is much different because of what happened. I realize the newspaper needs to heal and move on. I want to be the one that makes that happen. I want to be the person that makes a great newspaper even greater."

"You know, if I were to consider you as the interim publisher there would not be any pay increase unless you are named permanent publisher. There are other benefits, such as a country club membership and a company vehicle. You get to run your own show, and if you do well, a bonus program is available as well."

"Yeah, I understand all that, but money is not everything. I'm very interested and want the opportunity to be the publisher in Oakmont. I believe I'm the right fit to help heal the newspaper."

"Okay, I'll give it a lot of thought and give you my decision on Friday."

The week dragged on for Walt. Anxiety and anticipation consumed his every thought as Friday morning was his moment of truth. He wondered if he would finally realize his dream of being a publisher at a daily newspaper or not. Ten AM Friday had arrived, and he took the short walk down the hallway to Chad's office. Knocking on the door, which was halfway open, Chad looked up and motioned him to come in. He entered and closed the door behind him.

"Get yourself some coffee. I'll be with you in a minute."

Walt placed a Starbucks Caffe Verona K-cup, his favorite, into the brewing reservoir and hit the brew button. Once it finished brewing, he took his coffee and sat on the sofa. Chad had finished responding to an email, sat opposite him, and immediately explained his answer. "I have given your suggestion a lot of thought and discussed it with our COO, Gina Dickerson. Even though corporate had a few reservations, I decide what's best for the Kentucky Group." Walt nodded; a giddy smile grew across his face. Chad's last statement was very encouraging. Walt was feeling extremely confident even though corporate had reservations. He knew they always had reservations about everything and wasn't concerned about that. "I will give you a chance as interim publisher. We will meet each month and then at six months, at that point, I'll either name you publisher permanently or bring you back here. How does that sound? All the details are in this letter of intent. I just need you to sign both copies and keep one. I've already signed them."

As Walt signed both copies, he said, "Awesome. I won't let you down. When will it become effective?"

"A week from this coming Monday. We will travel in

separate cars as I will probably stay just a few days. Any questions?"

"When will I inform my staff as well as the other department heads?"

"We will do that next Friday. You can meet with your staff a few minutes before our meeting, and then join us."

Walt acknowledged him. Chad could see that Walt was very excited. Seeing a sparkle in Walt's eyes gave him a good feeling about Walt succeeding in Oakmont.

The week flew by, and before Walt knew it, he was meeting with his department just before the regular weekly department head meeting. After making the announcement to his staff, they were not surprised at all because they all suspected something was going on because of the way he had been acting. They also knew he wanted to be a publisher more than anything in the world.

The regular weekly department head meeting began as usual with every department head giving a short report on the previous week's activities. Chad liked short meetings, so each department head always kept it as brief as possible. With no questions, it was Chad's turn to speak. He started with the financial status of the company since everything was about money. The newspaper was doing very well as always.

He then talked about all the time he had been spending in Oakmont, and he still hadn't found the right individual until now. He said given the unusual circumstances, they needed an exceptional person to guide the newspaper and announced Walt as interim publisher of the *Daily Reporter* in Oakmont. No one was the least bit surprised and gave him a hearty round of applause.

The weekend couldn't go by quick enough for him as

he had to tie up loose ends at the paper and with his assistant, Myah Franconi. She had been with the newspaper for thirty years and could easily handle things in his absence, no matter how long that would be.

Finding a temporary home for his cat was a high priority. Vader, named after Darth Vader, was a shiny black cat with piercing greenish-yellow eyes. A very loving companion, in many ways, Vader was more like a dog than a cat. He was different. Sheila Hartley, known as Shi, a bartender at Roscoe's Bar and Grill, had watched Vader in the past and was his first, and only choice to take care of him.

CHAPTER 5

Interviews with all the movers and shakers in Oakmont yielded nothing vital enough for Carla to build her case on. Many people were on the receiving end of Mark Alison's columns and editorials, and expressed their disgust and dislike for him, but they also understood he was just doing his job. The case was getting colder and colder with each day's passing, and that didn't sit well with her. She was an excellent detective. However, this case was quickly dying, and time was paramount if she was going to solve it. Reviewing notes from previous interviews of the newspaper's employees, nothing stood out as well.

Carla's interview with Joanne Alison yielded nothing substantial except their affairs and probably on the surface, weren't particularly a motive for murder. She was hoping to question her again about them soon. From the transcripts of Dean Stephens' interview with Todd Hailey, editor of the *Daily Reporter*, nothing seemed to pique Carla's interest after reading them. However, her instinct told her differently, and he agreed to meet with her. She had heard newspaper editors knew everything—knew where the dirt was—and she was hoping to find out what he knew, even if it was old news.

Since her meeting wasn't till early afternoon, Panera Bread was one of her favorites for a quick and healthy lunch. While waiting for her order, she sat in a booth by a window watching people come and go. After a few minutes, her lunch order was ready for pickup. After she returned to her booth, she continued observing and studying people from all walks of life as she ate. Like any other day, everyone looked just like ordinary folks having lunch. Nothing caught her fancy as she continued eating her broccoli-cheese soup and French baguette.

Vacant seats were at a premium most of the time, and today was no different. A tall gentleman waiting for his order looked familiar to her, but putting a name with the face was not a strong suit of hers. After the man received his lunch, he noticed the only open seat was in the booth with a window view and a very stunning red-headed lady enjoying her lunch. As he approached the booth, Carla glanced up at him. The man stopped and asked, "Detective Carla McBride, right?

Casually and without making direct eye contact, she replied, "Have we met before?"

"Keith Edwards, manager at Alcom Industries. We met at a chamber function when I first arrived in Oakmont well over a year ago."

"Oh yeah, I apologize for not remembering you. Nice to see you again."

"Yeah, that's okay. I still have the same problem matching faces to names. May I join you since it's the only open seat in here?"

"Hm, you know, I'm already late for an appointment,

so, you can have this booth. Nice to see you again. Enjoy your lunch and have a nice day."

Visually disappointed, he replied, "Sorry that you have to leave so soon. I certainly understand. Have a great day."

As she got up and left, his eyes focused on her rhythmic, sensual movement as she opened the door and walked to her car. Once inside her car, it hit her. She remembered the uneasy encounter with him at the chamber function and felt his wandering evil eyes undressing her at every glance. Keith Edwards was definitely someone to keep her eye on.

Carla arrived at the *Daily Reporter* a little later than she planned. Identifying herself, the receptionist asked her to have a seat in the waiting area. A few minutes later, Todd approached the waiting area surprised at how hot she was. "Detective McBride, it's so nice to finally meet you. I've heard a lot about you."

"Thank you, it's nice to meet you as well."

Acknowledging her, he motioned for her to walk with him to his office. After taking a seat in front of his desk, she observed newspapers scattered everywhere, and how cluttered his desk was with just about everything you could think of. She wondered how he ever found things and shook her head back and forth.

Carla responded, "I apologize for being late. I know your time is precious. Shall we begin?"

"Sounds good. How may I help you?"

"Just start by recollecting the days leading up to Mark's murder, especially the day of the murder. I know you have been through this before, but I need to hear it from you, if you don't mind? Maybe something will come up that hadn't in the past."

Nodding, he explained that the week was like any other one in the newspaper business. Nothing was that different. Mark's demeanor was pretty much the same all the time. Carla listened intently to his description of the events leading up to the fateful day.

"Were there any issues that week that seemed to upset him?" Todd had answered these questions before shaking his head back and forth. "What about that morning? Did you see or hear anything suspicious?" Again, he responded with a simple no. "What time did he arrive?"

"Around 7:30 AM. It's the only day he arrived early. Friday afternoon is his day to golf with the movers and shakers in Oakmont. He always stopped to see me before heading back to his office. You know, the usual chit-chat about what's in the paper and what I thought about his latest column. And his wife Joanne would arrive around 8:15-ish for coffee as she did every Friday."

"I see. What time did the presses start that day?"

"I believe it was around 8:00 AM since Mark was a stickler about the presses starting on time."

"I see. I heard you didn't run Mark's last column, right?" He nodded. "What was it about and did you ever publish it later?"

"It was about a student housing development by a local contractor presented to the city planning and zoning board. He opposed it because it didn't pass the smell test, you know the 'Something Rotten in Denmark' test. No need to run it now since the planning and zoning board passed it anyway."

"What about any other of his columns?"

"Nothing stands out."

"So, none of his columns were worth killing him for."

"Nah, he just liked to stir things up, get people

engaged and, of course, sell papers. It worked as our audience continued to grow both in print and online. I know it's a crazy world, and people do stupid things, but I just don't think that's what got him killed. There were so many opportunities, that if the recipient of one of his columns wanted him dead, it probably would have occurred a long time ago."

"Yeah, I know, but if I don't check the usual suspects out, I may be overlooking something, so, let's start with the local contractor."

"Okay, suit yourself. Pete Garvin, he's the contractor." Reaching into his desk drawer, pulled out Garvin's business card, and handed it to her.

"Thank you, that should do it for now. Do you think I could take a look at his office and the back deck?"

"Shouldn't be a problem. It's not locked, and forensics has been through it and the outside many times as you know."

"Yeah, I know, but doesn't hurt to look at it again. Sometimes things get missed. I'm probably looking for a needle in a haystack, but I must do my due diligence."

He walked her down the long hallway to Mark Alison's office and stopped at the open door. Todd looked inside bringing back bittersweet memories of their last conversation that morning. "Here you go. Knock yourself out, and close the door when you leave."

Carla nodded, entered the office, and glanced around the room. The office looked lonely and forgotten; it begged for someone to bring it back to life. The office was large with a door at the rear of the office. Opening it, the large deck close to a densely wooded area running the entire length of the newspaper surprised her. Walking around the wooded area; there were no designated paths in or out. As she was returning to the deck, she noticed a bright reflection coming from underneath the decking. Approaching the deck, she kneeled down and inspected a shiny round object. A small round weathered disc was speaking to her.

Forensics missed it, but how she thought. Like the excellent detective she was, she put on a pair of latex gloves and picked it up staring at the blank, shiny side. Turning it over, a gold hat embossed on a blue background created a wondering curiosity in her mind. Placing it in the bag; her thoughts were everywhere. After taking a picture with her smartphone, she put it in her purse and headed back to Todd's office. Carla knocked on his partially opened door, he acknowledged her.

"Are you lost?"

"Nah, I have a couple of more questions. Do you know Keith Edwards, plant manager at Alcom Industries?"

"Strange question, know of him, met him once or twice, kind of different, if you know what I mean?"

"How so?

"I've heard he likes to look at the ladies when he is in a social setting, kind of undresses the hot ones. But I suspect he is pretty harmless."

"Yeah, probably so, has a new publisher been named yet?"

"Actually, they've just named an interim this morning, Walt Blevins from Altmont. He has been here several times working with Mark on marketing plans which are his specialty. He should be here next week. I've worked with him before, and he's a great guy, and I believe he is perfect for us."

"Great, I look forward to meeting him, thanks for your help."

Todd acknowledged her, and she left with new evidence, she hoped. Returning to the police department, she logged in the shiny gold disc as evidence. The male clerk identified it likely as a ball marker used in golf. Carla played a little golf but had never seen a ball marker quite like that one and wondered about its connection to Mark Alison's murder.

Back at her desk, Carla tied up loose ends and then was off duty for the weekend. Noticing her message light on her phone was blinking, she hit the voicemail button and listened as Laura Watson's message played in her ear.

"Hey Carla, you want to do dinner tonight, say 7:00 PM? Give me a call, love ya."

She hit the speed dial and waited for Laura to answer. After about three rings, Laura answered and asked, "Hey lady, you on for some great Italian food and wine tonight?"

"After this week, I'm ready for an evening out anywhere. Sounds great, where?"

"Pascali's. I'll call and make the reservations. See you at 7:00 PM."

"Great, see you then."

CHAPTER 6

While Carla had a habit of always being late, Laura, a promising attorney, believed in promptness and arrived a few minutes early for their reservation. She never quite understood how Carla managed to always be late, but she didn't mind since she was her best friend. In fact, they were more like sisters than friends. Like two peas in a pod, but very different peas all the same. Laura, refined and professional, dressed the lawyer part always in business attire expressing her professionalism and feminism. Carla, on the other hand, was outgoing and a down-to-earth gal, liked her denim and form-fitting blouse, a dark blazer, and designer sneakers. She always spoke her mind regardless of the situation. Carla finally arrived, and they greeted each other with a big sisterly hug.

The hostess escorted them to their table. As requested, when she made the reservation, a bottle of Da Vinci Riserva Chianti Classico and two glasses awaited them. The famous Black Rooster decal on the neck of the bottle guaranteed its authenticity from the Chianti Region in Italy. After being seated, the hostess poured a small sample of the wine for Laura to taste. Approving the bottle, the hostess filled their glasses with a generous pour. Glasses raised, simultaneously they cheerfully said, "La Dolce Vita." Glasses clinked together and after a long sip of the Chianti, 'La Dolce Vita' described the evening.

"What do you think of the wine, Carla?"

"As usual Laura, a nice red wine that I'm sure will pair well with our dinner. You always know how to pick the wines. You know I'm just a craft beer gal; however, sometimes I get a taste for Jameson Irish Whiskey."

"Whatever floats your boat."

Laura asked Carla how her case was progressing. Carla didn't have a lot to say about it, other than just to say it was coming along. She wasn't about to mention anything to her about the ball marker she found, catching up with each other was more important. The restaurant was getting busy as it always did on Friday night. It was buzzing with laughter and sounds of couples unwinding. It was as if no one had a care in the world except Carla.

Their server, a tall gentleman about six-feet, wavy black hair with a dark complexion arrived. He introduced himself as Ricardo. "Ladies, you both look beautiful tonight. I see you already have wine; so, may interest you in an appetizer?"

"Ricardo, thank you," Laura replied. "I don't think we'll need an appetizer, the bread and olive oil pairs well with our wine. We'll just order an entrée with salad."

"Very well, have you decided?"

Carla interjected, "Yeah, I'll have your house salad with the Italian house dressing on the side and Veal Parmigiana with angel hair pasta."

"Excellent choice."

"And you, my lovely lady?"

Smiling big, Laura responded, "Well thank you, Ricardo, I'll have the Caesar salad and five-cheese ravioli in marinara sauce."

"Great choice as well, I'll put your orders in right away, so please enjoy your wine. I will bring you more bread and olive oil right away."

Salads arrived with more hot bread and Pascali's special dipping oil as promised. While eating their salads, a party of four being shown to their table passed by them. One lady stopped to chat while they seated the rest of the party at the table behind them. The lady asked, "Laura, you look lovely tonight, how are you doing?"

"Very well, Mrs. Oliver, thank you. How is the clothing store doing?"

"We are doing quite well and thank you for your business. I see you have on that suit I sold you about a month ago. It looks lovely on you."

"Thank you. Have you met my good friend, Carla McBride before?"

Mrs. Oliver exclaimed, "No, I don't believe I've had that pleasure." She introduced Carla to Maggie Oliver, telling her what she did. Mrs. Oliver said, "Nice to meet you, Detective McBride, stop by my store sometime; we have a very nice assortment of business casual clothes as well."

"Nice to meet you as well, maybe, I'll just do that. Have a nice evening?"

"Thank you," responded Maggie. "I plan to, it's our anniversary."

Laura and Carla offered her their congratulations, and Maggie joined her husband and Janice and Mike Roberts already seated at their table. Laura explained to Carla about Maggie and her husband, Kevin, who was a political consultant. Janice managed one of the food banks in town while Mike was the County Judge-Executive who oversaw the county government. All of them were very upstanding members of the community. Laura informed her about Mike and Kevin and what's at stake for them both in the upcoming election. Mike's opponent is Willard Mackey, a very prominent and influential defense attorney in town. The race was very tight, and Mackey was the toughest opponent Roberts had ever faced in any of his re-election bids.

Kevin had always managed Judge-Executive Roberts's campaigns in the past and was an excellent political consultant. His staff rarely lost an election and didn't mind getting down and dirty if that ensured victory. Judge-Executive Roberts needed one more term in office to be financially set for life. The state retirement system for a judge-executive was very lucrative.

Carla after hearing all about Kevin and Judge-Executive Roberts said, "Wow, Laura. I wasn't aware of that. So, they both have a lot to lose?"

"Yeah, they do, and I wouldn't put anything past those two if it assured them of winning, if you know what I mean?"

"Did they know Mark Alison?"

"Absolutely. Let's just say those guys weren't necessarily bosom buddies if you know what I mean? In the last election, the paper endorsed his opponent. It's the same opponent Roberts is facing again. It's apparent that the newspaper's endorsement of Mackey had a huge impact on the last election that was extremely close."

"Interesting, how far would either of them go to win?"

"Hm, if you are referring to murder, uh, I don't think so. Why don't we talk about something more pleasant?"

Finally, their entrees arrived, and as usual, they were very enticing, and they dug right in. Ricardo poured them more wine as the Chianti complemented both their dishes very well. Laura and Carla talked about the good things in life and savored their pasta and wine. However, being the detective that Carla was, she kept an ear on the conversation the Olivers and Roberts were having behind them.

Mike asked Maggie, "Who are those ladies?"

"The dark haired one is Laura Watson, a lawyer in town. The other lady is Detective Carla McBride of the Oakmont Police Department. She is currently working on solving Mark Alison's death."

Kevin exclaimed sarcastically, "Well, good luck with that one. That may never be solved. Right, Mike?"

Playing the sarcastic card, Mike responded, "Probably not, he pissed-off a lot of people in this community including you and me. His killer could be anyone, hell, Kevin, it could even be you for all I know." Chuckles flew around the table, and they continued enjoying their wine and dinner and anniversary celebration.

Laura and Carla were finished and decided to pass on dessert. Their check arrived, and each reviewed it and placed their credit card with it. While they were waiting for their receipt and credit card to come back, Carla pulled out her phone and clicked on the photo icon. Since Laura was a golfer in college, she showed her a picture of the ball marker hoping she might recognize where it was from. "Laura, does this look familiar to you? It has a gold fedora embossed on it."

"No, but it's a pretty spiffy one. Probably from an elite club somewhere and certainly not from any country club around here or that I've ever played at."

"Really, where then?"

"Probably somewhere very expensive and exclusive, most likely in a gated community."

"Hm, I was hoping you would know where it came from."

"Is it related to the Alison case?"

"Maybe…hm, maybe not. We will leave it at that, okay?"

"Understood. My lips are sealed as always."

CHAPTER 7

After several months, the *Daily Reporter* finally had a publisher, albeit an interim one. Walt Blevins had accomplished his dream, and it ushered in a new era. He had the unique opportunity of healing the newspaper after the death of the former publisher, Mark Alison, and knew it would be a huge, but rewarding challenge. He was ready, but more importantly, prepared to heal the fractured newspaper.

The first day was a big blur in the review mirror. Meeting every employee and explaining his style of management to gain their respect, and their confidence was paramount in succeeding at the *Daily Reporter*. It was essential to take time with each of them to create a good working environment. The display on his office phone read 5:30 PM, his first day was over, and he could relax over dinner with Chad at the Red Lobster. Arriving around 6:30 PM, a hostess escorted Chad and Walt to a booth near a window overlooking the parking lot. A server quickly came and greeted them. After taking drink orders, the server went over the specials for the evening.

They both chose flounder stuffed with lump crabmeat hoping it would satisfy their appetite.

Two attractive ladies, one with fiery-red hair and one with long dark hair, on the other side of the restaurant grabbed his attention immediately. A sudden flirtatious glance in his direction piqued his interest. Being single and looking for his soulmate, he continued gawking indiscreetly much to Chad's chagrin. Recognizing a lack of attentiveness, Chad cleared his throat and squashed Walt's romantic fantasizing for the meantime. "I still can't believe you want to use Mark's old office. I just couldn't persuade myself to use it."

"You know, I don't think Mark's killer will ever return there. So, I feel I'm safe."

"Hope you are right. You know someone put a hit out on me while I was a publisher in Texas early in my career."

"Didn't know that. Why was someone out to get you?"

Chad explained that the paper had published a series on possible voting irregularities in the re-election of a prominent and influential city commissioner. His hard-hitting commentary got under the commissioner's skin enough he chose to do something about it. Although Walt's eyes were sneaking looks at the ladies, he was still intently listening to Chad's monotone explanation. The mysterious ladies met his flirtatious eyes with a brief smile, he smiled back and returned his gaze toward Chad. "So how did you find out about it?"

Chad explained that one day the local police chief met with him informing him that an undercover ATF agent had received an anonymous tip that a public official wanted to hire a hit man to take out a prominent local businessperson. Local law enforcement set up a sting operation, and the city commissioner took the bait. As Chad finished, Walt returned his attention to him. "Wow, that's some story, lucky for you the chief took it seriously."

Chad nodded, and his eyes shifted across the restaurant stopping for a brief moment at Walt's mystery ladies who were in a lively conversation. He had no interest in them as his wife of twenty years more than satisfied his inner desires. His eyes quickly returned to Walt as the server placed their salads in front of them. Eating in silence, the lady with long dark hair and blacked-rimmed glasses sent a sultry glance Walt's way. Walt smiled. The server cleared the salad dishes and returned with their entrées. A muted silence surrounded them as the crabbed-stuffed-flounder brought satisfaction to their growling stomachs. Declining dessert, Chad paid the bill, and they walked to the door. On their way out of the restaurant, Walt gave a passive final glance at the ladies. They smiled and laughed. Caught red-handed childish embarrassment covered their faces. A mental image of the two ladies was engrained in Walt's mind as he met the smell of Red Lobster in the outside air.

Back inside, the lady with the dark hair jokingly said, "Carla, you can't have the sandy-haired one. He's so cute, he's mine."

Carla just rolled her eyes and said, "Laura, honey, he's not my type anyway, so he's all yours. Probably you'll never see him again, anyway." She laughed and nodded as they finished their appetizers and beverages.

As Walt relaxed in his hotel room that evening, visions of a mysterious dark-haired woman bounced around in his head. Morning came quickly. He arrived at the *Daily Reporter* bright and early to a pleasing welcoming by those already hard at work. Much like his first day, Walt spent time with each employee getting to know them better. Chad's office had a wall of vertical windows which allowed him to see Walt in action. A smile crossed his face as Walt continued his interaction with the employees. He had a good feeling about making Walt the interim publisher.

Day two flew by, and Chad met with Walt telling him he was heading back to Altmont that night after dinner. Walt was not disappointed at all since he was confident and could handle everything, and if he would need Chad, he was just a phone call away. After dinner, Chad left as planned.

Day three would start with Walt having no one watching over him. He had a pretty set routine, up around 6:00 AM, hit the exercise room and pool, then breakfast. Arrive at the office around 8:00 AM, take care of only the critical emails, then out to the common area to interact with employees.

The rest of the week flew by, and Walt stayed in town to experience the pulse of his new community. Networking was essential to his success. Before leaving for the day, a visit with the editor, Todd Hailey, would help guide him in the right direction for his weekend in Oakmont. At a gentle tap on the office door, Todd waved him in. "Hey, I'm staying in town this weekend to get to know my new community. Where would you recommend I start?"

"McGruder's Irish Pub on Main Street! It's where the movers and shakers go, plus they have a great craft beer selection and sandwiches, especially the Rueben. You'll want to try it and the craft beer."

"Great, thanks, and have a great weekend."

"Will do, boss."

After freshening up and changing clothes, he was anxious about networking. A pair of comfortable black straight-legged Levi jeans with a *Daily Reporter* golf shirt was the perfect attire for networking at McGruder's. After slipping on his light-colored tweed sports coat, he was off to explore the sights and sounds of Oakmont's nightlife. Finding McGruder's was easy; however, parking was a different story. With no dedicated parking lot at McGruder's, it took a while before he found a safe spot for Old Yeller, his prized yellow Corvette.

McGruder's was hopping with activity. Open stools at the bar were a premium. As he scanned both sides of the entire bar area, he noticed someone had just got up to leave. He quickly walked to the open stool at the end of the bar next to a well-dressed gentleman. "Sir, is this stool taken?"

"Not at this moment," the man replied.

"Mind if I join you?"

"Not at all. Haven't seen you in here before. You new in town or just visiting?"

"Walt Blevins, interim publisher at the *Daily Reporter*. I'm new and visiting until I'm named permanently. I guess I'm a little of both."

Walt extended his hand, and the man reciprocated. "Nice to meet you, I'm Kevin Oliver."

"Nice to meet you as well, it appears they don't have my favorite beer here, what one would recommend?"

"Smithwick's Irish Ale, it's a big seller here, that's why they run out of it so frequently which pisses me off to no end. Let me buy you one." Kevin waved his hand at Sam, the bartender, to bring two more beers.

"Thank you, the next one is on me."

Kevin acknowledged him and started on his second beer in silence. Walt took a long-lingering sip. "Not bad, thanks for introducing me to it. You know, my favorite is Goose Island 312 from Chicago. You ever tried it?"

"Can't say I have. So, you are Mark Alison's replacement. He was a good friend of mine, we had our differences at times, but friends, nonetheless. We golfed each Friday afternoon at the country club and occasionally shared a drink or two right here, as a matter of fact, this same stool. I feel bad for his lovely wife. I can't believe someone wanted him dead."

"Well, me neither, I got to know him from my visits here in the past helping him with marketing initiatives. Never met his wife, but I heard she is a beautiful lady."

"Yeah, beautiful inside and out, a real head-turner. How about we change the conversation to something more pleasant?"

"You got it. You know a little about me, now it's your turn."

"I'm a political consultant, married, and an avid golfer. Played in high school, wasn't good enough to play in college though, but I still love to play just the same. You play?"

"Absolutely, I played at Marshall University many years ago."

"You don't say. I was ready to invite you to play in our Friday group. After hearing that, I'm not so sure, you may be too good for us."

"Nah, with handicaps, it's always a fair and equal game. Anyway, love to join you, that's if your group will have me. Who else plays?"

"See those two guys over there." Walt nodded. "The

tall one is County Judge-Executive Mike Roberts, while the short one is Oakmont Mayor Lester James. They're the real power brokers in town. They control all the government stuff and just about everything else as well. Part of the good old boy network as they say. You'll need to get to know them if you want to be successful in this town. That's what Mark did."

"Hm, who's the lady with them?"

"That's Vicki Montrose, Executive Director of the Chamber of Commerce, grab your beer, and I'll introduce you to the real power-brokers."

"Super, I appreciate that."

They mosey on over to where they are standing, and Kevin introduced Walt to the three of them. "Folks, he's all yours, I have other important business to tend to."

"Whatever," replied Mayor James. "Be that way!"

Mayor James introduced Walt to as many movers and shakers he could. Walt felt important and very appreciative. While making the rounds with the mayor, he had been keeping his eye out for the ladies he saw at the Red Lobster. Disappointment covered his face; the mysterious ladies were not among the crowd. After a whirlwind week and busy night at McGruder's, Walt returned to his hotel room and opened a Goose Island 312 to finish the night off. Relaxing in bed, he reminisced about his first days as a publisher. A few sips and his eyes began to droop, as he drifted off, the last thing he heard was the weather forecast for Saturday…sunny skies and pleasant temps.

CHAPTER 8

Saturday came bright and early for Walt, feeling well rested and ready for the day, he headed to the exercise room. His daily routine was very predictable which would make him an easy target if someone were out to get him. After his workout, he returned to his room for a quick shower and then off to breakfast before his tour of Avondale Country Club. The weekend breakfast menu was much lighter but still enough to jump-start his day. With breakfast finished, he grabbed a coffee and a copy of the *Daily Reporter* before hopping on the elevator to the second floor.

Back in his room, he sat on the sofa scanning the paper while his coffee was cooling down. Unless hard news warranted it, the Saturday edition was mostly human-interest fluff stuff. Not a big fan of comics, horoscopes were more to his liking and enjoyed reading them. Today's horoscope indicated an encounter with someone from his past. As intriguing as it was, he didn't give it much credence since he was new in the community and the chance of encountering someone from his past was improbable.

With a 10:30 AM appointment with Chris Abbott, general manager, and golf pro at the Avondale Country Club, he arrived a few minutes early. Entering the clubhouse, he immediately introduced himself to Duane, the person managing the pro shop. Asking for Chris Abbott, he was instructed to browse around while he made a quick call. Minutes later, Duane approached Walt, "Mr. Blevins, Mr. Abbott will be right over, his office is in the mansion. You know the mansion is an old southern style house with an exquisite dining hall, and a one-of-a-kind Sunroom."

"Thanks, glad to know that."

A man entered the pro shop and came over to him and extended his hand. "You must be Walt Blevins, I'm Chris Abbott, general manager, and club pro. Please call me Chris."

While shaking his hand, he replied, "Then Chris, it is. Nice to meet you, thanks for seeing me on Saturday."

"No problem; I'm usually around weekends unless I'm out of town, besides I like to welcome prospective members and personally give them a tour. We'll begin here and then end up with the tour of the grounds."

"Great, looking forward to it."

After a full tour of the clubhouse and pro shop, a tour the grounds and golf course ended at the eighteenth green. A tall, slender lady with long dark hair in a ponytail was eyeing up her putt. The attractive lady glanced in his direction and smiled. He remembered that smile and anxiety began to churn in his stomach. He turned to Chris and asked, "The lady with the ponytail getting ready to putt, do you know her?"

"Yeah, Laura Watson, an attorney in town and a damn good golfer as well. She is a consistent winner of the lady's club championship."

"Really, maybe you could introduce me to her someday?"

"I'm sure I can arrange that, now, let's go have lunch. I have a table reserved for us."

"Great, show me the way."

Chris had selected a table overlooking the eighteenth green. Menus and two glasses of unsweetened tea were waiting for them. After being seated, Walt's focus was on the mysterious lady on the eighteenth green and not the menu lying on the table. Within a few minutes, a server arrived to take their order. Walt ordered their famous cheeseburger with fries, while Chris ordered the house specialty, a club sandwich with a side salad.

"Walt, what do you think of the club?" Walt didn't respond immediately because his eyes were still on the mysterious lady. Chris cleared his throat to break Walt's fantasizing.

"I'm sorry, it's one of the nicest clubs I've ever been at. It has everything, and when I'm named permanent publisher, I will definitely be here a lot."

"Super, you'll love it here, and we are pleased that you want to become part of the Avondale family."

As Walt's cheeseburger was placed in front of him, Laura entered the clubhouse walking directly toward them. Recognizing the lady as the one he saw at Red Lobster on Monday, anxiety churned inside him as he watched her approach their table. She threw him a flirtatious smile which pushed his heart rate faster. Still smiling at Walt, she stopped and put her hands on Chris's shoulder and said, "How's my big brother today?"

Walt's face lit up with a smile of relief as he listened to their conversation. His pulse began to quicken as he waited to be introduced to her. Laura, still smiling at Walt replied, "I needed to sink that ten-footer to finish one under par for the round, but it lipped out on me, you know how that goes."

"Yeah, I do."

"Hey, you going to introduce me to your friend?"

"Sorry, sis, meet Walt Blevins, the interim publisher at the *Daily Reporter*."

Walt, a little jittery, stood up to shake Laura's hand, she firmly gripped his hand and said, "Nice to meet you, Walt."

Walt sort of stuttered at first. A feeling of puppy-love was painted across his face. Feeling flushed, he took a deep breath to calm his nerves and finally replied. "Uh, please to meet you as well, nice round. I played in college, maybe we could play sometime."

"Would that be considered a date?"

Walt not expecting such a forward response stuttered again, but a deep breath took care of that, and he replied, "A date, hm, no, just a round of golf for now."

"Well, how about tomorrow, then? Why don't you join Chris and I, maybe I can get one of my girlfriends to play, and we'll make it a foursome?"

"Uh, I'd love to, but I'm not a member yet."

"No problem, Chris will take care of everything including clubs if you don't have yours with you."

Well, that won't be necessary, clubs are always in my car, so if it's okay with Chris, I'm all in."

Chris, a little surprised by his sister forwardness as well, finally responded, "Sure, sounds like fun, I will take care of everything, tee off at 9:00 AM and once we are finished, lunch is on me. Laura, who are you going to try to get to play?"

"I'll try Carla first. Hopefully, she is not out chasing the bad guys, if you know what I mean?" Laura and Chris shared a quick chuckle, and she continued, "She is an average golfer, but loads of fun."

A little perplexed, Walt exclaimed, "Bad guys, what's that about?"

Laura and Chris shared another laughed before Laura responded, "Walt, she's a police detective that specializes in difficult cases like the death of Mark Alison."

"Hm, that's interesting, I'm sure it'll be fun, and I'm looking forward to meeting her. Uh, thanks for inviting me to play."

"I guess it's a date then, see you two in the morning."

They nodded, while Laura headed off for the ladies' locker room laughing. Walt continued to savor every bite of the club's famous cheeseburger, nice and juicy and cooked just the way he liked his burgers. Another bite and he was in cheeseburger heaven because he couldn't get his mind off Laura and wanted to know more about her. "So, your sister has a different last name than you, what's with that?"

"She tried marriage once, but didn't work out, ended in divorce. She is a workaholic and someday wants to be a judge. Her ex-husband couldn't adjust to her long hours, so they ended it amicably. They are still good friends, but there's no chance of them getting back together as he re-married and moved away. Not sure she will ever marry again. You married?"

"Nah, I've been single all my life. Had a few serious relationships, but never made it to the altar. Hopefully, the right lady will eventually come along and sweep me off my feet. What about you?"

"Haven't found the right lady yet as well."

After lunch, Chris explained the rules of the club. Walt thanked for him the tour, lunch, and especially for introducing him to his sister. Laura returned to the clubhouse restaurant and informed them that Carla would indeed join them in the morning. On his way to the Hampton Inn, all he could think about was playing golf with Laura and meeting Detective Carla McBride. Walt thought about his horoscope he read that morning and wondered whether he should put more faith in them. After all, he encountered someone from his past just like it stated he would, the lady from the Red Lobster.

CHAPTER 9

Avondale Country Club was buzzing with activity when Walt arrived at 8:15 AM Sunday morning. He didn't see Chris and asked for him. Within minutes, Chris came out of the assistant golf pro's office and greeted him. "Good morning, Walt. Are you ready for a great round of golf on this gorgeous day?"

"Absolutely, are Laura and Detective McBride here yet?"

"Yeah, they're in the women's locker room, I think they're planning their strategy."

"So, it's the guys against the girls."

"Yeah, it is. That's how Laura wanted it; she feels it would be fair considering we'll be using handicaps. Blue tees for us, while they will hit from the silver tees. On this course, that makes it an equal match."

"Sounds good to me."

While they were getting ready in the men's locker room, Laura and Carla were already on the practice range warming up. A few minutes later, Walt and Chris joined them where Walt met Detective Carla McBride.

Everyone warmed up, off to the first tee they went. Trees and rolling mounds guarded the first hole, a 340-yard par four dog-legged to the left. Being a guest, Walt would tee off first. Eying the fairway, Walt addressed the ball. His swing was very smooth and effortless, his ball flew down the center of the fairway landing eighty-yards from the green. After a fist bump from Chris, Walt locked eyes with Laura. She smiled and jokingly said, "Not bad, newbie."

Walt nodded and joined her as Chris went through his pre-shot ritual. Chris' ball flew off the club landing on the right side of the fairway about one-hundred yards from the green. Moving up to the women's tees; Carla's shot landed on the left side of the fairway about one-hundred-twenty yards from the green. Laura and Carla celebrated with a fist-bump of their own as she said, "Good ball Carla, you'll have an easy shot from there." Laura eyed the fairway, addressed the ball, and used every ounce of her one-hundred-pound frame to drive the ball down the center of the fairway just short of Walt's ball. Giving her thumbs up, Walt smiled and said. "Very nice, you have such a smooth, powerful swing."

"Thanks," replied Laura. Winking at him, she continued. "Your swing is sweet and smooth, too." Blushing with envy, he nodded.

Arriving at the green, each walked to mark their ball and repair any divots. Walking side by side, Laura and Walt, reached their respective shots. Laura marked her ball first while Walt fixed his divot before marking his ball. Satisfied with his repair job, he retrieved a round object about the size of a half-dollar from his pocket. Pushing on the center of it; a blue ball marker tilted upwards, and he marked his ball with it. Seeing Walt's ball marker, Laura did a double take. It appeared to be identical to the one that Carla showed her on her smartphone. Her mind was racing with all kinds of thoughts, good and bad.

Carla's ball was just two-feet to the right of Walt's ball marker. As she reached down to mark her ball, Walt's ball marker with an embossed gold fedora took her breath away. With eyes bulging, she remained calm even though her pulse was racing. Studying it carefully, so many thoughts and questions filled her head. After putting out, they reached the next tee in silence. With the group ahead of them still in range, teeing off would have to wait until the group was out of sight. While they waited to tee off, she broke the silence on the tee box. "Walt, that is quite a spiffy ball marker you have, where did you get it?"

"It's from a course in West Virginia called The Snead." While showing everyone what the entire ball marker looked like and how it worked, he continued. "Why do you ask?"

With a calm demeanor, Carla replied, "Oh, just wondering, never seen one like that before." Turning towards Laura, she continued, "Have you seen one like that before?"

Knowing Carla wanted Laura to play along with her, she responded quickly, "Nah, I haven't either, and I've played several courses in West Virginia before."

Carla, in detective mode, inquired further about the ball marker. "The gold fedora, what's it all about?"

"It's a tribute to the great Sam Snead, thus the name. He wore a straw snap-brim fedora with a puggaree which is a cloth wrapped around the crown of a fedora. It can be of any cloth, but usually it's made from Madras. The

Snead is an exclusive private club near The Greenbrier Resort in White Sulphur Springs, West Virginia."

Carla and Laura remained calm and reserved even though questions and concerns flooded their minds. The rest of the golf match went by quickly; however, it had taken a serious tone. Since seeing Walt's ball marker, it squashed fist bumps, friendly bantering, and high fives. Reaching the eighteenth green, Chris and Walt were up by two strokes and unfortunately for the ladies, it was too much for them to overcome. Walt and Chris celebrated with high-fives, while Carla and Laura walked off with a somber attitude. Losing was the least of their concerns. Carla was sure that Walt's ball marker was the same one found under the deck at the *Daily Reporter*. The possibility of Walt's involvement in the murder of Mark Alison weighed heavy on Laura's mind.

Chris had arranged for lunch on the outside covered deck. When they arrived at their table, house salads and sweet tea awaited them. As they ate, they reminisced about their round of golf and the great time they had. Laura and Carla bantered with Chris and Walt about the what ifs of the match. Before anyone could say anything else, Carla's phone rang. She answered and listened, then excused herself. Needing privacy, she went to the other end of the patio. A few minutes later, she returned and informed them she must leave because of an emergency. Carla's usual cheery face turned stone-cold, she apologized and quickly left the club.

Lunch continued without her. The atmosphere became subdued and funeral-like until Chris' phone rang. He answered and ended the call quickly. He excused himself to attend to a business matter. Taking advantage of the moment, Walt put on a charming smile and broke the somber atmosphere. "Laura, I would like to get to know you better, uh, would you have lunch or dinner with me sometime next week?"

Based on her brother's earlier comments about love, Walt expected a rejection; however, her response painted a giddy smile on his face. Still showing signs of anxiousness, he boyishly responded, "Well, I guess it would be a date."

"Great, I will let you know which day is best for me; hopefully, it will work for you."

Chris returned to the table where Laura and Walt were all smiles. Since he left, the somber atmosphere had changed. The server cleared the table and refreshed their iced tea. Even though they knew the look on Carla's face meant something terrible happened in the community, the conversation remained lively and casual as Laura and Walt could not keep their eyes off each other.

CHAPTER 10

As soon as Carla was out of earshot, she was in route to the home of Joanne Alison in pursuit mode. She wasn't exactly sure what was going on, just that the police officer investigating the crime scene ordered her there ASAP. Driving up the long driveway, the county coroner was already there. Pulling into the circular driveway, Carla was informed that Joanne Alison was found dead by her sister, Kathy Wilcox, who had arrived to help her with an open house. As Carla approached Officer Fred Jones, she knew by the expression on his face, something terrible occurred. Before she could utter a word, he began to speak. "I wanted you to see something before forensics tagged everything, it might be connected to your other case."

"What do you have?"

"Just follow me."

After reaching the den off the kitchen, Joanne's lifeless body was face up on the floor. Carla gasped as the bile rose from her stomach. Swallowing hard, she took a deep breath, the site of her body and the blood didn't shock her, but rather the round object lying on her stomach sent her pulse racing. A ball marker identical to the one she found under Mark Alison's deck was resting on her abdomen. It was very similar to the same one that Walt used today. So many thoughts clouded her mind at the moment. However, one thing was clear; the ball marker was a bad omen of things to come.

Seeing Carla near the body, the coroner walked over to her. "I'm estimating time of death to be about at least thirty-six hours ago or sometime late Friday night or early Saturday morning."

"Anything else you can tell me."

"Not at this point," said the coroner. "We will send her body to the state coroner's office for an autopsy. But there appears to be nothing missing or evidence of forced entry. It certainly appeared she knew her killer. Other than that, we will let forensics do their job."

Carla nodded and left to find Kathy Wilcox. She located her in the dining room towards the front of the house. Kathy, visibly upset, agreed to talk with her, anyway. Suggesting that the veranda on the second floor would give them more privacy, they walked up a stunning spiral staircase. Upon reaching the veranda, Carla immediately noticed two cats sleeping side by side at the foot of one of the wicker chairs. Taking seats opposite each other, Carla began her interview.

"Kathy, I'm so sorry for your loss."

"Thank you. Joanne was just starting to live again."

"I assume these are Joanne's cats?"

"Yeah, she asked me many times, if anything happened to her, would I take care of them, she loved them dearly, I'll give Hilo and Kona a good home. Now, what can I help you with?"

"So, you found the body. Tell me every detail you can remember. Take your time and if it gets too emotional for you, just let me know, and we will take a break."

"Joanne had an open house from 2:00 to 4:00 PM today. I agreed to help which makes it easier for her to show the house. I got here around 1:15 or so and rang the doorbell. Normally she would answer right away since she knew I was coming, but she didn't answer. After a few minutes, I walked around back and knocked on the back door, but still no response. I tried the back door, but it was locked."

Carla noticed tears starting to flow said, "Do you want to take a break?"

"I'm fine. At this point, I went back around front, found the spare key Joanne had hidden under a flowerpot. I opened the door and called out her name and still no answer. Her cats did not come to greet me as well, which was very odd. I decided to check each room and started with the kitchen. That's where I found her in the doorway leading to the den. She was lying in a pool of dried blood. Hilo and Kona were lying at her feet unharmed. A blue golf ball marker embossed with something gold was lying on her stomach. Didn't know what to think about that. I called 911 and went back to the front porch so I wouldn't contaminate anything."

"Okay, you did the right thing. I think that will do for now, I may want to talk with you again later, but I'll let you know. Once again, I'm sorry for your loss."

"Thanks, I hope you find the person who killed Mark and Joanne and see that justice is served."

She could tell that Kathy was angry; however, she

was a little surprised about her comment indicating the same person committed both murders. Questions started racing through her mind. Did Kathy know more than she was telling? Could she possibly be involved? Carla was confident she knew more, but that could wait for a few days. Carla knew Kathy needed time to grieve.

CHAPTER 11

The *Daily Reporter*'s chief photographer and photojournalist, Mikela Taggart, heard the news on the police scanner, and immediately, was in route to the Alison home. While on her way, she hit her hands-free phone and called Todd Hailey, editor of the paper. After a short discussion, the call ended. Within ten minutes, Mikela arrived first but could only get to driveway entrance secured with crime scene tape. Informed that it would be about a half-hour or more before the police would wrap things up, she waited for the officer in charge to hold a short press conference.

Arriving shortly after Mikela, she brought Todd up to speed on the investigation. While waiting for the officer in charge to appear, Todd chatted with some other officers securing the scene. He had a knack of getting information from people without them even suspecting it. He started with Officer Ted Walker. "So, I understand the victim is Joanne Alison."

Officer Walker said, "Although the coroner hasn't

officially confirmed the identity of the victim, there is only one body in the house that belongs to Joanne Alison."

"Hm, who discovered the body?"

"I understand that it was Kathy Wilcox, sister of Joanne Alison."

Todd said to himself, bingo. He had the answer he was seeking; the dead body belonged to Joanne Alison. Todd called Walt who was enjoying himself at the country club. Feeling his phone vibrate, Walt looked at the screen recognizing the caller ID. Excusing himself, he went to the end of the deck for privacy. He listened as Todd explained the situation at the Alison house. Walt returned to the table. Laura and Chris could see shock and disbelief on his face, and they remembered seeing a very similar expression on Carla's face before she left. They both could tell that something terrible had happened.

Deciding it was best to excuse himself, he kept everything he knew at this point to himself. He didn't know either of them very well and wasn't sure he could trust either of them. He apologized for the abrupt departure and left. He wasn't sure where to go. Should he go to the hotel? Should he go to his office, or should he drive out to the Alison home and wait with Todd? Those were all questions swimming in his mind. After much thought, he drove out to the Alison home. Walt knew he wouldn't be much use there, but at least he would be with someone he knew to deal with this senseless act. When he arrived at the Alison home, many more people were standing around since there was a big subdivision across from the driveway of the Alison house. Broadcast media had arrived and were ready to deliver the breaking news. He weaved his way through the bystanders and found Todd and Mikela at the crime scene tape.

"Hey, Todd. Do we know anything else yet?"

"Unfortunately, not. It's just a waiting game at this point." At that moment, the officer in charge came walking up the driveway. "I guess we will not have to wait much longer, here comes Fred Jones."

The crowd quieted down as Officer Jones addressed the media. "I will make a few comments, and I will not be taking any questions after I'm finished. I don't have much to tell you at this point other than Joanne Alison was found dead by her sister, Kathy Wilcox. We are treating this as a homicide as there no evidence present indicating anything other than that. Thank you."

Officer Jones began to walk away as Todd asked, "How did she die?"

He responded, "As I said, no questions, that's all we have at this time. A press release will be sent out to all media as we have more information to release." The short press conference was over, and police officers instructed the bystanders to return to their homes. However, all media remained hoping to get more information, but that would not happen as the officer in charge left to return to the house. Within minutes, the coroner's ambulance came up the driveway carrying the body of Joanne Alison and the many questions surrounding her death.

Todd instructed Mikela to return to the newspaper and pull file photos of Joanne Alison and her late husband, Mark. They would go with the information they had unless a formal press release from the police or coroner reached them before press time. The fact of the matter was that it didn't matter how much information was available for the front-page story in the *Daily Reporter*, the murder of Joanne Alison would send shock waves through the community once again.

CHAPTER 12

Carla remained at the crime scene hoping to find a clue that would help solve both murders. She was surer than ever the blue ball marker with the gold fedora connected the deaths of Mark and Joanne Alison and likely were committed by the same person. Before tagging it for evidence, Carla took a picture with her smartphone. She pulled up the image of the one she found at the newspaper crime scene. They were identical, and that kept her mind wondering what the hell was going on and who did it involve. Many questions swam in her head. However, one question was at the forefront, was Walt Blevins connected to either murder? He had a very similar ball marker, and he replaced Mark Alison as the publisher.

Given that Walt had the same ball marker, questioning him immediately was paramount. Hopefully, she could at least eliminate him as a suspect. Dialing Laura's number, she answered promptly but harshly. "Carla, what the hell is going on? First, you leave the table; when you returned, you looked like you had seen a ghost. Then

Walt gets a call and abruptly leaves. He looked like he had seen a ghost as well. I need to know what is going on, and now."

"Calm down, all I can tell you is Joanne Alison was found dead this afternoon at her house. I'm leaving here now, and I need to talk with Walt immediately. Do you have his number?"

"Yeah, but what do you want to talk with him about? Do you think he had something to do with her death?"

"Uh, I can't give you any specific information at this time. You'll just have to trust me on this, okay?"

"Okay, but you'll let me in on what you find out, you know you can trust me."

"Yeah, I know, and please don't worry, uh, I don't really think he is directly involved."

Walt, who was trying to process everything going on, was startled by his phone ringing. The caller ID read Carla McBride, and he let it go to voicemail. While waiting for his voicemail to ding, his phone began ringing again. The caller ID read, Carla McBride. He took a deep breath and finally answered.

"Walt, this is Detective Carla McBride, and we need to talk now."

Immediately, Walt knew by the tone of her voice, this was not a social call and responded, "What about?"

"I'd rather not discuss that over the phone. Where are you?"

"I'm at my office."

Before Walt could say anything, the call ended. He knew she was on her way. Leaving his office, he camped out by the front door to wait for her. Beads of sweat dotted his forehead as he paced back and forth. Ten minutes seemed like twenty minutes to him, but she finally arrived. Opening the door, she wouldn't let him get a word in edge-wise.

"Let's go back to your office, you don't want to make a scene out here, do you?"

Walt nodded, and he took a route through the press-room area so that Mikela and Todd hopefully wouldn't see them. He didn't want to disturb them or better yet, alarm them. Seeing Detective McBride might just create false suspicions or who knows what. Once in Walt's office and the door closed, she didn't beat around the bush. "Where were you on Friday night from 10 PM to 2:00 AM?"

"Seriously, what's this all about?"

"This is about Joanne Alison's death, believe it or not, you are connected to the crime scene whether you had anything to do with it or not."

"How so?"

"Walt, I don't like this any better than you do, so, just answer the damn question, okay?"

"Okay…okay. I went to McGruder's for a couple of beers. Met some community members, the mayor, the judge-executive and some political consultant named Kevin Oliver. And I met the chamber lady, uh, Vickie Montrose. I left around 10:30 PM and went back to the Hampton Inn. Then watched some television. Before falling asleep, I went to the breakfast area and got some creamers for my coffee the next morning. Then back to the room. You can check with the night manager if you like or check their security cameras."

"I'll do just that. Now, where were you when Mark Alison was murdered?"

Laughing sarcastically, he responded. "Seriously? Are their deaths connected?"

"Dead serious, now just please answer the damn question, and I will be out of your hair for now."

"Working my butt off in Altmont, as a matter of fact, I was in our department head meeting, just call my boss, Chad Atley, here's his business card."

"I'll do that as well. Walt, I don't like this any better than you do, I'm just doing my job, okay?"

"Yeah, I get it, uh, what's my connection to either murder?"

Evading the question, she broke eye contact with him. "That should do it, for now, thanks for being so cooperative, uh, I'll be in touch if I have any further questions."

CHAPTER 13

By Sunday evening, the death of Joanne Alison jolted the community. Shock and disbelief replaced a reverent atmosphere usually experienced on this day. By the time Monday's edition of the *Daily Reporter* hit the streets, aftershocks would reverberate through the community and rumors would run rampant, typical of small towns, where gossip spreads like wildfire. Speculation of why her beautiful life was so cowardly squashed dominated water-cooler conversations.

Mark Alison's death was initially pointed more towards his work as a newspaper publisher who shook things up and stepped on many individual's toes in Oakmont. However, his wife's death gave it a jigsaw puzzle like the persona of a real mystery novel of James Patterson proportions. After taking care of paperwork which, she dreaded, a visit to the Hampton Inn to verify Walt's alibi was first on her list because of the gold fedora ball marker. The security video footage confirmed his alibi. Chad Atley confirmed his whereabouts the day that Mark Alison died. She couldn't get it out of her mind that somehow this spiffy ball marker and Walt Blevins might be crucial in solving the death of Mark and Joanne Alison. In her mind, he remained a person of interest in both investigations. To ease his anxiety of being a suspect, she called him to ease his anxiety.

Although forensics had combed the Alison residence extensively, visiting again would satisfy her curiosity and unanswered questions. Still surrounded with the crime scene tape, the house was cold and lonely. Walking through each room, she hoped they would talk to her, that the spirits floating throughout the house would enter her subconscious and deposit clues. The walls were silent, nothing piqued her curious and investigative mind.

In the doorway from the kitchen to the den, stains remained where Joanne's spirit joined her husband in the afterlife. She imagined Joanne looking through the peep-hole, seeing someone she knew. Not afraid, she opened the door that ended her life. Food and water bowls were no longer in the kitchen, Hilo and Kona had a new home with Kathy Wilcox. After visiting every room, nothing seemed out of place, nothing was missing except for the life of a beautiful person. An eerie silence had painted the walls an invisible shade of death, and she wondered if they would ever breathe life again.

Focusing her efforts outside the house, she was hoping to find clues in the woods that surrounded the rear of the house. As she scanned the area, thoughts crept in her mind about the death of Joanne, and it was eerie similar to her husband's death. It was apparent to her that Joanne's death wasn't an attempted burglary gone wrong; someone had assassinated her, but why was the question Carla had to answer and by whom was the missing piece to her jigsaw puzzle investigation. Walking through the woods; nothing was catching her eye. Two paths lead into the woods ending at the same place, a county road where the killer presumably parked an escape vehicle. Although tire tracks were visible, they were unlikely to yield any clues. Back inside the house, the only thing she had going for her was the blue ball marker found at each crime scene. Her suspect list was blank, and her investigation looked as dead as the house.

Returning to the police station, she reviewed evidence collected by forensics. The only significant evidence was the blue ball marker, the one thing that continued to haunt her. It was the only thing that tied both murders together.

With no shell casings found at either crime scene or usable fingerprints on either ball marker, she had zilch to go on. Hoping that Kathy Wilcox could provide some new information, she scheduled a meeting that afternoon with her. In her initial interview with her, the comment made about Joanne's killer being the same person that killed Mark, nagged at her ever since that day.

Kathy agreed to meet Carla at a local coffee shop downtown in about an hour. Parking could be a nightmare in the afternoon, but today must have been her lucky day, and maybe that was a good omen. Finding one in front of the Parsons' Coffee Emporium, she entered and immediately noticed Kathy seated at a table near the back of the building. Ironically, it was the same table she interviewed Joanne several weeks ago. Approaching her, Carla greeted her and sat across from her.

"Kathy, how are you doing?"

"Much better. It's tough when you lose a family member, but I also know life must go on. I met with the funeral director this morning to complete the arrangements. Joanne wanted to be cremated just like Mark. I'll hold a memorial service at a later date, best I could do since she had no other family except me."

"I can't imagine what you are going through if there is anything I can do, don't hesitate to ask."

"Thank you. I appreciate it. What did you want to talk to me about?"

"When we talked on Sunday, you inferred that Mark and Joanne were murdered by the same person. You seemed certain about that, why?"

"Honestly, just a gut feeling I have. Joanne and Mark were so in love and kept no secrets from each other as far as I know. As sisters, we were very close and trusted each other. Whatever got Mark murdered, got her murdered, I'm convinced of that. Joanne had no enemies, she was well loved and respected in the community. Her death just doesn't make any sense."

"Murder never makes sense, but I guess at this point nothing can be ruled out."

"Is there anything else you want to ask me?"

"Were you aware that they both had affairs in Florida over ten years ago? That came out when I interviewed her several weeks ago."

"Wow, I didn't know that! I guess that's something they both wanted to be kept hidden for obvious reasons. Did she mention any names?"

"Nah, she was sure it wasn't important, and I never got the chance to question her about it again. Did they ever spend time at the Greenbrier Resort in West Virginia, or a golf course called The Snead near the resort?"

"Not that I'm aware of, they were supposed to leave that evening the day he was murdered. Why do you ask?"

"You remember the blue disc left on Joanne?"

"Yeah, what about it?"

"It's from a course called The Snead at the Greenbrier Sporting Club near the Greenbrier Resort. Based on what you tell me, it couldn't belong to either of them, since they hadn't been there yet. One last question, can you think of anyone who might want to harm Joanne or that she feared or was concerned about?"

"Well maybe, there was this couple that looked at her house, I don't think the husband would harm her or anyone for that matter; however, this guy gave us both the creeps. Joanne said she didn't care if she ever saw this individual again, she didn't care if they bought the house or not, that wasn't like her. Nicole and Keith Edwards is whom I'm referring to."

"Hm, I see. Thank you so much for meeting me today, that should do it for now."

Keith Edwards' name had surfaced once again. His actions toward the ladies were one of concern, Carla had felt it herself when she ran into him at lunch the other day. Her due diligence would be necessary to check him out; however, the big question on her mind, was he capable of murder and why kill both Mark and Joanne Alison?

CHAPTER 14

Still trying to process what transpired on Sunday, Walt worried about why he was still a person of interest. A person of interest in Mark Alison's death was plausible he thought because he always wanted to be a publisher, and eventually, he replaced him. He couldn't let this investigation consume his every minute, and he knew he must bury himself in his work. Fortunately, the nature of the newspaper business would make that an easy thing to do since the internet made the newspaper industry extremely challenging.

Wondering whether Todd or Mikela saw Carla visit him on Sunday, he paid Todd a visit to feel him out. Knocking on Todd's partially closed door, he heard a grumbled response. Peeking in, Todd motioned him in. A moment of silence lapsed as Todd went on about his editing as Walt asked, "What's going on?"

Casually, he replied, "Same oh, same oh."

"Really. Another murder and it's same oh, same oh."

"Yep. Hey, did I see Detective Carla McBride in here on Sunday?"

Walt got his answer, and there was no use in avoiding the subject. Pausing for a moment, he reluctantly replied, "Yeah, she was here. What I'm about to tell you is extremely confidential, and it must remain that way, okay?"

That got Todd's full attention and motioned Walt to close the door and take a seat. As Walt explained in detail his interrogation, shock and awe painted Todd's face. "Wow! That blows my mind. So, she is saying a connection exists between Mark and Joanne's deaths. And what is your connection?"

"I don't know, I asked that question several times, all I got was nothing. It's part of both ongoing investigations, wouldn't tell me anything else. I'm as stunned as you are."

"Hm, that's very interesting, I guess you've made a big splash in the community, but not in a good way."

"Guess so. My connection is really bothering me, but if I can help bring the murderer to justice, I'm all in."

Todd's mind wandered, and he seemed distant for a while because his reporter instincts were churning. Many unanswered questions raced through his brain. Walt could see that clearly on his face and asked, "What are you thinking about, you seem distracted, or your mind is somewhere else?"

"Oh, nothing. I agree, whatever we can do to help bring the individuals to justice, we will cooperate."

"There you have it. Remember, it is extremely confidential. I'll keep you updated on further information regarding me or the case as it develops."

"You got it, boss."

Back in his office, Walt buried himself in his work. He still had much to learn about being a publisher, he was working on new advertising strategies when his phone rang. Caller unknown stared back at him, he answered, "Hello, this Walt Blevins, publisher of the *Daily Reporter*, how may I help you?"

"Hey Walt, this is Kevin Oliver. We met at McGruder's on Friday night."

"Oh, yeah. How are you doing?"

"Very well, thank you. I know you are a busy man. So, I will get right to it. Would you like to join the Friday afternoon golf group at Avondale Country Club?"

"I'm not a member yet, but I'd love to, it will help me get my mind off all the stuff going on, you know newspaper stuff and of course the recent death of Joanne Alison."

"I understand, my friend. As for not being a member, you can be my guest."

"Thank you, sounds like fun. Who will be joining us?"

"You remember meeting Mike Roberts, County Judge-Executive and Mayor Lester James. You will be playing with us, while the other foursome will be Wylie Adkins, Keith Edwards, Jeff Walker, and Cliff Kagan."

"Great, I look forward to meeting the other guys. Thanks for the invitation, see you on Friday."

"You bet. See you around 12:30 PM on the practice range, we'll tee off at 1:00 PM."

"Thanks, have a great week."

"You, too."

CHAPTER 15

Taking a chance Keith Edwards was in his office today, Carla drove out to Alcom Industry hoping to interview him. Not sure what kind of business Alcom Industry was, she researched and found out they manufactured windows and doors. In the county industrial park, Alcom shared the complex with about six other companies. A perfect day for a leisurely drive, she wasn't in a hurry because the road would take her through some of the best farmland in the county. Entering the industrial park, a stop at the guardhouse to register was necessary.

After the car in front of her moved through the gate, she opened her window as she pulled to a stop. After standard procedures of security protocol, the guard waved her on, and off she went on a wild fishing expedition. She didn't think Keith had anything to do with either murder, but then again, she knew anything was possible in this whacky-sick world of the crime she had to fight every day. The plant was precisely where the security guard told her, and there was ample visitor parking right in front of the main entrance.

Entering through a set of double glass doors; the registration desk was directly in front of her. A beautiful blonde in her mid-thirties stood up to greet her. "Hi, I'm Kimberly Meadows, but everyone calls me Kimmy around here. Welcome to Alcom Industry, how may I help you today?"

"Ms. Meadows, I'm Carla McBride, is Keith Edwards in today?"

"Yes, do you have an appointment?"

"Nah, I was in the area, decided to stop in and see him, we are old friends."

"Hm, I see, let me buzz him and see if he is available to see you."

Dialing Keith's extension, Carla overheard Kimmy speaking with him. While eavesdropping on her conversation, Carla scanned the common area of the plant. After a long pause the call ended. "Ms. McBride, Mr. Edwards will be out shortly. Please wait in the customer lounge to your left."

While continuing to observe the hustle and bustle of the common area, out of her peripheral vision, Keith Edwards came strolling out like he was God's gift to women. He smiled at everyone he encountered and eyed the ladies in his path, especially Kimmy. She noticed Kimmy sent him a sultry smile. As he walked towards her, Carla stood up to greet him. Keith's eyes were moving up and down her body before he finally made eye contact with her. "Detective Carla McBride, what a pleasure to see you again. What brings you here today?"

"Oh, I was in the area, and I felt I needed to stop and

apologize for my abruptness the other day at Panera Bread, you remember, right?"

He acknowledged but knew damn well that she had something else on her mind, and so did he. However, not to cause a scene, he played along. "Oh, yeah, please follow me to my office where we can talk in private."

Walking together down a long hallway towards his office in the production area, she felt his eyes locked on her chest. Entering his office, a picture of the Greenbrier Resort on the wall behind his desk caught her attention. His office had a small casual seating area off to the right of his desk and motioned for her to have a seat. As she sat down, his eyes moved up and down her body. Fuming from his roving eyes, she cleared her throat breaking his sexual fantasy. "Mr. Edwards, you ever played a course near the Greenbrier Resort called The Snead?"

Keith thought it was an odd question and responded quickly. "Yeah I have, I have a friend that invites my wife, Nicole, and I up there each fall." Carla scribbled on her notepad as Keith talked about the course. "Now, Detective McBride, what really brought you here today? Am I any trouble I need to know about?"

"Nah, I just have a few questions regarding the death of Joanne Alison."

"Whoa, I don't know what help I can be since my only encounter with her is when my wife and I toured her house several weeks ago. We loved the house and were just about to schedule a second visit just before she died. Now, we have no interest in the house at all as you can understand."

"So, that is the only meeting you ever had with her?"

"In person, yeah; however, we chatted on the phone a couple of times after the first visit."

“Isn’t that a little unusual?”

“A little, but our agent wasn’t there for our tour, so she told us if we had any questions, to feel free to call her, so, I did.”

“May I ask you where you were last Friday night around midnight?”

“You think I had anything to do with her death?”

“If you will just answer the question, I’ll be on my way.”

“Okay…okay. Every Friday night Nicole and I meet friends at McGruder’s. We arrived around 8:00 PM and probably left around 11:30 PM. We then went home and watched a movie on Pay Per View on DIRECTV. If you need a copy of my account, I will be glad to give it to you.”

“That won't be necessary. I appreciate you seeing me today, I will be on my way now. Thank you.”

“I had nothing to do with her death, but if you have any further questions, please don’t hesitate to contact me.”

Although he was not a suspect or person of interest in the death of Mark Alison, due diligence was necessary. “Oh, I have one last question, did you know Joanne’s husband personally?” Hesitant to answer, a puzzled look plastered his face. “Mr. Edwards, would you please answer the question?”

“Sorry, my mind was somewhere else. Yes, occasionally, we were paired together in the golf league at the country club, but that’s it, we never had anything else in common.”

Walking together out to the customer lounge, she felt his eyes undressing her the entire time and she couldn’t wait to be away from him. Once outside the double doors, she turned around noticing Keith smiling and massaging Kimmy's neck and shoulders. Shaking her head, she knew he was a definite scumbag; however, a murderer, unlikely. He didn't fit the profile. Just the same she would check out his alibi at McGruder's and keep him on her radar.

CHAPTER 16

While enjoying the scenery on her drive back to the police station, one of her favorite country songs was playing on the radio. Kelly Clarkson and Jason Aldean were belting out *Don't You Wanna Stay*. Liking the song so much, she sang out loud, especially Kelly Clarkson's part. While getting lost in the lyrics thoughts about Keith Edwards swam in her head like an Olympian in a fifty-meter freestyle race.

She arrived at the police station hoping someone had called and left a tip which could lead to a break in the case. Her voicemail light on her phone was dark and lifeless, disappointment covered her face. Keith's alibi needed verifying, and McGruder's hopefully could provide that. She had never been to McGruder's, a hotspot for movers and shakers, even though she heard it was very law enforcement friendly. Arriving at the pub as it was opening for lunch, she sat at the bar where a young lady was prepping for the lunch crowd. The young lady noticing her at the bar walked over and greeted her with a friendly smile.

"What may I get you, Miss?"

"Hi, I'm Detective Carla McBride with the Oakmont Police Department, and I need some information."

"Hey, I just work here, I've done nothing wrong."

"Oh, honey, you are not in any trouble, what's your name?"

"I'm Samantha Lewis, but everyone calls me Sam."

"Okay, Sam, I didn't mean to alarm you. Do you have security cameras?"

"Yeah, we do. We have one at each door, and that pretty much covers the entire inside, and one outside on the deck as well."

"Do you know how to pull up video footage?"

"Absolutely, I'm studying to be a videographer and photojournalist. What are you looking for?"

"I'd like to see footage from last Friday night, around 11:20 PM to midnight. Just pull it up and if you don't mind; I'll review it here at the bar."

"No problem, detective." Sam left and returned with the business laptop. Working her skills on a laptop, she pulls up the video segment ready to be reviewed. "Here you go detective, just click on the play button."

Carla reluctantly acknowledged her and clicked on the video. She watched the video intently and around 11:35 PM, Keith, and his wife left together through the main entrance. His alibi checked out. Thanking Sam for her cooperation, she wished her good luck in her future endeavors. As she got up to leave, her stomach growled back at her. Having heard they had a great lunch menu, she decided to have lunch. Taking a table by a window facing a side street, she motioned for Sam. After finishing her prep behind the bar, Sam walked to the table where she was sitting. "Is there anything else I can help you with?"

"Yeah, lunch, what would you recommend?"

Without hesitation, she replied, "The Rueben, you will love it, or it's on me."

"Well, the Rueben it is. What comes with it?"

"Your choice of waffle fries or our famous homemade chips."

"Homemade chips and unsweetened iced tea with lemon, please."

"Super, I'll put your order in right away and be back with your tea, and refills are free."

"Works for me, thank you."

"You're welcome."

While waiting on her lunch, Carla paid more attention to the pub décor. Irish flags and numerous coat of arms flags hung from the ceiling while law enforcement badges filled every inch of wall space. It wasn't long before Sam returned with her Rueben and chips. The Rueben on grilled marble rye bread looked mighty tasty. All it took was one big bite, Sam was right, the Rueben was awesome. She tried one of the homemade chips; crunchy just how she liked them. As she enjoyed her lunch, she watched as the pub filled up quickly.

After downing her last bite, Carla noticed two businessmen taking a seat at the bar on the opposite side of the pub. One gentleman was wearing a gold-colored straw fedora, while the other was wearing a Cincinnati Reds baseball hat. Finished with her lunch, she motioned Sam to bring her the check. After paying her bill, she visited the ladies' restroom and passed by the two gentlemen on her way to the front of the pub.

When she passed them, their faces showed they were having a serious conversation while drinking Smithwick's Irish Ale. She overheard the man wearing the Cincinnati Reds hat calling the other one Spike.

Both men intently watched her leave the pub. Spike looked at his friend and said, "Rocky, wasn't that Detective McBride?" He nodded. "I guess we should keep an eye on her, right?"

"Seriously, my source at the police station indicates she is not even close to solving either case. Trust me, it's nothing to worry about, just lay low."

Spike took a long draw on his Smithwick's and gave a sigh. "Maybe so; however, I believe this is the first time I've seen her here."

"Come to think of it, you are probably right. Maybe Sam waited on her and can enlighten us."

"Let's ask her." Spike motioned Sam, and both held up their glasses. Sam understood and drew them another Smithwick's and placed them in front of them. "There you go, guys. Anything else I can get for you?"

Acting innocent and playful, he responded. "Yeah, there is, who was the red-headed chick that left a few minutes ago?"

In a jokingly manner Sam replied softly. "You know that will cost you if you know what I mean?"

Spike replied, "Honey, you know we always take care of you."

"Yeah, I know, just kidding with you. Some detective named Carla McBride, can't recall ever seeing her in here before. She wanted to look at some security video from last Friday night. We had no reason to contact the police, it was normal Friday night. So, I don't know what she was looking for, and I didn't ask."

"Anything else?"

The time frame was from 11:20 PM to midnight," said Sam. "Didn't say much or ask me any further questions. She moved to a booth, had lunch, and viewed the video. You guys ready to order?

Spike replied, "Of course, pretty lady."

"The usual, I assume."

Spike nodded, and an order for two Rueben sandwiches with chips was placed. Muted chatter bounced off the walls while they nursed their second beer. Just as their lunch was set in front of them, Spike turned to Rocky and asked, "Wonder what she was looking for?"

"Not sure, but whatever it was, we were gone by then. I'm not concerned, and you shouldn't be either. Detective McBride evidently didn't know us, or she would have said something to us a few minutes ago as she walked by."

"Yeah, you're probably right."

Spike motioned Sam to bring the check. Rocky patted Spike on the shoulder and left. A few minutes later Sam returned with the check and placed it in front of Spike. Checking it, he pulled a wad of money from his pocket. Looking directly in her eyes, he said. "If Detective McBride shows up again asking questions, please call me, okay?" Sam acknowledged him as he handed her his business card. He laid a fifty-dollar bill on the counter and left. Picking up the money and business card, she finally could put a real name to Spike. Jason Alexander Doyle, construction consultant.

CHAPTER 17

Over his anxiety of being considered a possible suspect, a person of interest concerned Walt just as much. It was a dark cloud hanging over him. Focusing on making the newspaper better and making as much money as possible brought his tension level to a manageable level. However, all work and no play made him an anxious man. Ever since meeting Laura Watson, he was looking forward to having dinner with her. Respecting her wishes, he resisted calling her as much as he could. Maybe it was karma, which he didn't believe in, or just dumb luck, but his phone rang as he pulled out her business card. The name on the caller ID put a smile on his face. After two rings, he answered in his usual professional manner. "This is Walt Blevins, publisher of the *Daily Reporter*, how may I help you?"

"Hi, Walt, this is Laura Watson. How are you doing today?"

"Busy as ever, and you?"

"Nose to the grind every day. I know it's short notice, but can we get together tonight at Pascali's Italian

Ristorante? We can make it a Dutch date if you don't mind."

"You sure? I'd be happy to buy you dinner."

"I'm sure; I prefer it this way until we get to know each other better. If the relationship grows, then you can foot the bill every time, okay?"

"Great, no problem, what time?"

"7:00 PM. okay?"

"Sounds great."

"Well then, I will call and make reservations, if you don't mind?"

"Not at all, see you at 7:00 PM. Thanks for calling and have a great day."

"You too. See you tonight."

After the call ended, he was beaming with joy, and it made the rest of his day much more enjoyable and fun. He always believed employees should have fun at work and that work should be fun as well because it fosters creativity and happier employees. After two meetings and a conference call, he would be free to enjoy the evening with Laura and getting to know her better.

She called and made reservations and to have a bottle of Chianti Classico and two wine glasses on their table. Never having had a problem with Pascali's before, she still arrived early to check on her reservation and her wine request. Wanting tonight to be unique, she wanted to make sure everything was perfect. When she arrived, the table she requested had a bottle of Chianti Classico open to let it breathe, and two empty wine glasses waited for some excellent vino to invade their space. After being seated, she poured the wine waiting for Walt.

Before she knew it, a hostess escorted him to their table. Taking a seat across from her, he smiled and thanked her for making reservations. Noticing the glasses of wine, he realized she was a take-charge lady. Some men might consider that as an attack on their manhood; however, he didn't mind because he found it to be quite sexy just like her. Raising her wineglass and looking at his deep blue eyes, she said, "To a great evening of food and wine."

While raising his wineglass, he stared into her mysterious green eyes and followed her lead. "Cheers. Here's to a great-looking lady, great wine, and us." A clink of the glasses occurred, and their relationship was off and running. Still focused on her haunting eyes, he said, "Laura, thank you so much for calling; I'm glad we could finally get together and get to know each other. I know this is just dinner, but the first time I saw you at the Red Lobster, my heart skipped a beat."

Like two teenagers in puppy love for the first time, they were timid and anxious at the same time. After taking a sip of her wine, she smiled as she reached for his hand and squeezed it gently sending a tingling sensation up his arm. Locking eyes with him, she responded, "Wow, I felt the same way when I saw you, too. So, tell me everything about you."

"Well, I was born and raised in Huntington, West Virginia. Stayed at home while I went to college at Marshall University. I was captain of the golf team and graduated with a degree in finance, with a minor in criminal justice."

"Hm, that's an odd combination, what made you go that way?"

"I've always liked law enforcement; however, I never wanted to be a police officer. I thought by getting a minor, maybe I could join the FBI and do something in financial forensics."

Still holding his hand, she looked deep into his baby blue eyes and said, "How did you get started in the newspaper business?"

"The FBI never panned out, so I tried the financial business, you know investments and insurance. Found out early on, it wasn't for me. I was kind of searching for my niche in life, and an old friend persuaded me to apply for a job in marketing at the local paper. I applied, and the rest is history."

"What about your family?"

"Well, I pretty much grew up in a single parent household," said Walt. "My father left us when I was seven years old, and we lived with my grandmother. My mom worked all the time to support raising five children."

"That must have been tough growing up in that kind of household."

"Yeah, it was. We were poor but didn't know it. My brothers and sister worked hard and managed to make it through college and into successful careers. Everyone is still living in the Tri-State area except me. Okay, it's your turn now, tell me all about you."

"Well, I'm a local gal. Born and raised right here in Bluegrass Region. Did undergrad at the university and then on to law school at the University of Kentucky. After graduation, I landed a job in my hometown, and as you say, the rest is history."

"What about your family?"

"You already know I have a brother and that's my family. My parents were killed in an auto wreck during my freshman year of college."

"I didn't know that; I'm so sorry."

"Thank you. It was a drunk driver, and that was the inspiration for me to go to law school. You're already aware I was once married for about a year. We both thought we were madly in love, but in the end, we were not a good match for each other. We parted ways amicably. He moved away, remarried and has kids now. And that's it."

"Now, that we got that out of the way, let's get down to ordering, I'm starved, and the wine is going straight to my head."

"Yeah, me too. This is one of my favorite places. I hear the lasagna made with Italian sausage is to die for, but since I'm a vegan, I've only had the vegetarian version, which was quite good. I'm sure the lasagna with Italian sausage is equally delicious as well."

CHAPTER 18

With their salad and entrée ordered, Laura and Walt could focus on each other. Their puppy-like behavior faded away as their conversation turned lively as though they had known each other much longer. As they finished their first glass of wine, their salads arrived. Noticing that their glasses were empty, Ricardo refreshed them and left. After another sip, Joyce Roberts and her husband stopped at their table to say hello. Laura and Joyce knew each other; however, she had never met her husband, Judge-Executive Mike Roberts.

On the other hand, Walt had met Mike but never his lovely wife. After informal introductions, Mike said, "Walt, can't wait to get you on the course this Friday. It's supposed to be a gorgeous day for golf, and we look forward to having you become a regular member of our group."

Walt responded, "Can't wait, looking forward to playing the course and being part of the group."

Addressing Laura, he continued, "Nice to finally

meet you. My wife tells me you are a lawyer. How's business going these days?"

"Nice to finally meet you as well," replied Laura. Mike nodded, and she continued, "Business is great, by the way; how's your re-election campaign going?"

"Great as always, I expect to win this one just like all the others," said Mike. "This election is the most important one to me, and nothing will get in my way of winning again if you know what I mean?" Mike and his wife let out a brief chuckle.

"Well, best of luck."

"Thank you, how did the two of you meet?"

"Avondale Country Club," said Walt. "I was checking out the club and noticed her on the 18th green. Her brother introduced us, and we played golf the next day. We both wanted to get to know each other better and tonight is just the beginning."

"Well, I see that your dinner has arrived, you two have a great evening; Walt, I will see you on Friday ready to take all your money."

Joyce and Mike let out another annoying chuckle as Walt nodded as they left to join Maggie and Kevin Oliver already seated at their table enjoying a glass of wine. With a concerning expression on her face, Laura asked, "Didn't know you were golfing with that group on Friday. You know Mark Alison played in that group."

"Yeah, I know. It's just a friendly golf game, and probably none of those guys had anything to do with Mark's death. I understand they were good friends as well."

"Just the same, be careful. As you heard Mike say, he would do just about anything to be re-elected. There is something about him that bothers me."

"He seems harmless and besides our food is getting cold, let's eat and get back to knowing more about each other." After a bite of the lasagna, a smile comes across his face as he savored its flavor and spiciness. "You were right, this is the best lasagna I've had in a very long time; the marinara sauce with Italian sausage is nice and spicy just the way I like it. How's your ravioli?"

"Great, as usual."

As they both continued to eat, a welcomed silence encompassed the table after their conversation with the Roberts. After they had finished their meals, Walt poured the rest of the wine, and the conversation became lively once more. "Laura, you know Carla came to see me last Sunday afternoon. She had just come from the crime scene to interrogate me or at least that's how I felt. It shocked me to know she considered me a suspect."

"Yeah, it's nothing to worry about, she is just doing her job."

"She said I have a connection to both deaths. I wonder what that could be, do you have any idea?"

Taken off guard by his comment. She asked, "What, did I hear you right, both deaths?"

"Yeah, she was specific about that, asked me for alibis for both murders."

With a surprised expression painting her face, she responded, "That's very interesting. Did she say why?"

"No, but something connects me to both murders."

She knew Carla wanted to talk to him about his gold fedora ball marker. Was there one left or found with the body of Joanne Alison? That had to be it, she thought. She promised her she would not mention the ball marker to anyone, not even him. With a blank expression on her face, she informed him they never mixed pleasure and business. Silence crept in, what had been a great evening, suddenly turned a little sour. Looking deep into her haunting green eyes, he wondered what she was thinking. He thought she knew something more but couldn't or wouldn't talk about it. He just knew it; he called it newspaper instinct. "I guess it's time to call it a night. I've had a wonderful time."

"Me, too, and I've got a busy day tomorrow, anyway. I had a great time as well. We should do it again soon, say same time next week?"

Those were the exact words he wanted to hear, and his mood improved immensely. "That would be great, but I get to pick the place."

She smiled at him adoring his beautiful blue eyes, probably the bluest she had ever seen, she touched his hand and said, "You're on, buddy. It's a date." Walking her to her car, she hit the key fob. He opened her door and extended his hand; she obliged extending her hand as they ended the night with a gentle, but sensual handshake. He wanted so badly to kiss her soft lips and hold her, but that would have to wait until the right moment.

CHAPTER 19

Rays of sunlight peaked through the plantation shutters in her bedroom. Stretching and yawning to chase away the remnants of a peaceful night's sleep, Laura squinted at her alarm clock. 7:00 AM glared back at her.

Turning over to shield her eyes from the bright sunlight forcing its will into the room, she smiled and moistened her lips. An erotic dream was still vivid in her mind. On a deserted island, she and Walt were making hot and sultry passionate love as waves crashed around them. One day that dream would turn to reality, or at least that was what she hoped would happen.

On the bedside table, the screen on her iPhone lit up, and Carla's assigned ringtone, *Girls Just Want to Have Fun* began. After a big sigh, she wondered what in the world Carla wanted. "What do you want this early, you woke me up from a really hot dream, if you know what I mean?"

"I take it your date with Walt must of went well. I

want all of the details, don't leave anything out or I will come over and interrogate the hell out of you."

Laughter rang out, then silence. "Dinner and conversation, and of course...wine. That's all there is to tell. He walked me to my car and like the gentleman he is, shook my hand. We have another date next week. I can't wait."

"That's it, I know you are holding out on me, I can sense it, now fess up."

"Yeah, that's it, except he did bring up your interrogation of him last Sunday after you finished at the crime scene."

"I wouldn't call it an interrogation, maybe more like a friendly conversation. What did Walt have to say?"

"Well, it sort of took me by surprise that you told him he was a person of interest because he was connected to both murders. I thought that was quite interesting."

"I don't recall saying that, maybe he misunderstood me."

"No, he was pretty specific about it. I think I know why you wanted to talk to him; it's the blue ball marker with the gold fedora, right? The one you showed me on your phone. Did you find one at the crime scene on Sunday?" Dead silence quietly filled the speaker. Caught off-guard, Carla wasn't sure how she should respond, she could try to change the subject; however, knowing Laura as she did, that wouldn't work. Impatient, Laura cleared her throat and lashed out at the silence with her courtroom tone of voice. "Are you there, The... Detective...McBride?"

Laura knew that would get under Carla's skin because she didn't like being called that or using that tone of voice. Of course, Laura knew that usually pissed her off and Carla would finally respond. However, Carla still hadn't answered her question. Carla knew the longer she kept silent, the more it would raise a red flag. Laura repeated the annoying phrase. Silence. "Dammit, Carla, answer..."

In a frantic tone of voice, Carla reluctantly responded, "I'll be at your office in one hour."

Before Laura could respond, the call ended. She knew once Carla arrived, she would get answers. They rarely discussed business, but since Carla opened the door by showing her the picture of the ball marker; she had to pony-up and confess. Keeping an eye out for her in the front lobby of the law office, Laura saw Carla parked in front of the law office. Once inside Laura's office, Carla had no choice but to come clean with her and put her faith and trust that Laura would not disclose what she was about to learn about both cases. Like an angry pit bull in a courtroom, Laura played offense addressing her quickly and directly. Laura was in courtroom mode. "Carla, I don't mean to pry. But you opened the door when you showed me the picture of the ball marker. When Walt used the same ball marker on Sunday, we both had similar thoughts swimming through our heads."

"Okay, you're right. Here's what I can tell you and it must stay extremely confidential if you know what I mean?"

"We've known each other for a long time, and you know you can trust me. Maybe, I can even help you solve these cases if you let me."

"Maybe, and I can use all the help I can get these days. I'm getting nowhere with everyone I interview.

Mark and Joanne Alison were very well liked. Mark shook things up, but nothing to get killed over and certainly not his wife, it must be something non-newspaper related. I've got to start thinking out of the box."

"Let's hear the whole story, maybe I can help."

Carla nodded, and after a detailed explanation, she sat silent. Laura wasn't surprised at what she heard; her innate deduction was a strong suit of hers. Breaking the silence, Laura continued her courtroom mode. "So, the two murders are connected as Walt alluded to at dinner. I can see why he has a connection, albeit a small one to Mark; however, not to Joanne."

"You're right, but I believe the blue ball marker is the key to breaking everything wide open."

"I'm afraid I won't be of much help then, but I know someone that will and so do you."

"Yeah, I know. I'm just not sure I want to get in bed with a newspaperman if you know what I mean."

In a kiddingly manner and to lighten things up a little, Laura sarcastically replied, "Watch it detective; he's all mine."

"Hell Laura, you know what I mean; symbolically, in bed with him?"

"Yeah, just joking; I believe he can be trusted, or I wouldn't be going out with him, he's so different from the other men I've dated. After my experience with marriage the first time, I'm very selective about men these days."

"Then, that makes me feel good. I'll give it serious consideration. Well, gotta run and do some more detective work. Thanks, see you soon. By the way, love your answer tone, *Girls Just Want to Have Fun*."

"All work and no play isn't much fun, you should give it a try, and I know just the person for you."

"We've been through this discussion before, I love your brother, but not in that way."

CHAPTER 20

After visiting McGruder's Irish Pub, the other day, Carla believed it had a connection to her cases. Maybe it was detective intuition or just a gut feeling she had, but she was confident that someone there was withholding valuable information. As Carla told Laura, thinking outside the box was necessary. Sam likely knew something, but Carla couldn't quite put the finger on it yet. Arriving at McGruder's shortly after they opened for lunch, Sam was behind the bar preparing for the lunch crowd. Sam noticed her entering the restaurant and approached her sitting at the bar. "Detective McBride, what brings you back here so soon?"

"More information, and your delicious Rueben."

"What kind of information?"

"When I was in here the other day two businessmen were sitting right here, who are they?"

With a concerned expression on her face, "I only know them by their nicknames. Spike and Rocky. Strange nicknames I'd say, locals and have always treated me good. Great tippers."

"No real names?"

Breaking eye contact with Carla, she changed the subject. "You want the Rueben with chips again for lunch? Unsweetened iced tea with lemon to drink, right?"

She knew Sam was holding back because she changed the subject quickly raising a red flag. She was sure that Sam knew their real names but played along with her and tried to catch her off-guard. "Yeah, that will do," she said. "Do they come here every day? Also, I need to review more video from last Friday night, 8:00 PM to midnight, if that's okay?"

"Not every day," avoiding eye contact, she continued. "Let me go place your order, and I will be right back with your iced tea. Then, I will work on retrieving the video footage you requested."

Leaving the bar area, she immediately returned with a big glass of iced tea with lemon and sat it in front of her without making eye contact. Quickly, she turned around and headed back to the kitchen since Carla was the only customer in the pub. Back in the kitchen she slipped out the service door to the deck, pulled out her phone, and dialed Spike's number. Within a minute, Sam ended the call.

Returning to the kitchen, she picked up Carla's lunch order and noticed she was no longer at the bar. Glancing around the tables, Sam spotted her at a table with a view of Main Street. Placing her lunch down, she responded in an uncharacteristic tone of voice. "Here you go detective, enjoy. I'll get the laptop and retrieve the video you requested."

"Thanks, bring the laptop here, and I will look at it while I'm eating, okay?"

Sam acknowledged and left. Moments later she

returned with the laptop, and the video file already queued up for playing. Carla knew the routine and pushed play. While eating, she let it play in regular time glancing at it from time to time. It was a fishing expedition and nothing else. She was hoping something would catch her eye the second time around. She wasn't paying much attention to the video since she planned to copy it to a flash drive before she left. After finishing her last bite of the Rueben, she downed her remaining iced tea. She stopped the video and motioned for Sam to bring the check. Sam cleared the table and left the bill without saying a word.

Inserting the flash drive into a USB port, within thirty seconds Carla removed the flash drive, mission accomplished. Sam was just a young college student and a little naïve; however, Carla was confident she was getting mixed up in something terrible. Not wanting to see her get hurt or something far worse, she left her business card tucked between a twenty-dollar bill with a message on it. She was hoping her detective intuition was right and Sam would heed her advice before she got in too deep.

Relieved Carla had left the pub, Sam noticed something, like a business card, tucked between the twenty-dollar bill. She picked it up and immediately went to the ladies' room to examine it. Once in the ladies' room, Sam pulled it out. It seemed like any other business card with contact information on the front; however, when she turned it over, she read the message written on it. She thought to herself, how could this detective know anything about what was going on with Spike, and why did she think she was getting into deep. And deep into what, was the question now upsetting her, consuming her thoughts. Looking at her reflection in the mirror; a colorless complexion stared back. She turned on the hot water, gently splashed it on to her face, hoping to bring color back to her face before she returned to the bar area. After another look in the mirror, she brushed her hair back out of her eyes and dried the tears of concern on her cheeks.

After finally regaining her composure, she opened the door from the ladies' room and let out a gasp. Spike's glare was frightening; a pale white complexion covered her face. Immediately, she filled a beer glass with Smithwick's and sat it down in front of him. Lying on the bar counter was a hundred-dollar bill. Not knowing what to think or say, she refused to make eye contact until he broke the unpleasing silence. "It's yours, pretty lady, take the beer out of it and keep the rest. I told you I would take care of you." As she picked up the money, he forcefully grabbed her hand scaring her. Trying to break free; his grip grew tighter as he continued. "Tell me exactly what Detective McBride wanted this time." Fear built in the pit of her stomach and her pulse was racing. Avoiding eye contact, she looked toward the kitchen hoping Silas, the day shift cook, was watching. Unfortunately, he was oblivious to her situation. Spike's grip grew stronger causing her to flinch. The fear inside her rose from her stomach. Breathing heavily, she hoped her fears would subside. Quickly glancing at him, his eyes were glassy and concerning. "You look like you have seen a ghost, what's going on?"

She knew she would have to respond soon, or he could get angrier, she had never seen him this way before, and it worried her. Still not making eye contact, she quietly replied, "Please let go of my hand, I'm just not feeling well today, and I'm concerned about an exam I have tonight."

He was a smart man and knew something else had upset her. Spike had had anger issues in the past, and he was running out of patience. "You'll do fine on the test, now tell me what Detective McBride wanted." As he released her hand, she looked deep into his eyes seeing something she had never encountered before, demon-like eyes were piercing her eyes. Fear and fright crept into her soul as she stared at the money lying on the bar. Still not making eye contact with him, his hand slammed hard on the bar startling her. "Dammit Sam, look at me and tell me everything…now!"

Fearing for her life, she glanced toward the kitchen hoping Silas was watching, nothing. Spike's forcefulness and tone of voice caused great concern. She didn't like his angry tone of voice nor the look on his face as his demonic eyes were on fire. Sam had now realized that maybe she had gotten herself into something she didn't plan on, but she had to talk soon, or he would get all the more furious. She finally responded, "Just as I told you on the phone, she wanted to see the video from last Friday night from 8:00 PM to midnight. She asked me your real names, but I didn't tell her because I don't know them. We didn't talk much at all. I saved the video file on the laptop and left it with her while she ate. I occasionally looked her way, and it appeared she didn't pay much attention to it at all. She finished her lunch and left. That's it, I swear."

"Interesting, may I see the laptop?"

Retrieving the laptop, she placed it in front of him and returned to the kitchen. He moved his finger on the mouse pad, in a few short moves, he found what he suspected, Detective McBride had copied the video. When she returned, he was gone. The empty beer glass sat on a hundred-dollar bill and a scribbled note. Picking it up along with the money, she put both in her pocket. The lunch rush would arrive soon and needing to compose herself before it got busy, she hurried to the ladies' restroom. Pulling Spike's note out, she read it. Fear had never left her body, and her pulse continued to race. Looking in the mirror; tears trickled down her cheeks. A knock on the door startled her.

Silas said, "It's showtime, Sam."

"I'll, uh be, uh, out in a minute, okay?" A deathly silence filled the ladies' room, the air was stagnant with fear. Splashing cold water on her face removed the tears of despair from her eyes. After several deep cleansing breaths, she met the lunch crowd with her usual cheery attitude and smile.

CHAPTER 21

After a restless night of intermittent flashes of Spike throughout the night, Sam rubbed her eyes hard to chase away the glassiness brewing in her eyes. Eliminating the Spike-infused fear controlling her subconscious was nearly impossible as his demonic eyes bored holes in her soul. Shaking her head, remembrances of Detective McBride's message attempted to pump up her spirit; however, the fear was winning the battle controlling her mind. Conflict and fear were consuming her every thought. Standing in front of her bathroom mirror, red-swollen eyes glared back at her, dousing them with cold water did little to erase the fright on her face, did little to ease the unhappy butterflies floating in her stomach. She had never experienced a feeling of this proportion in her life.

While getting ready for the day, Detective McBride's message continued its struggle to control her thoughts; fear was exploding inside her. Back and forth, Carla's note was taking hold of her. Without a doubt, she did not want to see Spike's demonized eyes cutting into her soul anymore. Putting her faith and trust in Detective McBride, she pulled out her business card and dialed her number. It immediately went to voicemail, she left a frantic message and hung up. Waiting for a return call; minutes seemed like hours as she waited for help. Tears were swelling her eyes. Her phone screen lit up, before one ring had finished, she pushed the answer button, but paused and took a deep breath. She could hear Detective McBride's voice. "Sam it's me. What's going on?" Silence. Her voice froze as Spike's angry grin flashed before her eyes.

"Sam, please say something."

Squinting her eyes, she chased the fearful vision of Spike into darkness. With a raspy voice, she cried out, "I need to see you, and now! Please help me."

"Come to the police station where you'll be safe, we'll talk then, okay?"

After a brief pause, silence took control until Detective McBride heard an unfriendly dial tone in her ear. Her pulse was racing now, she hit return call and listened. After several rings, Sam answered. The call was short, and Carla breathed a sigh of relief as the call ended. Sam locked her apartment door and hurried to her car constantly looking over her shoulder. Paranoia consumed her mind as she unlocked her car and started the engine. It softly purred as she scanned her surroundings. The police station was on Main Street but on the other side of town. She made a left turn onto Main Street and headed west. As she drove along Main Street, parked in her subconscious, paranoia waited for the right moment to rear its ugly head. She knew Spike was watching her somehow. Waiting for the light to change, she spotted him coming out of CVS. Sam did her best to avoid looking in his direction; however, her paranoia was real. His demonized eyes pierced her soul. As the light turned green, her tires squealed, raising more attention to the 2004 Jaguar speeding down Main Street. Beads of sweat dotted her forehead as Spike grew smaller and smaller in her review mirror.

Arriving at the police station; Sam entered through the main doors. A whirl of activity was going on, police everywhere, it made her feel safe for now. The main desk was straight ahead. After asking for Detective McBride, she waited impatiently seated with other people seeking help. Every time the doors opened, she flinched out of fear. She was oblivious to the fact she was now sitting alone waiting for help. The clock on the wall showed she had been waiting for only five minutes, it seemed like much longer. Sweat dotted her brow as she glanced at the doors once again. A tap on the shoulder startled her. "Sam, you look scared as hell." Sam could only nod her head. "Follow me where we can talk in private." Once inside a small interview room, emotions got the best of her as tears flowed down her cheeks. Handing Sam, a tissue, Carla continued. "It's okay Sam, you're safe now, now tell me what is going on?"

Tears were wiped away, but fear was still holding on as she began to compose herself. "You may be right; I might have gotten myself into something terrible."

"How so?"

"The day you were here, Spike and Rocky were seated at the bar. You walked by them, and they asked me what you wanted. I told them. Spike told me to call him the next time you came in, that they would take care of me. So, when you came in yesterday, I called him. Once again, he asked me what you wanted, so I told him."

Carla nodded as Sam continued, "After you left I went to the ladies' room, and I read your business card, I got concerned. I don't know him very well. I joke around with him occasionally, and that's all. What makes you think I'm getting in too deep?"

"Detective and female intuition. Now, what else?"

"When I came out of the ladies' room, Spike was sitting the bar. I drew him a beer and sat it in front of him. He had a hundred-dollar bill on the bar. He said it was mine for calling him. He then quizzed me on what you wanted. I told him the same thing I told him on the phone, but he got kind of angry and grabbed my wrist and wouldn't let go. I said that you didn't pay much attention to the video as you ate. He then asked to see the laptop and discovered that you copied the video file. That angered him even more, and I took the laptop computer back to the office. When I returned, he was gone. The money was still there with his note. The note said for me to call him again if you came around. What is going on?"

"Spike is a nickname; I need his real name if you want me to help you."

Reaching into her purse, she handed Carla Spike's business card. Reviewing it, she knew it was a simple business card created and printed on any old printer, nothing professionally done and that concerned her. It read Jason Alexander Doyle, construction consultant, and a phone number, nothing more.

Her tears had dried, her fears had not. Sam asked, "Why did you want to see the video from that night? Nothing happened at the pub."

"I was checking out an alibi of a person of interest."

"Person of interest, whoa, that sounds serious. Person of interest in what?"

"You know of the recent murder of Joanne Alison, don't you?"

"Yeah, do you think the killer was there that night or that Spike could be involved?"

"Don't know, anything else you can tell me."

"That's it."

"Okay, Sam, listen to me. I'll check out Jason Alexander Doyle and see what I can find on him, but I don't have a good feeling about him. If he gives you any more trouble, please call me right away."

Sam nodded. Carla walked her out to her car making sure she was safe. Sam returned to McGruder's beginning her shift, while Carla returned to her cubicle and searched all possible databases to find out just who Jason Alexander Doyle is or was. It didn't take long, and the news was disappointing, but as she suspected there was nothing on him. As far as the real world was concerned, Jason Alexander Doyle didn't exist, and that was a huge problem. She dialed his number, no answer. Finding Sam's phone number, she dialed it. It went straight to her voicemail; Carla left an urgent message.

Sam clocked in at the time clock in the kitchen at McGruder's and quickly visited the ladies' room where she listened to Carla's message. Tears flowed, and a deep concern for her safety overwhelmed her. A knock on the door startled her.

"Sam, are you okay?"

Tissues wiped away tears streaming down her cheeks. Splashing water on her face, she heard Greg's voice again. After a deep breath, she responded, "Yeah, I'm fine, I will be out in a few minutes."

"Okay, we'll probably going to get busy pretty soon, and there is prep work to be done."

"Got it, Greg."

Those few minutes passed by too quickly; she knew she had to get to work. After wiping a few more tears away, she exited the ladies' room and looked around to see if there were any customers yet. The place was empty, and that suited her fine. She prepped for the day and went to the kitchen to see if Silas had arrived. He was busy checking the freezer and she didn't bother him. Much calmer now, she hoped that the rest of the day would be better. Leaving the kitchen, she scanned the bar area and froze in her tracks. A pair of demonized eyes were shooting darts of fear in her direction. Spike was sitting at the bar, and she had no choice but to serve him. After drawing him a beer, she sat it down in front of him and turned to walk toward the kitchen. Sam could feel his eyes on her body. He cleared his throat, and she froze in her tracks, trembling from fear. "Hey pretty lady, don't walk away from me like that!"

"Is there anything else I can get you?"

"Where were you going this morning in such a hurry?"

Speechless and frightened, she responded, "The dentist, I was running late." Staring at her with his demon-like killer eyes, he downed his beer and sat the glass down with such force it sent chills up and down her spine. His snarling grin was the last thing she remembered as she sprinted to the ladies' room.

CHAPTER 22

Sam was foremost on her mind as Carla opened her eyes to the sound of a rooster crowing, she often wondered why she chose that sound for her alarm clock. A glance at the clock, in a bright crimson color, 7:00 AM was upon her. Her thoughts were still on Sam, and whoever, Jason Alexander Doyle, aka Spike was. The image of them were still hanging around her mind from separate dreams during her restless night. It was not important what happened in her subconscious mind; it was only important what happened in reality and that concerned her deeply. Not that the unsolved murders of Mark and Joanne Alison were not a priority to her, they were however, leads were drying up, and the only common denominator was a blue golf ball marker with a gold fedora embossed on it.

The only living person she knew who had one was Walt Blevins. Although his alibis checked out, he might be the only hope to solve these cases. Her case was like a dying person on life support and their family having to pull the plug ending their pain and suffering, and that's where she was. Laura had suggested working with Walt; however, crawling in bed with the media was a risk. She knew there was a constant tug of war between law enforcement and the press regardless of print, broadcast, or internet, they were always at each other's throat, per se.

Knowing unidentified people were out there with answers, finding them was difficult. Confiding in an interim publisher of the local newspaper was a risky venture. She trusted Laura, and although Laura trusted Walt, she wondered how much Laura's hormones affected her judgment because of her hot crush on him. If the information went public by an interim publisher's desire to become the permanent publisher, she could end up with egg on her face, and that wasn't something she wanted to experience. It was hard for her to trust him over a round of golf and substantiated alibis, but somewhere inside her subconscious, a voice urged her to follow her intuition. Sharing critical information with Walt was risky; however, the reward could even be higher, maybe even crack the case open. Mind made up, she took a deep breath, crossed her heart and walked through the main doors of the *Daily Reporter*.

The reception desk was straight ahead. A pretty brunette stood up to greet Carla. Her nameplate read Debbie Castle. Beside her in a chair, was a young girl exhibiting her coloring skills. As Carla approached, Debbie stood up to greet her. Carla responded, "I'm Carla McBride, is Walt Blevins in today, he's expecting me?" Debbie dialed his extension; Carla overheard her conversation and knew her moment of truth of trusting the media was near. "Mr. Blevins will be right out to see you.

Please sign in and have a seat in the waiting area, he said he would be right out."

"Thank you. Young lady, that's a pretty page you colored."

Debbie replied, "Shane, what do you say?"

"Thank you."

"Your welcome, sweetheart."

Debbie responded, "Bring your daughter to work day, she loves it."

"How old is your daughter?"

Before Debbie could answer, Shane spurted out, "I'm eight."

"Kids," responded Debbie as she rolled her eyes. "You have any?"

"Nah, not even married."

Debbie nodded, and Carla signed the visitor's log and sat in the waiting area and pondered her risky decision. Too late she thought as Walt greeted her and extended his hand toward her. On the way to his office, casual conversation helped ease her reluctance. Once inside the office, he closed the door and suggested they go out on the deck to discuss whatever was on her mind. After taking a lounge chair opposite each other, Walt asked, "Well, Detective McBride, I assume this is not a social call, correct?" She nodded but remained silent still contemplating how much she would tell him. Her mind was wandering in her silence. "Why are you here, detective?"

With her mind made up, she let her intuition fight off her emotional safeguards. "First of Walt, please call me Carla. And no, this is not a social call. However, I could use your help." Walt nodded with a giddy smile as she continued. "What I'm about to tell you is extremely confidential. Also, anything I tell you today is strictly off the record, and should this information ever get out; I will deny this conversation ever happened." He nodded, and she continued. Intently listening to the critical information, she was sharing with him; his eye contact never left her. Once she finished, he attempted to respond; however, she hushed him. "Now, you understand why I had to interview you the day Joanne was found dead. Only a handful of folks know about the ball markers. Laura knows, and she suggested I speak with you about them. She trusts you, so here I am."

"So, how do you think I can help. Just because I have one, and just about anyone who has played The Snead does as well; how's that going to help you?"

"I'm not sure; however, you have been there, and more likely the people behind these murders have been there as well. It's an exclusive place, and from what you told me before, you either live there or must be a guest of someone. So, how many people from Oakmont have likely been there, probably not many, wouldn't you say?" Walt nodded. "We just need to compile a list."

"Did I hear, we?"

"Yes, I said we. I know you want to catch the killer or killers, don't you?"

"Of course. How can I help?

"Wouldn't The Snead keep a log of who played there and their contact information?"

"Probably."

"You know someone at The Snead, don't you?"

"Yeah."

"Then that's where you start."

"Me?"

"Yeah, you. It would be better for a fellow golfer to inquire rather than a police detective, wouldn't it? We don't want to tip off anyone in case someone there might possibly be involved. Tell them you moved to Oakmont and wanted to hook up with other golfers that played The Snead. A piece of cake, Walt. You can do this. You're a newspaper guy, right?"

"Yeah, then what?"

"Simple, get me a list, and I can check each name out to see what turns up. Joanne's sister Kathy Wilcox said that Mark and Joanne have never been there together. They were heading there that weekend for their first visit."

"Okay, I will work on it, so, we're a team."

"I wouldn't go that far. Now, what about your date with my girl Laura. She wouldn't tell me much."

"Not much to tell. Dinner, wine, and conversation. A very nice evening with a lovely lady. We met there and left in separate cars. We agreed to go out again next week."

"Hm, that's just what Laura said, you two are so much alike, maybe it's a match made in Heaven. Thanks for your help and let me know what you find out."

He escorted her out to the main desk, and she left. Back in his office, he called The Snead to talk with his friend Carl Osburn. Locating the number, he dialed it, and waited for an answer. On the third ring, Carl answered. After catching up on each other lives and explaining his reason for his call, the call ended.

CHAPTER 23

As Walt waited for his Friday morning conference call, anxiety and several cups of strong coffee gave him an uneasy feeling. Swarming butterflies were making suicide dives inside his stomach. Playing golf on a Friday afternoon was nothing he never fretted about; however, add Mark Alison's golf group to the mix and the result was an anxiety-induced lack of confidence he had never experienced even as a collegiate player in a conference championship. Today was different; he was taking the place of his dead predecessor. His stomach continued to churn as he went through his usual routine; turning on the Keurig and then going to the press room to get a copy of that day's paper. Returning to his office, the Keurig was ready, and he hit the brew button. While waiting for his coffee to finish, he booted up his laptop. By the time his coffee finished, Microsoft Office had finished loading his email. Scanning his email; one stood out at the bottom of his list. His friend, Carl had come through as he promised.

Opening the email, he scanned it finally resting his

eyes on individuals from Oakmont that had played The Snead. As he suspected, the list was not a long one. He recognized most of the names; in fact, he was playing golf with all of them that afternoon except the last name on the list. Mark Alison was the final name on the list, he was dead. He thought to himself what was he doing on the list because he was sure that Carla told him that Mark and Joanne had never been there before. He called Carl to double-check the list. Carl confirmed that Mark had played at The Snead. Based on Carl's information, Mark had probably made a guy trip with the Friday afternoon group. And now he was taking Mark's place. With so many similarities between him and Mark, his swarming butterflies morphed into an eerie, eerie state of queasiness and uneasiness. Strange thoughts consumed his mind. Strangest of all, could he be playing golf with a killer?

Deciding to forgo forwarding the email to Carla at the moment, he would wait until his golf match was over. By doing this, he might have something interesting to tell her, besides, having her interrupting his afternoon of golf would help fuel the sleeping butterflies resting inside his stomach. Before he realized it, a reminder flashed on his laptop screen. Not wanting to be late, he locked his office and arrived at the club about twenty minutes early. He was all about making a good first impression with the movers and shakers in Oakmont. Inside the Pro Shop, he met up with Kevin Oliver, Judge-Executive Mike Roberts and Mayor Lester James with whom he would play. Walt met Jeff Walker, Wylie Adkins, Keith Edwards and Cliff Kagan who would make up the other foursome. Walt's group would tee off first with the second foursome to follow them. The mayor was the vocal leader of the group and said, "Walt, you know guests always have the honor of teeing off first."

"Yeah, mayor, I figured it would be that way, I'm ready, let's get it on."

Being first to tee off, Walt felt butterflies of a different kind come to life inside him. Butterflies of excitement and competition pumped him up. Teeing up his ball, he mentally pictured his drive. He slowly started his backswing, and then his powerful downswing took over. In a split second, his driver met the ball. Exploding off the club, the ball soared down the center of the fairway ending up seventy yards in front of green just as he imagined in his mind. After retrieving his tee, he turned around and addressed his playing partners. "There you go guys, game on, who's next?"

The remaining golfers teed off and landed in the fairway. Adhering to golf etiquette Walt would be the last to hit his second shot. Using a lob wedge; his shot stopped two feet below the hole. His playing partners were in awe of his shot-making. With everyone finally on the green, Walt approached his ball and marked it as his partners watched. Staring back up at them was a blue ball marker with a gold fedora embossed on it. Walt's playing partners stood like mannequins in a storefront window. They looked at him and then at each other. Anxiety and concern painted their mannequin-like faces. Silence surrounded them until Lester spoke, "Walt, where did that ball marker come from?"

"The Snead, a private club in White Sulfur Springs, West Virginia, near the famous Greenbrier Resort." Lester didn't say a word, just nodded at Walt. He continued, "Lester, you ever play there?" Once again, Lester just nodded and looked away. As each player marked their ball, they used the reverse side of their ball marker which had the initial of their last name on it. It was an odd way to use a ball marker, and he thought nothing more about it.

Mike would putt first and placed his ball in front of the ball marker. As he picked up his ball marker and attempted to put it in his pocket, the ball marker fell to the green landing face up. The same ball marker found at both murder scenes stared up at Walt. He glanced at Mike; however, neither said a word. Worried expressions painted the faces of the mayor and Kevin as Mike picked up the ball marker and placed it in his pocket. Although standard etiquette, while players are putting, is silence; however, the silence had a different meaning with this group. A puzzled expression crossed his face as thoughts and questions ran through his mind as each person finished putting. He sunk his birdie putt and on the way to the next hole, more questions kept surfacing. Did these guys have anything to do with either murder? Was there a conspiracy going on? Play continued with subdued bantering between the mayor, Kevin, and Mike. Although everyone seemed to have a great time, the ball marker was on everyone's mind.

With the front nine complete, Walt had played a fantastic round finishing two under par. Lester played well but was two over par. Mike and Kevin both shot their usual bogey golf and ended up at nine over par. As usual, a stop at the clubhouse was in order. A chance to get a beverage and a snack. Lester asked Walt, "What would you like to drink?"

"A water would be nice. I'll save the beer until after the round is over." Lester nodded and entered the clubhouse while Walt waited in the golf cart. Walt needed time to collect his thoughts and what he wanted to ask the mayor about their ball markers with the initials on the reverse side. Lester returned with two bottles of water and two packages of peanut butter crackers handing one each to Walt. "Thanks, Lester." He nodded and proceeded to the tenth hole. The mayor seemed like an honest man and Walt felt like he could get the real story about the ball markers. Arriving at hole number ten, they waited for Mike and Kevin to join them. After everyone had teed off, Walt and Lester headed down the left side of the fairway toward their respective shots. Feeling the time was right, he continued his conversation with Lester. "What's with the initial on the back of Mike's ball marker?"

Lester being very perceptive had been ready for more questions about the ball marker. "We all have one," said Lester. "We have a group that goes every spring to the Greenbrier Resort for golf and guy time. No wives, just golf. We always find a way to play The Snead."

Walt asked, "Who is in the group? And if I'm named permanent publisher, how do I join it? I love playing there."

Lester, surprised by the question, wasn't sure how to respond—reaching for his shot first gave him a little extra time to think about how he should answer Walt. Lester got out of the cart and took out a wedge for his shot. Based on his ability, this shot should be an easy one. However, the question laid on his mind; he lost his concentration and bladed the shot sending the ball over the green. A disgusted look painted his face as he mumbled something indiscernible. Walt just kept a straight face and didn't say a word. Grabbing his lob wedge, he walked to his ball. He surveyed the shot and promptly put the ball three feet below the pin making his birdie putt a relatively easy one. Lester picked him up and drove the cart toward where his shot ended up without saying a word. Walt continued his questioning of the mayor, "You never answered my question, who was in the group?"

Lester knew he couldn't remain silent any longer and responded. "Everyone playing today except you. Mark Alison was the other person in the group."

"Okay, what's with the initials on the back of the ball marker?"

Lester said, "We put initials on the back just for identification purposes. They had a sale on them when we were playing there, so we all bought extras in case we lost one, some of us bought extras to give to other friends as well since it's a special ball marker like The Masters."

Changing the subject hoping to catch Lester off-guard, Walt said, "That was terrible about Mark Alison, I got to know him pretty well when I worked with him on plans to grow his audience and readership. He had it all going for him."

Lester replied, "Yeah, it was a big shock to the community, he was very active and well liked. He pushed the envelope in his columns, I didn't always agree with him, but I respected his opinion. Did he piss-off someone enough it got him killed, that would be hard for me to believe?"

"I imagine when his wife was murdered, it was like an earthquake in the community."

"Yeah, and to make matters worse our police chief recently informed me they are nowhere close to solving either murder. Why don't we talk about a more pleasant subject the remainder of the round?"

Walt obliged, and the conversation turned to an upcoming charity event in the community. After the round was over, Lester honored his promise of buying Walt a beer. They chatted while drinking their beers and munching on snacks. Walt finished and thanked Lester, Mike, and Kevin for a fun round of golf and left. On the way back to the Hampton Inn, the gold fedora ball marker was foremost on his mind. The most important question of all, was the ball markers connected to the case? If so, he had probably met and golfed with the killer of Mark Alison, and likely his wife.

CHAPTER 24

With Laura out of town for the weekend, he planned a quick trip to Altmont to relax in his apartment with Vader. Maybe he would connect with a few friends, but mainly he wanted to relax and decompress from all the stress of being an interim publisher. While driving home on Saturday morning, Walt received a text from Chad. When he pulled into his parking spot at his apartment complex, he pulled out his iPhone and read Chad's note. As always with Chad, his message was short and sweet. *Will visit on Monday and leaving on Tuesday, have a great weekend.*

Knowing Chad's protocol, it wouldn't do any good to inquire about why he was visiting so soon and responded with a simple okay. Was his visit just his due diligence or was it the news he had been waiting and wanting to hear; that Chad would name him permanent publisher of the *Daily Reporter*? Just maybe, his lifelong dream of being a publisher was coming true. He wholeheartedly believed he had done absolutely everything necessary for him to reach his goal; however, he would have to wait until

Monday to find out. That meant a long weekend was in store for him. However, before he knew it, he was on his way back to Oakmont Sunday afternoon.

After a quick stop to the Hampton Inn to unload his belongings, he proceeded to his office to catch up on anything important before Chad arrived on Monday. It didn't take long for him to catch up on things and instead of heading back to the hotel; he enjoyed the sunny afternoon on the deck. After two hours outside, Walt called it a day, besides the coolness of an autumn day would soon invade the deck area. Walt had a smile on his face as he locked the doors to the main entrance. Walking to his car, Walt stopped and turned around admiring the newspaper name on the front facade. He had a gut feeling that tomorrow would be a great day, just maybe the best day of his life.

Experiencing a restless night, Monday morning eventually arrived for Walt. He kept his usual routine of exercising in the hotel. Once he was through, he would take coffee back to his room. While enjoying his coffee, his phone dinged. A text from Chad read: *Wait until I get there to have your department meeting.* He replied with a simple *okay*. Liking Chad's message, it created anxious feelings inside him. He emailed all department heads letting them know Chad was visiting today and the weekly meeting would start when Chad arrived.

Arriving at his usual time, he opened his office and turned the lights on, then the Keurig, and finally his laptop. In about three minutes, the Keurig would be ready to spurt out one tasty cup of coffee. With his Marshall University coffee cup in hand, he left his office and made his rounds through the newspaper plant. Usually, he visited editor Todd Haley's office first to see what the news of the day was. Todd's door was partially open, he tapped the door and entered. As usual, Todd greeted him with his usual good morning grumble.

"Back at you, what's the big news of the day?"

"It was a slow weekend, so we are using fluff stories we had archived. Great human-interest stories readers like to read. Hope they like them. Why is Chad visiting?"

"Not sure, maybe he will make me the permanent publisher here."

"Well, I hope so, we are getting back to normal here, and the employees love working for you."

"That's good to hear, guess we'll find out soon."

Leaving Todd's office, he visited each department head, and everything was going great, and no surprises should come up in the department head meetings. Entering his office, he noticed the door to the deck was open. He knew he hadn't opened it because it was a chilly morning and didn't know what to make of it being open. Approaching the door, Chad surprised him with a big grin all over his face.

Once back inside, they both took a seat at the conference table. Chad cut to the chase and reached into his briefcase and handed a letter to Walt. With his heart thumping, he read the letter slowly and then exclaimed, "Yes, yes, I accept the job offer of the publisher of the *Daily Reporter*."

"I thought you would. The details are straightforward; do you have any questions?"

"Nope, I'm ready to lead this newspaper permanently."

"What time is your meeting?"

"In a few of minutes, they should arrive shortly."

He was strict about being on time for meetings, and

the management team arrived one by one. Taking their usual seat around the conference table, each noticed that Walt was not in the room, the room felt like a funeral parlor where people grieved over the unexpected death of a loved one.

Suddenly, Chad stood up and cleared his throat. "I'm here today to announce the new publisher of the *Daily Reporter*." Puzzling glances traveled back and forth around the conference table. After a moment of silence, the door to the deck opened, and Walt entered smiling from ear to ear. Applause erupted, and high fives found their way around the table. His lifelong dream had finally come true.

CHAPTER 25

Carla turned on her iPad and then poured herself a cup of coffee from her four-cup brewer. Although it was old, it served its purpose many times over. She added non-fat hazelnut creamer to make it drinkable since she couldn't stomach black coffee. Taking a seat on the stool at the bar separating the living space from the kitchen, she pushed on the email icon. Her email loaded quickly; one message from Laura immediately caught her eye and opened it. Laura was informing her that Chad appointed Walt permanent publisher of the *Daily Reporter* and included a link to the website story. Carla had yet to take a sip of her coffee when her phone buzzed and flashed. She looked the caller ID; it was from the *Daily Reporter*. She answered it, listened and responded, "Well, I guess congratulations are in order, so congrats!"

Putting Walt on speaker, she took a sip of her coffee listening to him. "Thanks, can you do lunch on Wednesday, and I will fill you in on my golf outing with the

Oakmont Golf Mafia and the list of golfers who have played at The Snead?"

"Oakmont Mafia Group, what's that all about?"

"Just kidding, you on?"

"Absolutely, how about McGruder's?"

"Haven't been there for lunch yet, sounds great. Noonish, okay with you?"

"Works for me, see you then, and congrats again."

Following up on the email she received from Laura, Carla called Laura to let her know about the lunch meeting since Walt and Laura were a couple now. Calling her, Laura immediately answered as though she was expecting a call from her. "Hello, Carla, you are calling awful early, what's on your mind?"

"Shortly after I got your email, I received a call from your honey. Walt wanted to have lunch with me and tell me about his golf outing with the movers and shakers or the Oakmont Golf Mafia as he called them. I didn't want you to think I was trying to steal him."

"Nonsense, Carla. He called me as soon as Chad appointed him as publisher and told me about lunch to discuss what he found out. I told him I was fine with it, besides he's not your type."

"Really, what makes you say that?"

"Trust me, Carla, he's not. Gotta run, have a good lunch with him and solve a murder."

As Chad said in his text, he left on Tuesday afternoon. Walt was on his own and felt relieved that he was the one permanently in charge and not just a substitute.

As planned, Walt and Carla were meeting for lunch at noon on Wednesday at McGruder's Irish Pub to discuss what he had found out about the Oakmont Mafia Group that played at The Snead. Arriving first, he grabbed a table with a window in the front corner of the pub where they could talk in private.

As usual, Carla arrived a little late and spotted him in a corner booth and slid in opposite him. Looking around to see if she knew anyone; she didn't, and that pleased her. Walt had already scanned the pub with the same results. He didn't want rumors flying around about him meeting a hot lady who was also one badass detective.

Even though the pub was bustling with activity, an attractive young lady arrived to wait on them right away. Carla glanced up from the menu, and her face lit up. Seeing Sam standing at their booth thrilled her given their last conversation the other day. However, Sam's expression told a different story. "Sam, so good to see you, how are you doing and how's school going?"

"Things are great, and school is going just fine, thank you for asking. Are you ready to order?"

"First, let me introduce you to Walt Blevins, the new publisher of the *Daily Reporter*."

"Nice to meet you Mr. Blevins, have you guys decided what you want?"

Walt responded, "Yes, bring us both the Rueben with house chips and water with lemon."

"Great, I'll place your order and be back with your water."

Walt said, "Carla, I guess you know her fairly well. Is she always that cold and aloof?"

"No, normally she is very perky and friendly, something's bothering her."

"What do you mean?"

"It may have something to do with the cases I'm working on, besides aren't you supposed to be telling me what you found out from golfing with the Oakmont Golf Mafia, as you named them?"

"Yeah, I guess so. The information is interesting, but I'm not sure it will help that much."

"Let me be the one that makes that decision."

"Okay, here we go. Mayor Lester James, Judge-Executive Mike Roberts, Kevin Oliver, Wylie Adkins, Keith Edwards, Jeff Walker, and Cliff Kagan make up the Oakmont Golf Mafia, as I appropriately named them."

"Don't know all of them, is that it?"

"No, here's where it gets a little interesting. These guys, and get this, Mark Alison, always took a golfing trip each spring to The Snead. They all bought several golf fedora ball markers in case they lost one or wanted to give one out to friends. That means there are probably quite a few of those ball markers among the Oakmont Golf Mafia or floating around golf courses in Oakmont."

Before Carla responded, their orders arrived. However, it was not Sam delivering them and that concerned her. Asking where she was, the server informed Carla that Sam left abruptly for no reason at all. A concerned frown painted her face. Walt recognizing the frown on Carla's face said, "What is going on with you and Sam. From the look on your face, you are very disturbed that she left."

"Just let it go, Walt."

"Hey, no problem."

They ate in silence until Spike came through the door and took a seat at the bar. Carla eyed him and wondered where his friend was. Maybe his friend was just late. Pointing toward the man, she asked, "Walt, do you know that man at the bar?"

"Never seen him before; besides, I'm new in town. Obviously, you have, or you wouldn't have asked me."

"So, I guess he's not part of the Oakmont Golf Mafia."

"Correct, never saw him before."

"Just wondering, I've seen him twice when I've been in here. He gets really friendly with Sam."

"Does he have something to do with your case?"

Ignoring his question, she quickly changed the subject. "Well, I guess I better get back to the police station. Thanks for lunch and the information."

"You are welcome. Hope something turns up for you, and if I can be of any further help, please contact me."

Carla took one more glance at Spike at the bar and got up to leave. Walt followed and walked out with her. While outside shaking hands, and saying goodbye, Spike looked at them wondering what brought them here together. Spike caught the eye of the bartender who turned around to face him. Spike order his usual, Smithwick's and a Reuben. Before the bartender went to place the order, he asked, "Is Sam working today?"

"She was here earlier, but abruptly left after waiting on that couple that just walked out. She told me something personal had come up, and she'd be back later. That's all I know."

"Hey, thanks, will you let me know if she returns before I finish my lunch?"

"No problem, I'll put your order in and be back with your beer."

Spike wondered what Detective McBride might have said to her that made her leave so abruptly? His lunch arrived, and he ate in silence hoping Sam would return. With lunch finished, the bartender stopped by and asked

Spike if he needed anything else. Spike shook his head back and forth. Assuming that, the bartender had his check ready and laid it on the bar. Before the bartender left, he asked, "Sam ever return?" The bartender shook his head back and forth. Spike acknowledged, glancing at his check, he laid down twenty dollars and left.

CHAPTER 26

Although Sam entered McGruder's with her usually upbeat persona, inside her, fear was running rampant. She hid it well as her coworkers were oblivious to her inner self. Given there were at least two hours before the lunch crowd would arrive, Sam kept busy and to herself keeping her emotions in check. She hoped to make it through the day with no visits from Carla or Spike. Time passed rather quickly, and a few patrons arrived for an early lunch. Within a half-hour, an unusually large lunch crowd for a Thursday filled the pub. Although being table slammed, it kept her mind off the anxieties she felt inside, and to the patrons, she was her usual cheery and perky self. Before Sam knew it, the lunch crowd had left, and she hoped the rest of her shift would be uneventful.

Unfortunately, she spotted Carla walking through the main entrance and heading straight towards her, her pulse and respiration increased, she wiped away invisible sweat collecting on her brow as Carla took her place at the bar. Carla was trying to make eye contact with her, but Sam discreetly looked away toward the kitchen avoiding eye contact.

"Hey Sam, how are you doing? What happened yesterday, you disappeared. I didn't mean to disturb you, talk to me."

Meeting her contact, she reluctantly responded, "I had a personal situation to attend to at school. It was nothing. Today, I'm back to my normal self. Can I get you anything?"

"No, I just came to check on you. Have those two guys been bothering you again?"

"No, why?"

"Sam, the information on the business card you gave me is an alias Spike uses. I couldn't find any information about Jason Alexander Doyle, anywhere. I called the number several times, no one ever answered."

"Hm, is that a problem?"

"Just be careful and try to avoid him as much as possible. If you must wait on them, don't get personal or answer any of their questions. And if you ever need me, just call, okay?"

Sam nodded. Relieved that Carla was out of her hair, for now, Sam wanted to get through the rest of the day without seeing Spike. With about ten minutes left in her shift, she was still feeling relieved that she didn't have to face Spike, especially after yesterday's uncomfortable incident. The clock on the wall showed five minutes to go, and Sam wouldn't have to face Spike today. The minute hand reached twelve, her day had ended, she breathed a sigh of relief. Waiting for Mandy, the afternoon server, to come out of the ladies' room, Spike entered the restaurant and sat in his usual spot. She looked for Mandy, but she had not clocked in yet leaving her no choice but to wait on him. "Here's your beer, Mandy will take care of you, my shift is over."

Ignoring her response intentionally, he replied in a wolfish-like tone. "Fine, but where were you yesterday? They said you had to leave abruptly everything okay?" She gave him the same old story she told Carla and hoped that would take care of his curiosity. Unfortunately for Sam, he wouldn't let that end there and continued, "Has Detective McBride been in to see you?" She quickly shook her head back and forth. Sensing she wasn't telling the truth, slapped his hand on the counter. "If you know what's good for you, don't lie to me!"

Almost in tears, she said, "Okay, she came in today to see how I was doing, and that was it. She asked me if you were bothering me, but I told her no, and that was the end of the conversation, and that's the whole truth. After that, she left."

"That a girl, there's nothing to worry about; I would never harm your pretty face."

After downing his beer, Spike slammed a five-dollar-bill down hard on the bar startling her. He stormed out of the pub. Fear captured her body as she trembled inside, scared as hell, she ran to her car and sped home. Pulling in her dedicated parking space, she turned off her car and sat in silence. Emotions were erupting inside as she scanned the parking lot. Nothing, there was no one in sight. She breathed a sigh of relief and exited her car. Before unlocking her apartment door, she spotted a figure in her peripheral vision. She couldn't make out who it was. The man entered the far end of the parking lot; he stopped and stared in her direction. With her keys in hand, she fumbled putting them in the lock as she was keeping an eye on the man.

Finally, she found the keyhole and turned the key unlocking her apartment door, she quickly entered, slammed the door, and dead-bolted the door. Standing against the metal kitchen door; her respiration grew heavy as panic infused bile made its trek upward. Muted shades of darkness created a haunted-house-like atmosphere, while shadows drifted across the walls of the kitchen. An eerie quiet silence whispered throughout her small apartment. A dull thud-like noise traveled to her from the front of the apartment. A scream filled the apartment. Tears of uncertainty rolled from the corner of her eyes, she wiped them away repeatedly to no avail. Knowing she left a knife on the counter before going to work that day, she found it, clutched in her hand creating a white-knuckled grip. Quickly taking a deep breath and exhaling, she flipped on the light in the kitchen, peaceful fluorescent light surrounded her.

With her heart thumping, she walked to the entry to the living room. With adrenalin controlling her every movement, she was ready to use the knife and kill, if necessary. Silently counting to three, she flipped on the living room light. Nothing, the room was silent and peaceful. Walking to her bedroom, she flipped on the ceiling light. A set of bi-fold doors to the closet were on the wall opposite the bedroom door. Approaching them, she prepared to defend herself. She swung them open expecting the worse. Her dry cleaning hung on the clothes bar undisturbed, she moved them apart, nothing. After a big sigh, she locked her bedroom door and placed a chair under the doorknob hoping that would be enough to save her. Feeling a cold dark sensation invade her body; emotions finally exploded releasing the pent-up fear for the moment. Placing the knife on the bedside table, she collapsed on her bed.

Uncontrollable weeping filled her bedroom and shivering catapulted throughout her body. She pulled her knees to her chest as though she was in her mother's womb before birth safe from harm. Her emotions finally succumbed to a deep sleep. Emotionally drained and breathing heavily, cold sweat cooled the temperature rising in her body until the ringing of her doorbell woke her. As the ringing subsided, fear and paranoia were retaking control of her soul. Remaining in a vulnerable fetal position, she pulled a comforter over her for warmth and safety. Praying again; a peaceful silence enveloped her as she drifted back into a deep sleep only to wake up from a terrorizing nightmare. Spike, standing over her with her knife, was ready to strike, to carve her up. A banging noise coming from her back door stole her breath away, she gasped breathing heavily and exhaling. Her fear was real.

Grabbing the knife from the bedside table, she hid in the pitch-black closet praying the banging would stop. Cell service inside her apartment was spotty; however, she dialed Carla's number anyway and waited, and waited. Although the screen on her phone showed the call was going through, call failed reared its ugly head. She tried again, the same result. The banging continued as she crouched in her closet. Deafening silence pounded the walls until a sound similar to glass breaking exploded throughout the apartment.

CHAPTER 27

With Walt settled as publisher of the *Daily Reporter*, he was looking forward to his date with Laura. When he called her to inform her of his good news, she suggested they celebrate. Both were looking forward to spending intimate time together since he would be living in Oakmont permanently. With reservations at 7:00 PM at Avondale Country Club, she suggested he arrive at her townhome by 6:30 PM for a ceremonial glass of wine. As he approached the door, she was waiting to greet him. Before he could do anything, she flung her arms around him. Returning her embrace, he could feel her firm breasts tantalizing him. Before he could even say a word, she released her sensual embrace, caressed his face gently, and planted a passionate, but gentle kiss on his lips. It was a very tender soft kiss he willingly returned. Peering in her haunting green eyes; his hormones rage inside him.

"Wow. What was that for?"

"Let's just call it a congratulatory kiss."

"Well, that's the best congratulatory kiss I've ever had."

"Good answer and the right one, Mr. Publisher," Laura said with a sneaky grin on her face. "We should have time for a small glass of wine before we go, okay?"

Although his hormones were looking for more, he nodded. Laura already had two glasses of Chianti Classico poured. She went to the large island bar and picked up both glasses of wine and joined him on the love seat. He swirled the wine around and around smelling the aromatic nuances of the wine permeating from the glass. Taking a sip, he savored the wine on his palate. An excellent tasting wine he thought, but not as tasty as her soft lips.

"Walt, let's make a toast."

"Hm, a great idea."

"Here's to us, may we share many more glasses of wine together and grow our friendship even further?"

"I'd like that very much, thank you."

They both raised their glasses and softly clinked them together. After another sip of the wine, Laura placed her wine glass on the table and took his drink out of his hand and placed it on the table. A little surprised, he studied her haunting green eyes. She smiled, leaned in and kissed him again. This time it was more than a soft kiss sending his hormones into action. Returning her passionate kiss; the chemistry inside his body was erupting. Longing for more of him; her kisses went deeper tasting his sultry-hot sweetness. Pulling her close to him; he felt her passion and heat as her firm breasts moved against his chest. Although he was longing for more, he didn't want to take advantage of her and pulled away from her. Picking up his wineglass, he tasted the wine and then sat it down. "I think it's time we went to dinner. I don't want to rush things, you know."

"Yeah, I guess we better go, or we might not leave at all, besides I am getting hungry, we can finish our wine later."

Arriving at Avondale Country Club about ten minutes late wasn't a problem since she had reserved the private Sunroom. A bottle of Chianti Classico and two wine glasses were waiting for them as she requested. Almost immediately their waitress, Carrie, arrived and greeted them. Carrie recognized Walt from his picture in the paper, and introductions weren't necessary.

"May I pour you both some wine?"

Laura said, "That would be great Carrie, thank you."

"You are welcome," replied Carrie. "I'll give you both some time to look the menu over, and I'll be back in a few minutes to take your order."

The Sunroom, as it was so appropriately named, was just off the side entrance of the Victorian style mansion that housed the main dining room. Even though windows surrounded the room that looked out over the main parking lot and grounds, it still provided a romantic and intimate setting for any occasion. Unfortunately, anyone entering the mansion through the side entrance could see inside the Sunroom, but that didn't matter to anyone. Carrie returned and took their orders, then left. Within minutes, salads and fresh bread arrived. The conversation was lively and intimately personal. Walt couldn't keep his eyes off her stunning beauty and her undeniable sexiness. Not wanting to appear like a gawker stalking her, he broke eye contact with her scanning the parking lot seeing a couple walking toward the side entrance. As they got closer to the building, the man looked very familiar to him. Laura noticed she had lost Walt's attentiveness and tapped him on his hand. Feeling a little embarrassed, he took her hand in his and kissed it gently.

"Laura, I'm sorry. I didn't want you to feel I was gawking at you, but you are so damn beautiful and sexy."

"Thank you, but you can gawk all you want."

As the couple walked up the steps to the door, the man locked eyes with Walt. It was then he remembered where he saw this man. Noticing that Walt kept staring at the couple, she tapped him on the arm and said, "Walt, do you know him?"

"No, I've just seen him before, and I now remember where. He was at McGruder's when I had lunch with Carla. It's obvious that you don't know him either since you asked me. Do you know the lady with him?"

"I don't know her personally, but I believe I've met her before around the courthouse. I think she works for the family court system. However, I don't know her last name though, but I think her first name is Lana." Intimate conversation filled the Sunroom, and it was apparent that they were enjoying each other's company by the laughter emanating from the Sunroom.

Meanwhile, the hostess seated the other couple in the main dining room where Carrie waited on them. The lady ordered a glass of Alpha Omega Unoaked Chardonnay from California while the man ordered a Smithwick's Irish Ale.

The man said, "Lana, thank you for bringing me here. I've never been here before. This is a real classy place."

"You are welcome, Jason. And yes, this is a very nice country club, isn't the mansion beautiful?"

"Yes, it's quite a place. Did you notice the couple in the little room at the side entrance?"

"Oh, you mean the Sunroom. Yeah, the lady is a lawyer in town, and the man is Walt Blevins, the new publisher of the *Daily Reporter*. I've seen the lady around the courthouse. I believe her name is Laura. However, I don't remember her last name. Why do you ask?"

"Hm, no reason. Maybe our waitress knows her last name. She seems to know everyone here, and it shouldn't be a big deal to find out, right?"

"I don't want to pry, can we let it go, okay?"

Lana thought it was strange that Jason was so interested in finding out Laura's last name. She was getting to know him but also didn't want to chase him off. Lana felt Jason's dejected expression. Carrie arrived to take their orders and noticed that Jason's glass was empty. "Sir, may I get you another beer?"

"Please, I guess I'm thirsty tonight, thank you."

"You're welcome. I'll be right back with it."

Carrie walked away when Lana said, "Carrie, may I ask you a question?" She nodded. "The couple in the Sunroom. I've met the lady before, isn't that Laura, can't seem to remember her last name?"

"Yeah, I'm not good with last names either. It's Watson, Laura Watson. She's an attorney in town and her brother, Chris Abbott, is our GM and golf pro here at Avondale."

"Yeah, that's right. Laura Watson, she is stunning. Thank you!"

"Hey, no problem."

Jason smiled and thanked Lana. He had a way of getting what he wanted, something he learned from his days in the special forces. Their meals came, and they ate in silence as his mind was somewhere else.

Finished with their meals and the bottle of Chianti Classico, Laura waved at Carrie for their check. While on the way to her townhome she broke the silence in the car. "Hey, the night is still young, you want to come in and finish what we started before dinner?"

Hearing such a question, he smiled as hormones danced in veins. "What do you mean?"

"You know, finish our wine, what did you think I meant?"

A little embarrassed and disappointed, the rest of the drive to her townhome was in complete silence. Walt didn't know what she meant since their time together before dinner went a little further than he planned. He liked her a lot and didn't want to move too fast. Once inside her townhome, he sat on the loveseat, while she grabbed the wine glasses. Although the wine was open for several hours, it surprised him at how good it still tasted. Knowing he should call it a night, he finished his wine and put his wineglass on the table.

"Laura, I think I better leave and get a good night's rest, I have a busy day tomorrow."

"Hm, Mr. Publisher has to get his beauty rest, does he?"

"That's right. I had a fantastic evening with you, thank you."

"Ditto that…Mr. Publisher."

Walking him to the door, she hugged him tightly. Gazing into each other's eyes, she leaned in, kissing him goodnight. Her passionate kiss excited him. Returning it with a long and lingering one, she searched deeper and deeper for more. Feeling her firm breasts against his body sent his hormones searching for more. Her breasts were firm, and her nipples craved his arousing touch.

Feeling his primal urges against her body, her kisses went deeper and deeper swallowing the hot passion boiling inside him. Burning desires were running rampant throughout them. Grabbing his hand, she led him to her bedroom and closed the door. Heat and passion exploded as their bodies moved naturally and rhythmically extinguishing the fires inside their soul.

CHAPTER 28

While reviewing evidence and interview transcripts of her two unsolved cases, Carla's cell phone rang. Not recognizing the number, voicemail picked up the call. Within seconds, her voicemail icon lit up. Putting the speaker on, she listened to the message. "Detective McBride, this is Greg Fields, from McGruder's. I'm sorry to bother you, but I didn't know who else to call. I'm concerned about Sam. Please call me or stop by the restaurant as soon as possible so I can tell you more. We are not open just yet, so call me at this number when you arrive, and I will meet you at the main entrance. Thanks."

With the speaker off, her mind raced with all kinds of horrible thoughts. Her heart thumped hard and loud as she took several deep breaths trying to ease the anxiety erupting inside her. Ever since she discovered that Jason Alexander Doyle was an alias that Spike used, she had a great concern for Sam's well-being. Grabbing her purse, Carla made a B-Line to McGruder's. Not open for another hour, she parked in front of the restaurant and dialed the number left on her voicemail. Within a minute, Greg Fields appeared at the door. Flashing her badge; the door opened, and she entered.

"Detective McBride, thanks for coming right away."

"What is going on with Sam?"

"Follow me back to my office where we can talk privately." After they entered his office, he motioned her to take a seat. "You were here last Wednesday having lunch with the new publisher, Walt Blevins, weren't you?" Carla nodded. "She waited on you, took your order and immediately left; you remember?" Once more she nodded. "On Thursday after you were here, that man she gets chummy with showed up. That's the last time she's been at work. She hasn't called to let us know anything, I'm really concerned something has happened to her, this is not like her at all, she's very responsible."

"Did you call the university to see if she is attending classes?"

"Didn't have to, they called me. Sam was to cover some big event on campus that evening but didn't show up. With no immediate family, McGruder's was the only emergency contact listed on her school records."

Getting more concerned by the minute, she asked, "Has anyone been to her apartment to check on her?"

"Mandy, one of our other servers, drove by and knocked on her door, but Sam didn't answer."

"Was her car there?" Greg shook his head back and forth. "Is there anything else you can tell me? Anything at all?"

"Hm, not really. Is Sam in any danger?"

"Possibly, if she reaches out to you, please have her call me immediately? Would you give me her address, I will run by and check things out?"

With the address in hand, Sam's apartment was near the university and close to McGruder's. The University Terrace Apartments contained eight ground-floor units. Knocking on Sam's door several times, silence and uncertainty responded loud and clear. With no one stirring around outside, she knocked on each apartment door hoping to find out something. Striking out, she assumed that all the tenants were students and likely in class. As she stared at Sam's apartment door, a sickening feeling erupted in her stomach. Noticing a sign on the front of the building with a phone number, she put her phone on speaker and dialed the number. It rang and rang and rang. Ready to end the call, a man finally answered and identified himself.

"Rick, this is Detective Carla McBride with the Oakmont Police Department."

"Okay, what's going on, I don't want any trouble."

"I need information, that's all. I'm trying to locate the young lady in apartment four, Samantha Lewis. She hasn't been to work since last Thursday and didn't show up to cover a big important event on campus. Have you seen or heard from her?"

"Nah, but I rarely have any contact with any tenants unless their rent is late, or something needs repairing."

"Is there any way you can let me in her apartment to look around, I think something terrible may have happened to her."

"Sorry detective, under strict orders, you'll need a warrant and probable cause. I know the law."

"I'm sure you do, sir. Time is important here, so can you bend the rules for me?"

"Sorry, I follow the rules, don't want to lose my job, if you know what I mean?"

"Right, I'll get the warrant and get back with you. Can you tell me what kind of car she has?"

"Let me look at her file." Over the speaker sounds of a file cabinet drawer opening and closing tested her patience. "Here we go, according to her file, she drives a white 2004 Jaguar X-type."

"Thanks, you've been a big help."

Rick hung up without saying another word. Scanning the streetscape in front of the apartment complex, no Jaguar in sight. At the end of the complex, a driveway went around to the rear of the building. Taking the driveway to the back of the apartment complex, the sight of a white Jag in front of the rear entrance of apartment four sent her pulse racing. Walking over to the Jag, she tried the doors, all locked. The hood of the car was stone cold heightening her concern.

Scanning the parking lot, she looked for anything that might help determine her whereabouts; however, nothing immediately caught her eye. The back entrance to Sam's apartment had a solid metal door with a small square window. Walking over to the door, she peeked through the small window and gasped. Queasiness in her stomach slowly moved up to her throat. Taking a deep breath, she swallowed hard forcing the uneasiness back down for the moment. Immediately, she re-dialed Rick's number putting it on speaker. After a few rings, he answered.

"Rick, this is Detective McBride again."

"Look, detective, I told you to get a warrant."

"Sir, I looked through the window in the rear door of her apartment, the apartment appears ransacked. You better get down here, there is no time to get a warrant. I'm calling for backup now and a forensics team."

"Damn, I'm on my way, ten minutes, tops."

Returning to the front of the apartment complex, Carla waited for backup to arrive. After several minutes, two patrol officers arrived at about the same time as Rick. Carla and Officer Pete Wiesmann escorted Rick around back to see the damage inside the apartment. The other officer secured the front entrance of Sam's apartment. With the owners of the apartment complex notified, Rick unlocked the door. Ordered to stay a safe distance from the building, Rick sauntered to the far end of the parking lot.

"Officer Wiesmann, we go in on my count, okay?" He nodded. Weapons drawn, Carla counted to three, and Officer Weismann cautiously opened the door stepping inside scanning the small kitchenette. All clear and motioned her inside. A barstool tipped over on the floor laid on several broken dishes. Down a short hallway, the main living area awaited them. Officer Wiesmann scanned the living room, all clear again. A modern glass table smashed on the floor laid on several pieces of shattered glass covered with dried blood heightening Carla's concern for Sam.

Only one room remained. Pulse racing, the door to the bedroom was closed. On her count, Officer Wiesmann opened the door seeing her clothes scattered everywhere. The doors to the closet were wide open, recent dry-cleaning hung neatly on the clothes bar. On the floor, a bedside table lamp laid, the shade bent beyond repair. The door to the bathroom was closed. Opening the door; her personal items neatly displayed on the vanity made no sense. A colorful shower curtain spanned the width of tub and shower enclosure. Pulling it back, Carla let out a big sigh of relief.

Sam had disappeared. The walls swirled around her

as fear exploded in her soul. Several deep cleansing breaths calmed her pulse but did nothing to ease the guilt and anxiety rocking her soul at the moment. Returning to the parking lot, she scoured the area looking for anything out of the ordinary while forensics arrived to collect evidence inside her apartment. Near the end of the building, she noticed a shiny reflection on the ground near apartment number eight. Walking toward it; a small shiny disc glared up at her sending her pulse soaring. With a gloved hand, she stooped down to examine it. Picking it up and turning it over, she'd seen it before, and it spelled trouble.

Assuming it belonged to whoever lived in apartment eight, Carla knocked on the door several times, no answer. A white shade covering the small window in the door blocked her view of the inside. Officer Wiesmann, standing nearby, watched her frustrations crashed against the door repeatedly. "Detective, is everything okay?" he asked. Shrugging her shoulders, she walked away mumbling four-letter vulgarity under her breath as she massaged her angry-looking fist.

Pondering about the ball marker she had just found; she knew one thing for sure. Two people were dead, and now Samantha Lewis was mysteriously missing. The same ball marker found at each crime scene connected her to the killer without a doubt.

CHAPTER 29

The police scanner at the *Daily Reporter* was buzzing with normal activity as usual; however, police and crime reporter Marshall Robinson picked up on something more interesting about an apparent break-in and a missing person at #4 University Terrace Apartments. Known as Marsh, he was a veteran reporter with many awards. He grabbed his backpack which contained his iPad and camera and out he went. When Marsh arrived, it was still an active crime scene. He spotted Detective Carla McBride talking with several patrolmen. Crime scene tape was covering the front door of apartment four, but nowhere else. The door was open, and Marsh could see a flurry of activity inside. He saw Detective McBride coming towards him and braced himself for what was to come. "What are you doing here?"

"Just doing my job, like you are. What do we have here? I heard on the scanner something about a break-in and maybe a missing person. Who is missing?"

"You know I can't tell you anything until our investigation is complete. Then, I'll send you a press release like I always do. For now, stay out of our way and let us finish."

Marsh knew the drill and wandered around taking several photos of the building. Walking around back, he found the same thing. Crime scene tape strung across the parking lot from Sam's rear apartment door. Shooting a few more pictures, he spotted a man standing at the far end of the parking lot. Maybe just an innocent bystander; however, he would find out just the same. Putting his camera in the backpack, he sauntered over to the man. "What's going on here?"

"Apartment four appears ransacked, and the tenant has not been to work or school since last Thursday."

"Hm, whose apartment is it anyway?"

"According to our records, Samantha Lewis, a college student. I also understand she works at McGruder's. That's about all I know."

"Is that her car there, the white Jag? I've always wanted one of those. Do you mind if I take a picture of it?"

"I believe it's hers, but not sure. Take all the pictures you want."

Marsh took his iPhone out and shot two photos of the rear of the car capturing the license plate. Then a couple from the side and the front to make it look like it was a personal thing rather than a newspaper reporter probing. With all the information he needed, he proceeded to the front of the building looking for Detective McBride. Informed she was still inside, he returned to the newspaper to work on his story. Back at the *Daily Reporter*, he told Todd about what was going on. In the newspaper business, they had seen this many times before, so it was not a big news story at the moment. Marsh called a friend at the Department of Motor Vehicles to see if he could find out who owned the white Jag. Marsh called and asked for Myra. After bantering with his wife, he got what he wanted. Smiling over the phone, he said, "Love you, too. I won't be late since we are having my favorite dish tonight, pork ribs, sauerkraut, and dumplings."

Once finished with his story, he emailed it to Todd. A few minutes later, he went to Todd's office to let him know about the email he had sent. When he arrived at his office, Marsh knocked on the half-opened door. Todd motioned him to come in. Marsh opened the door fully seeing he was meeting with publisher Walt Blevins. "I finished the brief about the possible missing person even though we haven't received a press release from Detective McBride yet. Once we get it, we will be ready to roll with it."

"Got it, keep me informed."

Walt had been listening intently to their conversation, and after Marsh left, he asked Todd what was going on. Todd informed him that a local employer had reported to the local police that one of their employees had not reported to work or been to school since last Thursday. The individual had returned no phone calls and did not answer her apartment door. He explained this happens a lot and usually the person finally shows up, and all ends well. Todd explained to him they would wait on a press release from Detective McBride before deciding where to place the story.

When Walt heard Detective McBride's name, his ears perked up, and his eyes opened wide. "So, this could be something bigger?"

"Could be, just depends on what they find out in their investigation."

"I thought it was just a missing person report."

"It is for now; however, they entered the individual's apartment, and it resembles a break-in. Things tossed around, broken glass, the usual things. The individual's vehicle is still there, her phone, her clothes, and personal items were still in her apartment. It certainly appears like an abduction, but you never know these days."

"So, the individual is a female. Do you know her name?"

"We don't have official confirmation yet; however, the owner of the car in the parking lot is Samantha Lewis, a college student that works at McGruder's."

"Oh, I've met her before. I had lunch with Detective McBride there, and she waited on us, friendly and pretty."

Surprised at Walt's answer, he asked, "You and McBride an item. I thought you had a few dates with that female lawyer, Laura Watson?"

Walt had yet to inform Todd about what was going on; that he had been doing some investigating on his own. He planned to get to that eventually, but not until there was something substantial to tell him, so he had to come up with something quick. Walt responded with a short laugh before answering. "Oh, Laura and Detective McBride are like sisters. She wants to throw Laura a surprise birthday party; you know the big 4-0 is coming up soon."

"Well, you know, it wouldn't look good if the publisher of the newspaper was dating hot-shot Detective McBride, would it?"

Walt laughed. "Probably not. Guess I should get out

of your hair and let you get back to work. Would you mind letting me know of any further developments on this missing person story?"

Todd nodded and thought to himself, something is going on other than Walt and Detective McBride planning a birthday party.

CHAPTER 30

Day by day, Walt was getting more comfortable as a publisher and his fears slowly subsided. The employees at the *Daily Reporter* were getting more comfortable with his management style as well. He believed in his heart that being in Mark's office was the right thing to do and that has helped the healing process move along.

His relationship with Laura blossomed quickly. Their love for each other wasn't just puppy love or a strong physical attraction. It was real and becoming the talk of the town given his high-profile position in the community. Their relationship almost mirrored Mark and Joanne Alison's life. Walt felt like life couldn't be any better, just maybe he had met his soulmate in Laura Watson. They liked being seen together in public and being active in the community.

With the annual charity ball, a black-tie formal affair, several weeks away his presence was mandatory. Needing a tuxedo and all the accessories, he asked Todd where was the best place in town to buy men's clothing.

Todd informed him Amsbury's Fine Clothing had been around for a very long time and had the best women and men's apparel in the city. With several black-tie events he would attend, purchasing a tuxedo rather than renting one made common sense. The charity ball would be the first of many black-tie events to attend as publisher. Having a very light day since the month had ended meant he would have free time to visit Amsbury's Fine Clothing that afternoon after lunch with Laura. She would help him choose the right tuxedo.

Amsbury's, located across the street from the Apollo Café, had the finest men's clothing in Oakmont. Walt called and made a 12:30 PM reservation just in case Apollo's Café was extremely busy. Arriving a few minutes early, a hostess escorted Laura to the table Walt had reserved. Several minutes later Walt came, and the hostess escorted him to his table. As he suspected, Apollo's was very busy, and he was glad he made that reservation, he never wanted egg on his face in her presence. Walt leaned over and greeted Laura with a kiss on her cheek and sat down across from her. With their lunch order in, he looked deep into her eyes. "You are going with me to Amsbury's and help me pick out a tuxedo, right?"

"Of course, thank you for asking me, I had some free time after lunch, I don't have another client until 3:00 PM, should be fun, can't wait."

Lunch arrived, and they ate while having a casual conversation about the upcoming charity event. After they finished their meal, they made the short walk across the street to Amsbury's. Entering through a single wooden door with glass inserts reminiscent of old classic downtown buildings built over one-hundred-years ago; a chime rang out. They could see a man, presumably the owner, waiting on a customer sporting a gold fedora. The owner glanced their way. "Just browse around, and I will be with you shortly."

Walt nodded but took notice of the gentleman he was waiting on; he knew had seen him somewhere before but couldn't remember where. A blank stare painted the face of the customer. He heard the owner tell the customer it would be about a week before his suit would be ready. The customer just nodded and walked toward the door, he paused and locked eyes with Walt momentarily before he quickly left the store. The owner walked over and greeted them.

Walt said, "Hi, nice to meet you, Mr. Amsbury. I'm Walt Blevins, publisher of the *Daily Reporter*, and meet my girlfriend, Laura Watson."

"It's a pleasure to meet you both. What are you looking for, Mr. Blevins?"

"I need a tuxedo, a dark suit, and all the right accessories for the charity ball."

"Ah yes, the charity ball. You've come to the right place. Do you want to buy or rent a tuxedo; we do both?"

"Since there are several black-tie events I will attend, buying one is the smart thing to do."

"Make sense. If you wear it three times, you've paid for the cost. Have you picked out one already?"

Walt walked with Mr. Amsbury over to the rack of tuxedos, pointed out which one. Returning to the counter, Mr. Amsbury took Walt's measurements. He picked out the dark suit he wanted and all the accessories for the tuxedo. Walt paid for his clothes, and Mr. Amsbury inquired if he could help either of them with anything else, Walt shook his head back and forth. Mr. Amsbury informed him he would call him when his clothes were ready.

As Walt and Laura walked toward the door, the thought of Spike entered his mind. He turned around and said, "Oh, I have one more question. The previous customer, I've met him somewhere before, but don't recall his name. Do you mind telling me his name in case I see him again?"

"No, not all, Jason Alexander Doyle."

"Yeah, that's right, thanks. Would you happen to have Mr. Doyle's phone number? I want to call him and apologize for not recognizing him today."

"Sorry, he didn't leave one. Paid for his suit in cash up front. If he doesn't come back, I'm not out anything."

"That's okay, thanks."

"You are welcome. Thank you for your business."

Walt nodded, and they left the store. He walked Laura back to her office since it wasn't far and was on the way to where he parked. He seemed preoccupied as they walked back, and it concerned her about what was bothering him. "Walt, is everything okay? You seemed a little different after leaving the store. Did I do something wrong?"

"Nah, you did nothing wrong, sorry for worrying you. I see we're at your office now, I'll see you later. Thanks for helping me pick out the clothes."

She nodded and gave him a hug and kiss and went inside her office to get ready for her afternoon appointment. Walking back to his car; what just transpired with Jason Alexander Doyle, aka Spike consumed thoughts. Arriving back at the newspaper, Walt still couldn't get him out of his mind. Coming face to face with Jason was a little unnerving and queasiness settled in his gut.

Unsure of what to do caused even more uneasiness in him. Confronting him was risky. Although his newspaper instincts were telling him to try meeting up with him when he picked up his clothes, the fearful common sense in him said otherwise.

He dialed Carla's phone number hoping for answers and guidance. Several rings, she finally answered. "Do you have a few minutes to talk?"

"Sure, what's up?"

After a short pause, he explained to her he had a run-in with Jason at Amsbury's. Walt held the phone away from him as the four-letter expletives exploded from the other end. During Carla's tirade, Walt could only nod his head during her tongue lashing. The call ended without a goodbye. His face flushed, he got her message loud and clear and certainly didn't want to be on her shit list. Also, he didn't want to endanger himself or especially, Laura.

Carla immediately left the police station and paid a visit to Mr. Amsbury to see what help or information he could give her. Anything would be helpful. It was a short drive, and maybe she could get lucky and find a parking place close. Luck was on her side that day seeing a space right in front of the store. When entering the store, she heard the doorbell sound and Mr. Amsbury looked her way. She walked toward him glancing around the store and noticed a surveillance camera on the ceiling at the rear of the store. He greeted her and identified himself. Flashing her badge, she said, "Mr. Amsbury, I'm Detective McBride of the Oakmont Police Department, and I would like to ask you a few questions about a customer of yours that was in this afternoon. Do you remember a Jason Alexander Doyle?"

"Of course, may I ask why and how you knew this man was even in here today?"

"That's not really important, he was in here today, right?"

Mr. Amsbury nodded and explained what Walt had already told her. "Does that camera work?" He nodded. "Great, may I see the footage of when he was here and if possible, get a still shot of him and at least a copy of the footage?"

She followed him to his office where his laptop was already open and monitoring the store. After putting in the timeframe for the search, they watched the sequence of events unfold just as Walt had explained. After the video finished, she requested a copy and, still shot of Jason, if available. Five minutes later, she left the store with the video on a flash drive.

Across the street near city hall, a man stood watching her as she left the store, got in her car, and drove off. Jason Alexander Doyle, aka Spike, knew why she had been there. Not liking what had just transpired, he sent a text to Rocky: *We need to meet and have a talk but not at McGruder's, somewhere else we haven't been before.*

Rocky replied: *There's this local neighborhood bar called Whisman's Beer Joint on Adams Avenue on the other side of town. Never been there before but heard it's frequented by ordinary local folks, not in the know. Let's meet in an hour.*

Spike replied ...*Great, see you then.*

CHAPTER 31

Whisman's Beer Joint was just as Rocky described it. On the corner of Adams Avenue and Short Street. Constructed of cinder blocks and painted white, one end of the building curved instead of the typical square ninety-degree angle. In the curved section, it had a car-hop window for walk-up customers. Having two doors; windows flanked the main entrance while the other door, near the back of the building, appeared to be for employees and deliveries only.

Spike parked across the street, walked over and entered through the main entrance surveying the place. To the left were booths bordering the walls all the way to the bathrooms which were straight ahead. Centered in that area; a pool table sat. To the right was the bar area. Except for two guys sitting at the bar having a Bud Lite, Whisman's was empty. Rocky hadn't arrived yet, so, Spike sat in the booth in the corner at the front of the building. The place smelled like a beer joint, cigarette smoke, stale beer, and that dreaded greasy food smell of burgers frying on the flattop—classic old-time beer joint atmosphere.

After a few minutes, a waitress came over and identified herself as Daisy. In her forties, she was in great shape. With a pretty face surrounded by short brunette hair, he envisioned how she might be for a one-night stand. With all the right stuff in all the right places, Spike knew she could easily quench his primal desires and urges. Even though he had gone out with Lana a few times at Avondale Country Club, she was a lovely lady; however, nothing intimate had occurred between them. That was not his agenda. Spike was using her to get information on Laura Watson and Walt Blevins. He informed Daisy that he was waiting on a friend and wanted to look at a beer list while he waited for him.

Daisy left and returned handing Spike a beer list. "Honey, don't think I've ever seen you here before. Is this your first time here?"

"Yeah, a friend told me about it, and he should be here soon. When he arrives, bring us each a Smithwick's Irish Ale."

"Will do, honey."

Spike watched her walked toward to the bar area, before she disappeared, he moistened his lips and smiled. It wasn't long until the main entrance door flew open. Rocky spotted Spike and approached the booth and slid in across from him. Noticing that Spike's friend had arrived, Daisy opened two bottles of Smithwick's, approached the booth, and sat them on the table. Daisy, making eye contact with Rocky, smiled and said, "Welcome to Whisman's. Never seen you in here before either. Anything else I can get you all?"

Spike replied, "No, beer is all we need. Thank you,

Daisy. Please give us privacy; if we need another beer, I will wave my hand, okay." She nodded and walked away.

Rocky looked Spike right in the eyes, at first, Spike glanced in Daisy's direction. Rocky intentionally cleared his throat demanding Spike's attention, his focus returned to Rocky. "What's so damn important that we had to meet again?"

"I went to Amsbury's Fine Clothing to buy a suit, and as I left that new publisher, Walt Blevins came in with this lawyer girlfriend. He locked eyes with me, and I'm sure he remembers seeing me at McGruder's and at the country club where I had dinner with a lady name Lana."

"Yeah, so what."

"About an hour later I had just come out of city hall and was looking down the street when Detective McBride came out of Amsbury's. I know she didn't see me because she got right in her car and left. Because she didn't have any packages, it was not a shopping venture. I believe Walt Blevins told her about our unexpected run in."

"I think you are just paranoid, are you taking your medications as prescribed?" Spike nodded and glanced toward the bar area. "Listen, that detective is no closer to solving either case or anything else. You need to cool it for now, and things will blow over, trust me on this, okay?"

"Yeah, you are probably right, thanks for meeting me."

Waving at Daisy, she delivered two more beers and sat them on the table. Silence filled the booth while they enjoyed their beers. With nothing else to discuss, Rocky finished his beer and left. Daisy's shape and flirtatious mannerism aroused Spike, and he was hoping to get her phone number. Catching Daisy's eye, she sauntered over to the booth. As she approached him, his eyes focused on her sexiness. A tight pair of casual jeans and a very slim-fitting knit blouse accentuated her most enticing features. As she leaned down on the booth, Spike felt a warmness growing in his body. Her perfume was sensual, and he liked everything else about her.

"Yeah, honey, what do you need?"

"Well, how about another beer and your phone number?" A little taken by his forwardness, she walked away. Spike's lust quickly turned to ice. Returning with a Smithwick's, she sat it down on his coaster. Her perfume lingered, he took a deep breath letting it float throughout his body tantalizing his wants and needs. He sent a charming smile toward her. Taking a short sip of the Smithwick's, he made direct eye contact with her flirtatious smile. "Thank you, darling, no phone number?"

"Listen, I don't give it to just anyone. How about a name, first?"

"Hm, tell you what, I'm gonna assume that Daisy is a nickname, so will my childhood nickname be enough to get your phone number?"

"Well, hm, let me think for a minute…yeah, I can work with that."

"Then, Spike, it is. Maybe we could get a drink sometime and see where that goes?"

She nodded, pulled a piece of paper from her back pocket and replied, "Call me sometime and we'll see where that goes."

Giving her a charming smile, he downed his beer. As she walked away, he pulled out a fifty-dollar bill, left it on the table, and stepped outside meeting the smell of Whisman's permeating from the rooftop exhaust vents.

CHAPTER 32

After Carla returned to the police station, she took out the flash drive that contained the video file and inserted it into her laptop. She then clicked on the video file; her eyes focused on the screen as though she was in a hypnotic trance. Carla had already seen this movie once, but just like seeing a movie the second time around, she was hoping to notice something she didn't see the first time. After watching several times, nothing different stood out. Jason Alexander Doyle, aka Spike, had been very careful to avoid the video camera in Amsbury's. It would not be easy to get a clear still shot of Spike since the video file was in black and white with poor lighting, but she knew the techies in forensics would do their best to produce a still shot of her "person of interest" in Sam's disappearance and maybe more. Before she took the flash drive to forensics, she saved it to her laptop and sent a copy to her smartphone.

Knowing it would take time for forensics to produce a still shot, she went to McGruder's to find out if anything new had surfaced regarding Sam. After that,

Walt would receive a stern Irish piece of her mind. As usual, McGruder's wasn't busy this time of the day. She entered and looked around hoping she would see Spike, aka, Jason Alexander Doyle, but he was not in the bar. In fact, there were few people there and none she recognized. A new person was behind the bar, likely Sam's replacement. The young lady, another college student, noticed her standing at the bar, approached and greeted her. Flashing her badge to identify herself, Carla responded, "Nice to meet you Mandy, is Greg in?"

"Sure is, detective. I'll get him right away and tell him you are here to see him. That way he won't screw around as he does when someone wants to see him."

"Thanks, I appreciate that."

It wasn't long until Greg came lumbering out of his office greeting her with a husky handshake. He suggested they go back to his office where they could talk privately. Mandy was new, and Greg didn't know her that well even though she came highly recommended by Career Services at the university. Once reaching his office, he motioned for her to take a seat as he began. "What brings you here today?"

"Just following up leads and information on Sam's disappearance. Have you heard anything since the story ran in the newspaper?"

"Wish I had information to share with you, but I don't, and nobody seems to be talking about it around here."

"I will show you a video of a man from a local clothing store that may have had something to do with Sam's disappearance. His nickname is Spike but also uses Jason Alexander Doyle as an alias."

She handed Greg her smartphone with the video playing. He watched the video intently, and once it ended, he played it a second time. When it finished, he handed the phone back to her. She asked, "Do you know this individual, or have you seen him in here lately? I know Sam knew him because she came to talk about him before her disappearance. She knew him by his nickname of Spike until he gave her a business card with the name of Jason Alexander Doyle. She always seemed to wait on him and his friend. So, I believe there is a connection between them."

"I'm not out in the bar area that much, so I may not be much help. I recall seeing her wait on him a lot but paid no attention since she was very friendly to everyone she waited on. She knew how to charm people with her friendliness, especially the men, and that's what earned her a lot of tips."

"Do you recognize the name, Jason Alexander Doyle?"

"Sorry, doesn't ring a bell with me either."

Although Carla was focusing on her cases and Sam's disappearance, she was still fuming over Walt's stupidity trying to interact with Spike and was ready to nip it in the bud. The newspaper wasn't far from McGruder's and arrived in about ten minutes without notice. Entering through main doors, she checked in with the reception desk which was being attended by someone different. She wondered if Debbie was off today, or maybe her daughter was sick. After signing the visitor's log, Carla proceeded directly to Walt's office. With the door wide open, she stood in the doorway glaring at him. Walt motioned her in, and she slammed the door closed. Ready to blast him for his stupidity, his expression stopped her in her tracks. He rubbed his watery eyes.

"Walt, did something happen to you and Laura, you look down?"

"No, um, one of our employees died this morning in an accident. Debbie, our receptionist, was ran off the road and hit a tree, died at the scene."

"I'm so sorry, what about her daughter?"

"Debbie had just dropped Shane off at school, and she was on her way here. A person living near where the accident happened saw a black Toyota Camry was in the area just before it happened, anyway, but that's all they have to go on. It appears to be an unfortunate accident."

"Is there anything I can do?"

"Nah, what did you want to talk about?"

"Nothing, you have enough to deal with, it can wait till another day."

CHAPTER 33

Jason, aka Spike, didn't have to pick up his clothes from Amsbury's Fine Clothing for a few days, but his encounter with Walt and Laura along with seeing Detective McBride at the store all on the same day continued to bother him. He couldn't get it out of his mind regardless of what Rocky told him. Because he would be in Oakmont today, he thought it couldn't hurt to drop in and see if his clothes were ready. Doubting it, Spike would use it as an excuse to get more information about what transpired the other day. He entered the store about 10:05 AM and just as he suspected; it was empty. The familiar doorbell sound filled the stillness of the store. Seeing the camera on the ceiling the other day, he wore his dark fedora with a gold puggaree today. He wore it tipped-down to cast a shadow on his face making a video identification a little more difficult. Mr. Amsbury immediately came out of his office and approached him. "Let's see, Mr. Doyle, right?"

"Right. In town today, I decided to stop by and check

on my clothes. I wasn't sure when they would be ready or not."

"Sorry, it will be late Friday afternoon."

"That's what I thought, thanks."

"Is there anything else I may help you with today?"

It was just the segue he needed to inquire about Walt and Carla. "As a matter fact, there is. When I was here last week, there was a gentleman with a beautiful lady looking around before I left. I recognized them, but just couldn't put a name to the face. You know how that is, don't you?"

With a grin on his face, he replied, "Yeah, I do. What's interesting is that man said the same thing about you. Said he had met you but couldn't put a name to the face. He wanted your phone number. He said he was new in town, you know, the publisher of the newspaper, Walt Blevins."

Playing along, he said, "Yeah, that's it. I met him before. And the pretty lady?"

"Um, Laura Watson, a lawyer in town."

"Hm, anything else?"

"Nah, that's pretty much how the conversation went."

"Okay, thanks, he replied." He turned around to leave and wasn't sure how he would address Detective McBride's visit. He thought a moment and turned back around and said, "A little later that afternoon, I was walking down the street and saw this nice looking red-headed lady come out of your store. Do you know her, I thought I had met her about a year ago as well?"

"Hm, yeah, I remember, that was Detective Carla McBride with the police department."

Trying to bait him, Jason replied, "Yeah, that's right, I met her at some chamber event a while back. I noticed she wasn't carrying any packages, guess she found nothing she liked that day?"

Retaking the bait, he replied, "You know, the funny thing is she was asking about you, asked to see video footage from our surveillance camera. Not sure what she was looking for but requested a copy of it and I gave her one."

"Oh, guess I'll see you on Friday to pick up my clothes, thank you."

"You bet."

Jason got what he wanted, and his anxiousness grew stronger. Rocky accused him of paranoia, but this was getting to be a big problem for them. Detective McBride wasn't even close to solving the Alison murders, so, all these inquiries must have something to do with Samantha Lewis. Based on what he found out at Amsbury's, he knew Walt called Detective McBride and told her about seeing him there.

He thought about paying a visit to McGruder's, but that could be very risky; besides what he might find out there, he already knew. Being an excellent detective, Detective McBride would have already been back there to inquire about Sam. She seemed to focus more of her efforts on her disappearance rather than the murders. He didn't know quite what to think about that. He immediately sent a text to Rocky. *I'm not paranoid...we need to meet again...Whisman's in an hour, okay?*

Rocky answered... *Really, see you then.*

CHAPTER 34

Arriving a few minutes early, Rocky entered Whisman's scanning the entire confines of the local neighborhood bar. It was pretty much like it was last week, mostly empty which was what he wanted. From his research on the bar, Jack Whisman opened it in the 1940s, passing it down through the family to its present owner, Gabe Whisman. The bar was an iconic pillar in this section of Oakmont, and it had stood the test of time. Rocky had his pick of booths to sit in, the one in the corner they used before was perfect and chose it. The older man working the bar acknowledged him and quickly approached the booth introducing himself as Gabe Whisman. Rocky ordered two bottles of Smithwick's as Spike would arrive soon. Gabe left and returned with the beers as Spike entered and went to the corner booth.

Sitting opposite Rocky, they raised their beers and toasted each other; it was a ritual from their Alpha Tango days. Spike took a swig of his beer and swallowed hard, making eye contact with Rocky, he felt the glare of Rocky's eyes in his mind. Spike wasn't expecting such a greeting from his partner and glanced toward the bar looking for Daisy. Rocky chugged his beer almost finishing it; Spike knew he pissed-off Rocky. "Spike," he said. No response as Spike focused on the bar area. "Spike, she's not here, look at me dammit." Spike reluctantly forced himself to meet him eye-to-eye. "What is so damn important that we had to meet again so soon. I told you to play it cool, what the hell is wrong?"

Breaking eye contact, Spike responded in a crackly tone. "Maybe I'm paranoid or whatever you call it, but I paid a visit to the clothing store to check on my clothes. Anyway, I asked a few questions about Walt Blevins and Detective McBride, about the day I was there. Walt asked the owner for my phone number which I didn't give to Mr. Amsbury. Also, Detective McBride asked to see video footage of when I was there, and the owner gave her a copy."

"Slow down and take several deep breaths, bro. So, they are inquiring and have a video of you buying clothes, that's not a crime. Are you taking your meds?"

"Yeah, it's not that but what if Detective McBride shows it around town? She knows we got friendly with Sam. You remember she saw us there one day."

"Yeah, so what. I've never asked you before, but did you have anything to do with Sam's disappearance I've been reading about?" Spike hesitated for a moment and broke eye contact with him again. Rocky knew Spike had lied to him before and wondered whether he told him the truth about Sam's disappearance. Also, he wondered whether if Spike took his meds for bipolar disorder and PTSD. Spike was not religious about his meds and lost control occasionally in the past. "Spike, did you hear me?"

Still not making eye contact, he reluctantly replied, "Hm, I don't know what happened to her. I may have scared her the last time I was in there since I know she went to see Detective McBride about me. I was using Sam to get information and her disappearance, more than likely, is why Detective McBride is so interested in me."

Questions filled Rocky's mind; concern was always on his mind regarding Spike because he was the weak link in the tightly knit Alpha Tango unit. At least for now, he knew he would have to trust that Spike was telling the truth this time. "Okay, but I think you need to cool it and stay away from the city for a while, especially since you resolved the other issue the other day. I know you have an office there, but why not work out of your home for a while? You know out of sight, out of mind, might be the best thing for you and me, there is too much at stake."

"Yeah, you're probably right. I'll pick up my clothes on Friday and then disappear until this blows over."

Rocky nodded and downed his beer and left. Needing another beer to calm his nerves, he signaled Gabe. Within a few minutes, Gabe placed another Smithwick's in front of him. He inquired about Daisy. Gabe informed him she was working the night shift and should be in anytime. Nodding, Spike asked for the check. Hoping Daisy would arrive before he finished his beer, he nursed it while chatting with Gabe. Daisy had been on his mind since meeting her and he had visions of an intimate interlude with her. More now than ever, he was ready to ask her to have a drink tonight hoping that drink would lead to something more intimate. Entering through the employee door as he finished his beer, he watched Gabe speak to her. Within a minute, she was standing at his booth; that brightened his day. She leaned on the table; her cleavage sent his hormones dancing. Moistening his lips, her beautiful eyes met his. She said, "What are you doing here? Thought I'd never see you again, why haven't you called?"

"I've been busy, but I have been thinking about you a lot, and I mean a lot. How about that drink after you get off tonight?"

"It'll be late, probably at least 1:00 AM or so. Why don't you come in around 12:30, have a beer, we'll go from there?"

Instead of responding, he nodded and smiled, as she walked away. Her sexy motion tantalized his every hormone as he drained his beer. After leaving Whisman's, he met its smell once more emanating from the rooftop vents. He breathed the air in hoping one drink would lead to a night of hot sex needed to clear his mind and relieve his stress of meeting Rocky today.

At Midnight, Spike entered Whisman's primed and ready for action. It had been a slow night for the locals, only one patron remained sitting at the bar finishing his beer. Noticing that Spike had arrived and was sitting in the same booth he was earlier that day, Daisy ended her conversation with Rufus and promptly delivered a Smithwick's over and sat across from him. "Hey, a little early, aren't you?"

"Didn't want to be late for such a pretty lady, you know?"

"Right, shouldn't be too much longer, as soon as he finishes his beer, then I should be able to lock up and call it a night."

About fifteen minutes later, she gave Spike the

thumbs-up gesture. Turning off the lights, she locked the doors and activated the alarm. Hand in hand they walked to her apartment engaging in casual conversation. Spike had forgotten about his uncomfortable afternoon with Rocky. Entering her apartment, Spike surveyed the surroundings and felt a relaxing atmosphere.

Family pictures stood out on several sofa tables while two pictures graced each side of the mantel framing a fireplace. Walking over and observing them, Daisy said, "My mom, she was not only my mom, but she was also my best friend and died too soon. Breast cancer, that's why I'm a big supporter of the breast cancer movement, why I enter the local Hospice event each spring."

"I'm so very sorry, I didn't know."

Touching his hand, she acknowledged his concern and sympathy. He faced her and drew her against his body hugging her, rubbing her back as she released a few tears that always welled-up when she talked about her mom. He released her momentarily, looking deep into her eyes, she leaned in and tenderly kissed his hardened lips. A kiss that lingered, he wanted to taste more of her sexiness. He went after it with a long passionate exploring kiss, and she melted in his arms. Their bodies pressed hard against each other; hormones were erupting within their yearning bodies. Pulling away from him, she grabbed his hand and led him to her bedroom. A bedside nightlight cast muted shades of light on the floor and walls. Extinguishing the nightlight; primal urges exploded as their bodies moved in perfect rhythm.

As soothing rays of sunlight crept into the room, Spike relaxed as Daisy slept in his arms. He felt like a new man, and he believed his relationship with Daisy could be much more than a one-night sultry interlude, he smiled at that possibility. Staring at the ceiling, Spike wondered if that would be even possible. It reminded him of one particular relationship many years ago to a beautiful young woman. As soon as his clothes were ready, he'd disappear and let things cool down. Forgetting Daisy, and the time they spent together, would not be easy. His military training taught him never to let his emotions affect business decisions. Out of sight, out of mind was best, besides he trusted Rocky's opinions. As he left her apartment, he silently said goodbye to her forever.

CHAPTER 35

Apollo Café was a perfect setting for Laura and Carla to catch-up on each other's lives over a late-afternoon lunch. Carla was very interested in Laura's relationship with Walt. Laura had been very vague when talking about her relationship with Walt, and Carla hated that, since they were besties. Laura and Walt were becoming very serious, and as best friends, Carla didn't want Laura to get hurt or want their relationship to change.

Arriving first, Laura picked a table for two near the front window. A few minutes later, Carla entered the cafe taking a seat at the table with a view of the street. Laura ordered a glass of chardonnay while Carla ordered a local craft beer. While enjoying their lunch, and catching up with each other, Carla noticed a man entering Amsbury's across the street. Under her breath, she murmured something. Spike entered Amsbury's and gave her the opportunity to confront him. Not to alarm Laura what was going on across the street, she glanced at her phone as though she'd received a text. "Laura, something has come up, and I must leave. I'm sorry, please take care of my bill, and I will pay you later."

"Is everything okay?"

"Yeah, I need to go check something out now, you know, police business that never ends."

She quickly left and headed straight for Amsbury's. Instead of going inside, she peeked in the window and saw Spike at the counter waiting for Mr. Amsbury to return with his clothes. Moments later he returned and handed him his clothes. They exchanged small talk, and he was on his way out of the store. As Spike opened the door, seeing Carla blocking his path surprised him. Panic set in, and he froze in his tracks, she had caught him with his guard down. He didn't know what to do but running would not help him.

Flashing her badge, "Spike, or is it Jason? I'm Detective Carla McBride with the Oakmont Police Department, but you already know that. I want to ask you a few questions. We can do it next door at the coffee shop or go to the police department; you choose which one."

Still stunned and with nowhere to go, he finally replied, "Detective, what's this about?"

Pulling up a picture of Sam on her phone, she continued, "Does she look familiar? What do you say, next door at the coffee shop or the police department, your choice?"

"Okay, next door, but I've done nothing wrong."

She motioned for him to go next door and they entered the coffee shop which was very busy, and they took the only table left in the rear of the building. She thought this was a perfect setting to question him. Showing him a picture of Sam, she said, "You know her don't you Jason? Her name is Sam…Samantha Lewis. What did you do to her?"

Knowing Detective McBride already knew he knew her, replied, "I only know her from McGruder's, but you already know that since you've seen me there talking to her. She just waited on me, and we got to be friendly and all. She was a sweet young lady. What's this got to do with me, anyway?"

"Sam is missing, but you already know, don't you? She came to see me about you and told me you frightened her. Sam gave me your business card. I searched for a Jason Alexander Doyle, and he doesn't exist. So, let's have a real name, or we go the station, and I will hold you as a person of interest for at twenty-four hours until we find out everything about who you are and what you've been up to."

With a concerned look all over his face, he replied, "Okay, okay. My real name is Frank Ramsey. I'm an accountant, and I have an office here in Oakmont. I live in Carysville and work out of my home, too. Here's my business card. Check it out, I have nothing to hide."

She took a quick look at the business card and returned her gaze to him. "Don't worry, I'll do just that. Why do you use an alias?" While waiting for him to respond, she did a quick search on her smartphone, and the information seemed legitimate for a Ramsey Accounting Firm with offices in Carysville and Oakmont.

"I only use it at McGruder's. I thought it was a cool name that I read in a book once. The guy was a ladies' man and used a lot of aliases to meet young women. I know it sounds corny, doesn't it?"

Detective McBride just rolled her eyes. "Okay, Frank, don't leave the area, you got it."

"Am I free to go?"

"Yeah, but don't disappear because I'm sure I will have more questions for you." He nodded and got up, but Carla said, "One last question before I let you go. What about your friend I saw you with at McGruder's, what's his name?"

Silence, he needed a moment to collect his thoughts and replied, "Jack Davis, he uses Rocky, an old childhood nickname. We have lunch and drinks together sometimes, and that's it."

"Does he live in Oakmont and how can I reach him?"

"Yeah, but I don't know where. We communicate by texting, here's Jack's business card. May I leave now?"

"In a minute," she replied. She pulled out her iPhone and clicked on her photo icon. Selecting the photo of the blue ball marker, she continued, "You ever see this before?"

He glanced at the photo very quickly and responded, "What is it?"

"It's a golf ball marker."

"Oh, I don't play golf, are you done with me, I have to get back to work."

Carla nodded, and Spike left quickly. She thought to herself what an idiot he was. Maybe he had nothing to do with Sam's disappearance, and in her opinion, he didn't fit the profile of a murderer. Returning to the police station, she rebooted her laptop and searched for a Frank Ramsey in Carysville. It didn't take long, and detailed information for Ramsey's Accounting Firm loaded. Everything looked legitimate until she opened the website for the accounting business. A picture popped up, and it wasn't the man she questioned at all. "Shit," she murmured to herself.

She searched for Jack Davis, and the results revealed about ten in the area, all to be checked out later. A search on the phone number showed it was for the local food bank on Main Street. She called it, and no one had ever heard of a Jack Davis, aka Rocky or Jason Alexander Doyle, aka Spike. Carla thought she had made progress in interviewing Spike. However, in hindsight, she should have hauled him back to the police station to hold him for twenty-four hours. Unfortunately, Carla didn't have any concrete evidence of tying him to Sam's disappearance or anything else to warrant such action. She was now back to square one, and neither investigation was going anywhere.

Mad at herself, she stormed out of the police station heading for downtown, specifically, Ramsey's Accounting on Main Street hoping to catch Spike at his office, to catch him off-guard. Climbing several flights of stairs, she found the door to Ramsey's Accounting office. Knocking on the door, she waited for someone to answer. Grabbing the doorknob, she tried to turn it. It jiggled a little but didn't open. Calling the number for the Carysville location, it went straight to voicemail. Closed until further notice; the greeting stated if an emergency existed, to call the Oakmont location. Dialing that number, she heard it ring several times before going to voicemail. Suddenly, a door slammed inside the office.

Hanging up, she hurried down the stairs. Outside on Main Street, she looked up, and down the street for Spike, or whoever he was, she saw no one. Noticing a walkway between the buildings, she sprinted to the back of the building. As she reached a small parking lot, she heard squealing tires in the alleyway. Drawing her service weapon, she ran into the alley and noticed a black Toyota Camry fishtail around the corner. Unable to see the license plate, she stood with her hands on her knees gasping for air.

CHAPTER 36

Disappointed that the man she questioned was not Frank Ramsey found on the internet, Carla was still in good spirits when she returned to work on Monday. Before going to her desk, she picked up her mail. A plain white envelope, with an out-of-town postmark, greeted her. It didn't have a return address on the front or back. Taking it back to her desk, she opened it. A short letter she read to herself resulted in cursing tirade interrupting the morning tranquility in the station. Letter in hand, Carla made a B-Line to see Chief Evans.

After showing him the letter, Carla requested a squad car to follow her out to 1028 Wiltshire Drive. She wasn't sure what she would find or encounter there and wanted to prepare for the unexpected. Twenty minutes later, Carla pulled into the long gravel driveway of 1028 Wiltshire Drive. As she continued up the driveway, she could see that the front door was open creating an uneasy feeling inside her. She pulled to a stop and got out of her car and waited for two police officers accompanying her to exit from their car. With their service weapons drawn, they were ready for whatever was inside the house. Detective McBride silently motioned one officer to go around the house to secure it from the rear.

The other patrolman, Officer Pete Wiesmann, followed her lead and crept slowly toward a small porch where the front door stood wide open. Carla glanced inside the house, on the floor, a body laid in a pool of blood. Sunlight casted muted shadows on the body, a flip of the wall switch illuminated the room. Spike, aka Jason Alexander Doyle, stared blankly at them. Carla checked for a pulse, nothing. No gun was present near the body.

A small round shiny disc laid on Spike's white polo shirt stained in crimson-red, she'd seen it several times at the other crime scenes and near Sam's apartment. It was another bad omen. Stepping around the body, they searched the rest of the house, all clear. The coroner and a forensics team were in route to the crime scene.

While she waited for the coroner and forensics to arrive, she put on latex gloves to examine the shiny disk on Spike's body. After taking several pictures from different angles, she picked it and turned it over. The uneasiness she was experiencing turned to anxiety and disbelief. A blue ball marker quickened her pulse rate. Breathing deeply, she swallowed hard pushing the bile from creeping up to her throat. Taking a long deep breath to calm the anxiety building inside her gut, she placed the ball marker it in a plastic bag and walked back toward Officer Wiesmann. Knowing she couldn't hide it from him, she let him inspect it. He nodded and didn't question her about it. As her rosy cheeks turned a pale shade of white, a soured expression painted her face. Officer Wiesmann noticing an abrupt change in her demeanor expressed his concern. "Detective McBride, you look like you have seen a ghost. Are you okay?"

"Yeah, I'm fine, seeing a dead body gets no easier. Seeing it right after my breakfast bagel, well, it evidently upset my stomach a little. I'll be fine in a few minutes."

Officer Wiesmann nodded and joined his partner securing the crime scene at the driveway. While the coroner and forensics did their job clearing the crime scene, she sat silently in her car staring at the blue ball marker. Joining the forensic team in the house, she trolled carefully not to impede their collection efforts. Off a small mudroom, a door opened to the garage. In the garage, a black Toyota Camry sat. It was similar to the one that sped away from her in the alley, and its hood was cold. Just like the inside of the house, the car was spotless inside and out. The registration and insurance card found in the glove box stated that the vehicle belonged to Frank Ramsey, Sr. of Carysville, Kentucky. She remembered that name from the business card Spike gave her.

Knowing she could not be of any help at the crime scene, her attention moved to Frank Ramsey, Sr. in Carysville. After a thirty-minute ride, she found his house on Main Street. Operating an accounting firm out of his house, he also had an office in Oakmont apparently was being used by his son. Turning into the driveway of the home, she noticed the business sign in the yard. The house was similar in an eerie kind of way to the house where Spike lived. Pushing the doorbell button; it was answered promptly as though the individual was waiting for her. A lady with grayish-silver hair in her mid-sixties opened the main door and stood behind a storm door.

Flashing her badge, Carla said, "Good morning, I'm

Detective Carla McBride with the Oakmont Police Department, is Frank Ramsey, Sr. at home?"

"Yes, he is. I'm his wife, Elaine. What's this about?"

"I need to ask him a few questions about his office in Oakmont, an attempted break-in occurred last night."

"Oh dear, please come right in, I'll take you to his office."

Detective McBride nodded and entered the main living room and once again, it reminded her of the house she just left sending chills up her arms. As she followed Elaine down a hallway lined with pictures, she examined each of them hoping to see a picture of Spike. To her disappointment, he was not in any of the photos. At the end of the hallway, she could see Frank's office, an older man with thinning gray hair was sitting behind a modest desk. File cabinets that appeared modified lined the walls along with bookshelves full of books.

Elaine knocked on the office door, and her husband looked up at her. "Honey, this is Detective Carla McBride from Oakmont, an attempted break-in occurred at the office there, and she needs to ask you a few questions."

He wheeled himself away from his desk toward Detective McBride who was standing just inside his office. As she scanned his office, she understood why his desk, cabinets, and bookshelves were modified.

"Nice to meet you, Detective McBride, but why send a detective from Oakmont to let me know about a break-in at my office in Oakmont. A phone call would have made much more sense, don't you think? So, why are you really here?"

"Okay, you are right. I'm not here for any break-in, your office is fine. I just didn't want to alarm your wife with the questions I need to ask."

"What kind of questions?"

"A few days ago, I interviewed a man in Oakmont that we had been watching as a person of interest in a young college student's disappearance, he said his name was Frank Ramsey, and he gave me a business card, well, your business card in fact. That man was found dead this morning, and the death is classified as a homicide. I found his body at a house on the outskirts of town. The address is 1028 Wiltshire Drive. Registration and insurance card found in a 2007 Camry states it belongs to you." At this point, Elaine teared up, while Frank's face remained expressionless. Carla put two and two together and knew the answer to the next question she had to ask. "Is that your son we found? Is that your house and car?" Elaine couldn't hold back the tears any longer and broke down. She walked over to her husband and hugged him tightly as more tears flowed. Frank, Sr. remained expressionless. Trying to show as much compassion as possible, she gave them a few moments to console each other before continuing her questioning. "I'm so sorry for your loss. I know this must be difficult, but I need for you to tell me everything you can about your son."

In a raspy, broken voice, he said, "After graduating from high school, he joined the Army. I don't recall how many years he was in the Army or even what he did. He never talked about what he did, and it didn't matter, anyway. Once he got out, he went to college at some community college in Florida. He lived most of his life in Florida and worked as an accountant, mostly in the newspaper business. He…"

"I'm sorry to interrupt, what newspaper?"

"I don't know, he moved around a lot in Florida, he worked for a newspaper group, don't remember the name either. An only child, he was a very private person and never married. My son moved back to Oakmont when a car wreck several years ago left me paralyzed from the waist down. He took over my office in downtown Oakmont to serve our clients there. The house and car in Oakmont belong to me as well. We didn't talk much, and when we did, it was strictly about business. Frank, Jr. was, for the most part, a loner but never got into any trouble as far as I know. I can't believe someone murdered him."

"I know this is difficult, but the quicker I get answers, the quicker we find who did this." Frank, Sr. dried his eyes and nodded. "Now, what about his personal life? Any friends or girlfriends? Did he play any sports such as golf? Did he have a childhood nickname?"

"As I said, Junior was a private person. He brought no one over when he visited which wasn't often. We usually communicated by phone or email. I'm not aware of any sports. Like I said before, he was a loner. Just did his job and led a simple, and quiet life. As far as a nickname, as a child we called him Spike because his love of trains, you know railroad spikes, a strange nickname isn't it?"

"I see. Do you have any recent pictures of your son for identification?"

His eyes welled up as he turned around a framed photo on his desk of him and his son in front of the business sign in the yard. Each had a big smile on their faces. Taking a picture with her smartphone, she gave it back to him. It evidently meant a lot to him, and it was the only picture on his desk. "That should do it, for now, I'll let myself out, and once again, I'm sorry for your loss."

CHAPTER 37

When Carla returned to the police station, Marsh, crime reporter of the *Daily Reporter*, had left her a voicemail message. He wanted more information regarding the unidentified male found dead at 1028 Wiltshire Drive. Even though Marsh was at the crime scene, the police didn't announce the identity of the deceased or manner of death. She didn't want to call him but knew he was relentless and would continue to annoy her, so she dialed his direct line. Answering immediately, he said, "Detective McBride, thanks for calling me back. What have you got on the man found dead yesterday at the house on Wiltshire Drive?"

Wanting to make the call short, she told Marsh the newspaper would get a press release later in the day with all the information. He informed editor, Todd Hailey, he should receive a press release later in the day and to keep space open for a story. Two hours later, the press release and photo were in his email inbox. Todd found Marsh, who was in the break room getting coffee and informed him about the press release and photo. Returning to his desk, Marsh opened the email and began working on the story. Walt happened to walk by his workstation and noticed the picture Marsh had up on his monitor. After a double take, Walt asked, "What's that all about?"

"We finally received the official press release regarding the man found dead on the outskirts of town the other day. Frank Ramsey, Jr is the younger man while the older man is his father, Frank Ramsey, Sr. Classified as a homicide investigation; this story will be front page tomorrow. As soon as I get the story written and have comments from Detective McBride; the story will be on our website. I sure Todd sent you a copy."

"Thanks, I'll check it out."

Walt returned to his office and closed the door. He sat down at his desk and put his hands to his face and rubbed his temples. Pulling up Todd's email, he opened the press release with the picture of Frank Ramsey, Jr., aka, Spike, aka Jason Alexander Doyle. His face turned a ghostly shade of coldness, his pulse began to race, and sweat dotted his forehead. To calm his nerves, he brewed a cup of strong coffee. After reading the press release several times, he called Carla to find out just what was going on. Recognizing the caller ID for the newspaper, Carla immediately answered and lashed out at Marsh assuming it was him.

"Carla, this is Walt. I received a copy of your press release and saw the picture of the man found dead. It's the guy we saw at McGruder's and the same guy Laura, and I ran into at Amsbury's and was at the country club. What the hell is going on?"

"I wish I knew, but yes, it's the same guy. Classified as a homicide, and the manner of death is the same as

Mark and Joanne Alison. Two shots to the heart at point-blank range. He died within minutes of being shot. That's all I can tell you at this point."

"So, what now? Wasn't he your person of interest in Sam's disappearance?"

"Yeah, but now he is dead. I've got to run, say hello to Laura for me. Also, stay out of trouble, and let me do the police work."

"Don't worry. I hear you loud and clear."

Entirely composed now, Walt knew he needed to focus on running the newspaper. The strategic plan was due to Chad in two weeks giving him plenty of time to put it all together. He held brainstorming sessions with each department head, and each had to submit their department plan from their meetings with their staff. Walt dug in and pieced it all together as the day flew by very quickly. Before leaving for the day, he backed up his laptop on a flash drive and dropped it off to the business manager as required by company policy.

Since being name publisher, he was enjoying one of his perks, a company car. The Chevrolet Impala was not as much fun as driving his Corvette, but it allowed him to keep the miles low on the Corvette which he liked. The Impala had all the bells and whistles and was a comfortable driving car. On the way home, the car felt like it was pulling to the right, the tire pressure monitor lit up on the dashboard. As he pulled into his parking spot, the steering was hard to turn, but he eased the car into his parking spot without incident. After gathering his briefcase, he walked around to the passenger side and looked at the front right tire. A flat was all he needed. Wanting to take care of it right away, he did a quick-change clothes and went out to change the tire. With the trunk open, he raised the mat covering the spare tire well. Front and center in the spare tire well was a mini-laptop with a charger cord. Thoughts were running rampant in his head about why it was there and who did it belong to? Because changing the tire while there was enough daylight was foremost on his mind, examining the mini-laptop would have to wait till later.

Thirty minutes later, he was back in his apartment taking a shower before he had to leave for his dinner date with Laura. The mini-laptop had mystery written all over it. Curiosity was getting the best of him, and he opened it up. Pushing the power button, it didn't light up. Dead battery he assumed. Attaching the charger cord, he plugged it into an electric outlet. Pushing the power button again, it lit up, and the mysterious mini-laptop hummed. Within a minute, the screen lit up and reared its ugly head. The cursor flashed asking for a password. Frowning with utter disappointment; the cursor continued its annoying blinking. With no idea what the password could be, he closed the laptop to charge it overnight. A night with Laura was more important than the mystery laptop.

CHAPTER 38

An evening of wine and hot passionate sex was the perfect remedy for the stress and tension that Walt experienced yesterday. Laura had fallen asleep in his arms, so he just enjoyed the warmth and silkiness of her body next to his until morning arrived. He arrived at the newspaper a little later than he intended. Walt was a different man, all cheerful, walking around the newspaper plant with a smile on his face on the way to his office. Once in his office, he started the Keurig and as soon as it was ready; he put in his favorite K-cup pod. After the coffee finished brewing, Walt took his mug and went to see Todd. He tapped on the partially open door and entered his office. Todd motioned him to sit down.

"Good morning, what's going on this morning?"

"We're just following up on the murder story. It's received tons of page views as it should, and I expect our single-copy sales will be through the roof. We'll try to get more information from Detective McBride, but she has been a little hush on this one. Not sure what is going on, but something definitely is, I can smell it."

"Sounds good, keep me informed."

"You got it, boss."

Back in his office, he stared at the mini-laptop and wondered about its contents. Flipping it open, it came to life, and once again the annoying cursor blinked asking for a password. KT, the business manager, was the keeper of all passwords and everything else. Taking the mini-laptop, he knocked on her door. Staring at the mini-laptop in Walt's hand, she gave him a quizzical look and motioned him to sit down. There was a moment of silence before Walt asked, "I had a flat tire on the way home last night, and when I went to get the spare out, this was in the spare tire well. Do you have the password?" Handing it to her, she inspected it and returned it to him. A little dumbfounded, Walt asked, "Well, may I have the password?"

"Sorry, it's not ours."

"Then who does it belong to?"

"Mark Alison was the only person that drove that car. Even when Chad was here, he never used it. I would assume it belonged to Mark, not sure why he would have had it, must have had personal reasons because as you know, it's against company policy to have personal information on a company computer, laptop, tablet, or phone."

He nodded and returned to his office dejected because he knew the mini-laptop was useless without a password. The password could be anything and discovering it might take some luck. After opening the laptop, the annoying flashing cursor continued to challenge his mind and test his patience. Randomly, he keyed in passwords hoping one of them was right. As he tried one, he wrote it down. Nothing worked. Joanne, newspaper, golf, publisher; the guessing game went on and on. Frustrated, he turned on the Keurig for a cup of coffee. When the Keurig was ready, he placed a Starbucks Caffe Verona K-cup in the brewer and pushed the brew button. Two minutes later, he sat on the sofa savoring the robust aroma coming from his cup. His mind took him back to when he was visiting the *Daily Reporter* and helping Mark with his marketing initiatives. He spent many hours brainstorming over coffee in the morning and sometimes out on the deck. He tried to recall anything Mark said or did that might help him discover the passwords. Remembering when he arrived for his first day as publisher, water and juices stocked the dorm-sized fridge. Starbucks Caffe Verona was the only K-cup in the coffee drawer.

A light went off in his head, and he took his coffee to his desk and stared at the mystery laptop. The flashing cursor continued to haunt him. Not knowing what might be on the computer, he felt it must be something very private. Keying in starbuckscafeverona, he hit enter and waited. The flashing cursor continued to blink; the wrong password. To his dismay, it did not open the laptop. Walt thought for a moment and got up to take another look at the K-cup pod and brought it back to his desk. Discovering he was missing an additional letter "f" in the word cafe, he entered starbuckscaffeverona and hit enter again. Wrong, he cursed at the annoying cursor.

Again frustrated, he stepped out on the deck to breathe fresh air and clear his brain. The password could be anything, and should he discover it, there might be nothing of value on it. He returned to his desk and sat down glaring at the blinking cursor. About to give up, he rubbed his temples and ran his hand through his hair. Looking around the office, he was hoping something would grab his attention. Nothing, he reviewed all the previous passwords he had tried. He looked at the used K-cup again and noticed the K-cup pod's name was in all caps. It was worth a try he thought. He entered STARBUCKSCAFFEVERONA. He paused for a moment and said a short prayer. He hit enter and waited. The blinking cursor disappeared. Within ten seconds, a picture of a young boy building a sandcastle on a beach filled the screen. Juno email loaded showing a list of old emails in the inbox. Ironically, the last email was on March 31, the day before Mark Alison died. Opening that email and reading its contents, he noticed Mark sent a reply. As he continued to read the rest of the emails, shock covered his face.

The email discovery was enlightening enough. Wondering what else was on the laptop, Walt pulled up a directory of the hard drive and its files. It listed a few Word documents; however, one PDF file name "G" at the bottom of the list immediately grabbed his attention. He double-clicked it and waited for it to open. Within twenty seconds, the document appeared on the screen, amazement covered his face. After closing it, he returned to the directory of the hard drive noticing a single Excel spreadsheet file. Double-clicking on it; the spreadsheet filled the screen. A simple spreadsheet, he thought. He wasn't sure what it was for, but he knew for certain, it had nothing to do with any newspaper business at the *Daily Reporter*. He pondered about what he should do about his discovery. The investigative person in him told him to run with it by himself; however, the common-sense person told him to let Carla have it. The mini-laptop and its content could be the key to solving the murders of Mark and Joanne Alison and bringing the people responsible to justice.

CHAPTER 39

With Frank Ramsey, Jr., aka Spike, aka Jason Alexander Doyle dead, Detective McBride's investigation into Sam's disappearance was on life support. These cases were turning out to be the most difficult ones she had ever tried to solve, but she was not giving up. Failure was not in her vocabulary. No matter how difficult things were, she always believed in staying positive. Retrieving her mail from the in-house mailbox, one piece of mail looked very familiar, she had seen it before, that sent her pulse racing. It appeared to be identical to the one she received last week with no return address. Postmarked from a town at least fifty miles away; however, it was a different town this time. Returning to her desk, she opened it. Taking out the letter out, she unfolded it and read it silently.

Good Morning, Detective Carla McBride,

Hope you are having a great day. I am. I see you found Spike; sorry he couldn't talk to you. I suspect you have a lot of unanswered questions like who killed him.

That one is easy–I did. Spike got careless because I could no longer trust him. Too bad, he was like a brother to me.

Now, about that missing college student, Samantha Lewis. Spike told me he had nothing to do with her disappearance; however, I don't believe him because he has lied to me several times before.

Now, for your other unsolved murder cases. Who killed Mark and Joanne Alison…that, too, is easy. Frank Ramsey, Jr., aka Spike, aka Jason, did it. If you go back to his house and find the fourth brick in the row four from the top of the porch and just to the right of the steps, it's loose and the murder weapon used to kill them is there.

It is in a plastic bag, take the brick out and put your hand through the hole. I guarantee it will be an exact match to the bullets taken from their bodies. Of course, that doesn't prove that Spike killed them, only that you have the murder weapon and my word he killed them.

I can only assume I've answered all your questions now, except one…and that is…who am I?

Game on…are you up to it…Detective McBride?

A loud smashing of glass on wood disrupted the unusually quiet morning atmosphere in the station. Forty sets of eyes glanced in her direction as her hand still held her ten-year anniversary paperweight. Immediately grabbing the other anonymous letter in her desk, she headed to Chief Evans' office. She pushed open his partially open door and stood at his desk. On the phone, he motioned for her to have a seat. His call ended and his eyes locked with her, and his face tensed. "What's this all about, Carla? Lucky for you it was just my wife I was talking with."

Without saying a word, she handed him the anonymous letters and breathed deeply calming her anxiousness. Minutes passed as he intently read each letter not making eye contact with her. His face remained flush as beads of sweat surfaced on his brow. Finished with them, he handed them back to her and responded, "What the hell is going on? Do we have a psycho on hands? And, what's this game-on shit about?"

"Hell, Chief, I don't know, but I'm going out there to find the damn murder weapon. Let me take Detective Bernie Kowalski, since he is not working a dedicated case currently, and in case we run into any trouble."

He made a quick phone call. Within minutes, Detective Bernie Kowalski entered the chief's office. After a short conversation, she and Bernie left for Frank's Ramsey's house. The crime scene tape still blocked the small porch and front door. Pulling up to the house, they got out and immediately located the brick identified in the letter. It was a tight fit, but after much patience and wiggling, she got it out. Using a flashlight, she shined it through the open space, but couldn't see anything. Reaching in with her gloved hand and feeling around, she finally located a plastic bag. Being very careful, she grabbed the plastic bag and pulled it out through the opening. Just as the letter had stated, the gun with four spent shell casings was in the bag, but it was the other items that caused her respiration to race. Two blue ball markers with an embossed gold fedora stared back at her.

Returning to her car, a noise in the brush that surrounded the house stopped them in their tracks. With weapons drawn, they turned around to see a small dog wagging its tail. A sigh of relief came over them. Bernie glanced at the large picture window of the house seeing movement among the blinds. He tapped her on the shoulder and pointed toward the window. They approached the house with weapons drawn and flashlights ready. On the count of three, Bernie opened the door shining his flashlight toward the blinds discovering a stray cat sitting on a table. Wondering how it got in the house, they searched each room discovering an open window in a bedroom. Bernie closed the window and went to shew the cat away. Reaching the living room, the cat had already disappeared. After the front door was closed, they entered her car and drove up the long driveway to the street and headed back to the station. After returning to the police station, she logged in the gun, shell casings, ball markers, and the brick as evidence.

Carla brought Chief Evans up to speed on everything. She would just have to wait for the results from forensics on the evidence brought from the house. She prayed that they would come up with something that could jumpstart her cases. Later that afternoon, Sherry Caudill, the forensics specialist, brought her the report of her findings. As the anonymous letter showed, the gun matched the bullets taken from Mark and Joanne Alison. However, the gun did not match the bullets taken from Spike even though they were of the same caliber. The blue golf ball markers were identical to ones already in evidence. As she read on, hope was fading about finding something new. Feeling depressed, she smiled as she read the last paragraph of the report. They found two sets of prints. One belonged to Frank Ramsey, Jr., which made perfect sense, while the other belonged to an undetermined individual. They ran it through all criminal databases with no luck.

Carla was no further along in solving each case. The

only thing she knew was that it was very likely Frank Ramsey, Jr. murdered Mark and Joanne Alison, but why? She knew her interview with Frank likely got him killed, but why? Carla also knew the blue ball marker meant something, but what? Wondering what would happen next in this game, she prayed that whatever turned up would be the key to answering all these questions ending this psychotic game of murder. Carla loved challenges; however, this game was becoming extremely dangerous for her, and anyone connected to her. Searching all government agency databases, state, federal, and military for a match to the fingerprints would take time. Forensics would begin the process while Carla waited impatiently for a break in her cases.

Carla's patience was wearing thin, and thought to herself, just how long does it take to run fingerprints through a government database, especially military databases. Picking up her phone to call Sherry in forensics, she noticed her walking toward her with a file folder in her hand. She held her breath as Sherry approached her desk. Carla impatiently asked, "What have you found?"

"It's your lucky day, McBride. We got a hit on the fingerprints when we ran it through the military databases and got a match. One belongs to Frank Ramsey; the other belongs to Wylie Adkins."

"Shit, I've heard that name somewhere before, great job, what else?"

"He was in the Army, Special Forces to be exact. The interesting thing is that Frank was in Special Forces as well. What's more interesting, they apparently were in the same unit at the same time."

"Now, isn't that interesting? Anything else, like where I can find this character? What does he do?"

"Only known address is a PO Box in Oakmont."

"Great work! Now, I have to track him down."

"You are welcome, let me know if I can be any further help."

She nodded and turned her attention to where she had heard or seen that name again. She went to see Chief Evans; his door was open, and he motioned her in, and she took a seat. "You ever heard of a Wylie Adkins? His fingerprint was found on one of the golf ball markers. The report lists he was in Army Special Forces years ago and now in the construction business. Only contact information is a PO Box in Oakmont."

"Can't say I know him."

Back at her desk, she remembered where she heard that name before, and immediately dialed Walt's number. He answered after two rings. She put him on speaker. "Detective McBride, how are you doing?"

"I'm fine, you know you can call me Carla, don't you? Anyway, remember the list you showed me of the golfers from that golf course in West Virginia? You called them the Oakmont Mafia Group, wasn't one name Wylie Adkins?"

"Yeah, it was. What do you want with Wylie?"

"Let's just say he is now a person of interest in the murder of Frank Ramsey, Jr. I need to find him; do you know where he lives because all I have is a PO Box in Oakmont?"

"From what I remember, he is in the construction business and works out of town a lot, mostly in Florida. Your best bet would be to contact Keith Edwards. They were in the same foursome and had much in common. If anyone knows, he will."

"Great, and thanks. How's our girl Laura?"

There was a moment of silence before he responded but finally said, "Um, she is doing just fine. Carla, I believe we need to meet at my office today."

"Really, what's this about?"

"It's imperative, and I'll tell you when you get here. Are you coming or not?"

"I hope it is important because every minute I waste puts me further behind in solving all the cases."

CHAPTER 40

Walt mingled with several employees in the common area of the newspaper waiting for Carla to arrive. While speaking with KT, the business manager, a tap on his shoulder startled him. The receptionist informed him Carla was in the waiting area. Spotting Carla standing there, he motioned her to follow him to his office. Once they reached his office, they entered, and Walt closed the door. He motioned for her to take a seat on the sofa. She noticed a mini-laptop and some printed material on the table. He offered her something to drink; she declined. Walt put the Foglifter in the Keurig, and it spouted the rich, robust coffee. When it finished, he sat beside her. She asked, "What are those papers lying on the table?"

"We'll get to that a little later, why do you need to see Wylie Adkins, has he done something wrong? He seemed like a very nice guy, maybe a little rough around the edges. I didn't quite understand why he was in the golf group to begin with, he just didn't fit, if you know what I mean?"

"As I said on the phone, he is a now a person of interest, and I need to ask him some questions."

"A person of interest regarding what, Sam's disappearance?"

"Yes, but maybe even more serious stuff; can we quit screwing around with the twenty-question game, okay?"

"Patience, like I told you on the phone, go see Keith, he probably knows how to contact him."

"I'm not so sure that's a good idea. I've already interviewed Keith once regarding the death of Joanne Alison, and that didn't go so well."

"Now, that's funny."

"Just following up leads or hunches. Didn't I interview you, Mr. Big-Shot Publisher for the same thing!"

"Interrogate me, don't you mean?"

"Okay, Walt. Let's not get in a pissing match, let's try to help each other to solve these murders. We must trust each other, deal?"

"Deal. Let's talk about Wylie first since you contacted me and then I will let you know what I found out."

"Okay, but what goes on in here stays in here. There is too much at stake, got it?"

"Yeah, you can trust me. So, let's get started."

"Walt, this is some heavy shit, and I can't believe I'm getting in bed with the media to help me solve all this shit." Sighing, she continued. "Based on all the evidence I have, this is my theory of who killed who and what happened to Sam. Here we go."

"Hold it a minute. You may not like what I'm recommending, but I think it's time to bring my editor Todd Hailey in on this. He is not aware of our discussions to this point, but I know he will help us make sense of this information. What do you say?"

"Sure, we can use all the help we can get."

Walt dialed Todd's extension, and within a minute, he knocked on Walt's door and entered. Surprised to see Detective McBride sitting in Walt's office, a puzzled look came over him. Walt motioned for him to take a seat across from the sofa. "Todd, I know this will be all new to you, and I apologize for blindsiding you on this, but Detective McBride is here to talk about the Alison cases and Sam's disappearance. I have discovered information on a secret mini-laptop that belonged to Mark I found in the spare tire well of my company car. Anyway, I felt you should be part of the discussion since you knew Mark better and longer than us. Just listen, take notes, and anything discussed in here stays in here."

Todd acknowledged, and Carla began by letting them read the anonymous letters she received over the past ten days. While reading them, facial expressions showed concern for her. They returned the letters and waited for her next move. "Not to bore you with all the little details, forensics found two sets of prints from the bag and its contents. One belonged to Frank Ramsey, Jr., while the other belongs to Wylie Adkins. Walt, that's why I need your help in finding Wylie Adkins, I believe he is key in breaking these cases wide open. I've had a run in with Keith Edwards before, and I don't think he will cooperate with me on this. We may have a better chance of him cooperating if you contact him to get a phone number or address for Wylie. Maybe you can let Keith know you need some home renovation done and wanted to talk with Wylie since you played golf with him a few weeks ago."

"Yeah, I can see where Keith might clam up, and

your idea just might work. I can try it and see what happens."

"Great, now what about your discovery?

"I'll get to it in a minute; I need more coffee after all of that. How about you, Carla? Todd, can I get you anything?"

Carla replied, "Water, please."

Todd responded, "Foglifter will be fine."

After a brief break with coffee and water, they were ready to hear what Walt wanted to discuss with them. "Before I let you both look at what I've discovered, let me tell you how I discovered them. It was plain dumb luck. I'll make it as short as I can."

Carla and Todd nodded, and Walt began. After telling them the story of finding the mini-laptop and solving the password enigma, he handed them the spreadsheet and explained what it meant. Carla said, "Maybe blackmail, but his joint account showed none matching that type of activity. There must be another account somewhere." Walt continued as he handed them the second item he printed. It was copies of email correspondence between Mark, and someone named Bruno. They were all brief, but the last one from Mark to Bruno is particularly interesting, it was the day before he died.

Todd, who had been listening intently the whole time, jumped in with information supporting the email correspondence and said, "Sounds like he owed money to a big-time bookie, like he was big into horse racing. He mentioned it to me several times, dropped a lot of money at Keeneland and Churchill Downs."

Carla added, "If he owed that kind of money to a big-time bookie, that could have got him murdered. What makes little sense is killing Joanne for the same reason.

Mark hid this from her. I really believe her death was simply collateral damage thinking whatever Mark knew, he confided in Joanne."

Walt handed the final item to them. A copy of a letter Mark received from someone known as "G," and was important enough to scan and save. After Carla had finished digesting the contents of the letter, she interjected, "I remember when I interviewed Joanne, she came clean that both had affairs while living in Florida. She told me that Mark wanted kids, she didn't. That caused them to drift apart. Don't know who it was because Joanne said it meant nothing to either of them and was adamant about someone murdering him over it. I wanted to address it with her again at a later time; however, I never got that chance. Wonder what the gift was that she treasured and what did she mean to leave the skeletons in the closet?"

Todd chimed in, "One time when Mark had too much to drink, he alluded to the affairs but mentioned no names; however, it was really none of my business so I never pursued the subject again."

Walt said, "Those are all interesting questions and observations but look at the wallpaper on this mini-laptop, and we'll go from there." He turned the mini-laptop toward them. The wallpaper was a photo of a young boy making a sandcastle on a beach somewhere. Eyes were wide open, and the expression on their faces showed their minds were deep in thought. "What are you thinking?"

Todd replied, "Looks like the gift he gave 'G' is the young boy, why else would he put it there?"

Carla replied, "I think we need a breather to digest all

of this info; how about we step outside and get some fresh air for a few minutes?"

Todd said, "Yeah, sounds good, and I need a smoke, anyway."

Stepping out on the deck and breathing the fresh air of the afternoon. Most of the time, Carla, Todd, and Walt just stood in silence and enjoyed the solitude. A thought hit Walt, and he said, "How ironic it is to be relaxing at the original crime scene that started this mystery with pieces just like a difficult jigsaw puzzle, quite eerie, don't you think?" Carla and Todd acknowledged him. Returning to Walt's office, they all sat staring at each other waiting for someone to break the deafening silence in the room. Walt broke the silence. "We've heard a lot and seen a lot today, Todd, what do you make of it since you've known Mark the longest?"

Carla interjected, "Yeah, tell us everything you know even if it seems trivial. It may just help."

"Okay," said Todd. "I knew they both had affairs when they lived in Florida, and I already mentioned that. One night Mark and I went out for a beer since Joanne was out of town. He had one too many and talked about the affairs. I told him how lucky he was to have a wife like Joanne. He said he just about lost her because of his affair. Mark said he told Joanne about it, she felt jilted, and had an affair of her own. He didn't toss out any names. Mark told his wife he got drunk and told me everything. That's why she didn't like me. I knew about the skeletons in their closet. I've already told you he loved the horses and was a heavy better. That's pretty much it." Carla and Walt acknowledged him. "May I leave now, I've got a newspaper to put out, and I have nothing further to add?"

"Yeah, that's fine. Carla and I will continue brainstorming about where we go next with the information, and if we need you, I'll let you know."

After Todd left and closed the door, Walt said, "This was a lot to digest today. Why don't we get together again tomorrow away from here and see what we can come up with?"

"Yeah, but there is just one thing, Walt. The mini-laptop just became evidence, and I will need to take it and let our techies see what they can come up with. You understand, don't you?"

"Yeah, I figured that, but I need assurance that when this all breaks, and it will, that we will get the scoop first and on our publication cycle. Solving these murders will be a huge story, maybe the biggest ever for the *Daily Reporter*."

"You have my word on it; nothing gets released until you have it and publish the story. One other thing, as farfetched as this might seem, for some odd reason my gut tells me there's a connection between Debbie Castle's accidental death and Mark and Joanne's deaths."

A puzzled expression grabbed Walt's face. "How so?"

"A black Toyota Camry seen in the area; Spike drove the same car. Was Debbie single?" Walt nodded. "What else do you know about her?"

"She grew up in Florida, then found her way here."

"I think you should talk to her parents. You have a single mother, and there is a father somewhere. It's worth checking out, might be nothing but you never know."

CHAPTER 41

Daisy didn't keep up on local news all that much because she felt it didn't affect her. Reading the newspaper much was not a habit of hers, however, if a patron would leave one, she would take it home. Spike hadn't been around lately, nor had he called her, and that bothered her. She felt they connected, both physically and personally. Even though they had only one night together, Daisy thought it could blossom into something much more. While cleaning off tables, she grabbed a newspaper left by a customer. Before tossing it in the trash bag, she did a double take. A photo on the front page of the *Daily Reporter* punched her in the gut. Opening the folded newspaper; Spike's picture took her breath away. The big bold headline sent chills through her soul; tears welled in her eyes.

After reading the first two paragraphs of the story, chills in her body morphed into shivers of fear, and her rosy cheeks turned a pale shade of fright. Taking the newspaper, she put it next to her purse to take home.

With no patrons in the bar, and not feeling well, she informed Gabe she needed to leave. Not living far, she ran all the way to her apartment. Once inside, she locked the doors and closed all the blinds. After reading the entire story, emotions erupted inside her body. Two nights ago, she was having hot passionate sex with Spike, and now he was dead. Shivers traveled up and down her body. Pouring herself a double-shot of Jack Daniels, it went down harsh. After several more, her shivering and shaking subsided. Fright, fear, and too much Jack, she passed out on the bed.

Waking up the next morning; a monumental hangover ravaged her body. After brewing some robust coffee, she forced herself to reread the story. She could not believe what she was reading about Spike, that he was Frank Ramsey, Jr., an accountant. At the end of the story, it said if anyone has any information about him to contact Detective Carla McBride at the Oakmont Police Station. Scared shitless, she was unsure what to do. Stay or run. Remembering the man Spike met there concerned her deeply. Although she couldn't afford to quit her job, endangering herself or her co-workers began to take its toll on her. After several cups of coffee and aspirin, Daisy realized she couldn't just ignore the possibilities and would contact Detective Carla McBride. After that, choosing whether to stay or disappear would be much clearer.

Feeling much better mentally and physically; a scalding shower helped relax her. It also washed away the scent of a dead man that still lingered inside her body and soul. Composed, she made an appointment with Detective McBride. Although the police station was only fifteen minutes away, and she drove there as fast as she could out of fear. After entering the police station, the receptionist escorted her to Carla's desk where she sat beside the desk. Carla ended her phone conversation and turned her attention to a lady that appeared frazzled and scared.

In a weakened-frantic tone, Daisy said, "Um, I'm Wanda Jordan, but I'm known, as Daisy where I work. Whisman's Beer Joint on the other side of town, Adams Avenue. It's a friendly local neighborhood bar if you know what I mean?"

"Hm, what brings you here today, Wanda?"

"Um, call me, Daisy, please. Is there somewhere that is a little more private where we can talk?"

"Yeah, just follow me." They entered an interrogation room, and Carla continued, "This is as private as it gets. So, what's this about, Daisy?"

"Hm, you know, Frank Ramsey, Jr., aka, Spike, the man murdered a few days ago, well, I met him at Whisman's Beer Joint. He and another man that went by the name Rocky met there at least two times and had a few beers. I could tell that it was serious stuff since they didn't want me bothering them unless they wanted another beer. Anyway, Spike asked me for my phone number. Eventually, I gave it to him, and he met me one night after work. Probably the night before someone murdered him. We ended up back at my apartment and spent the night together if you know what I mean? I wondered why he never came back or called me. I thought we hit it off pretty good. He was really a nice man, at least to me, guess I was wrong about him."

"Anything else you can tell me?"

"Well, neither lived in the neighborhood and had never been there before, and that's about it. It was like they wanted to remain invisible to the rest of the world like they had something to hide."

"What about the other man, has he been back? Can you describe him?"

"Never been back as far as I know or at least not when I was working. As far as what Rocky looked like, well, uh, he was about 6'2", thin with brownish hair parted on the left side. Am I in any danger?"

"Maybe, I think Rocky, as you call him, may have had something to do with Spike's murder or maybe even the one that killed him." Hearing that comment from Carla, Daisy's expression grew more concerned, and tears trickled down her cheeks. She wiped them away. "Daisy, I'm sorry to frighten you, but I can't sugar-coat the situation, you may be in danger. Now, can you think of anything else; anything would be helpful?"

Taking a deep breath to calm her down, she replied, "Well, I did notice they both had tattoos on their left forearm. Come to think of it; they were identical. I didn't recognize it, but Spike told me it had something to do with when they both were together in the Army, I believe he said they served in the same unit."

"Okay, do you think if we put you with our sketch artist you could help her create an image of that man?"

"I'll do anything to help catch Spike's murderer."

"Great. I'll bring our sketch artist, Patsy Groves, in and once she finishes, you're free to leave. Here's my contact information. If you need me, call me anytime, okay? Be diligent and safe, okay?"

Daisy nodded, and Carla left the room to find Patsy. Daisy sat alone in the room pondering her fate. Several minutes later, Carla returned with Patsy and made introductions. Twenty minutes later, Patsy's sketch displayed a likeness of a man known as Rocky. Daisy studied it for a brief moment and nodded. It was a perfect resemblance of Rocky.

CHAPTER 42

Carla arrived at Walt's office holding a copy of the sketch created from Daisy's description. She explained to him that a waitress named Daisy came to see her because she met Frank, aka Spike at Whisman's Beer Joint where she worked. They hooked up, and he spent the night with her. Carla informed him that another man, known as Rocky, met Spike at the bar and appeared to be having a very serious conversation and didn't want Daisy to bother them. She handed him the sketch.

Without hesitation, he responded, "That's Wylie Adkins, it's almost a perfect resemblance except for maybe the thickness of the hair, but that's him. What's next?"

"I want to get it out to the public. I'm just not sure how I want to present it just yet. Let's go over the information and then we can talk about it. There was one thing that Daisy mentioned that might be important. She said both Frank and Wylie had identical tattoos on left forearm. Daisy wasn't sure what it was, but Frank told her he got it while he was in the Army. Do you recall if Wylie had one?"

"Yeah, I recall seeing one on his left forearm the first time I met him but didn't pay much attention to it nor did I ask him about it."

"Did you call Keith Edwards yet?"

"Yeah, Keith bought it and gave me Wylie's cell number. He thought Wylie was back in Florida working on new development. I called that number several times, no answer, went straight to voicemail. I left a message but doubt I will ever hear from him."

"Yeah, probably not, thanks for trying. What do you make of all this information? The anonymous letters I received and the secret files you found."

"I've given it a lot of thought and here's what I've come up with. It's apparent that Mark had an affair with someone married to a high-profile politician. Mark gave her a special gift, not sure what that could be, and maybe he fathered a child. She wanted to keep their secrets hidden which usually means something very serious was at stake. Now, as for the spreadsheet, I think it's a record of blackmail money, the problem is who is blackmailing who and where the money is going. Maybe the big-time bookie or her? I know this sounds way out in left field. Let's hear your thoughts?"

"Walt, not as far out as you think. The two letters I received referencing a 'game on' between me and who killed Frank. It appears that must be Wylie, aka Rocky. However, not sure what the 'game on' means. I wonder if the ball marker was merely a diversionary tactic, maybe to get me thinking a serial killer scenario exists? You know, get the public in a panic, if it got out."

Walt agreed and responded with his two cents, "It

appears Frank and Wylie go way back since they have tattoos alike and were in the same Army Special Forces unit together. They both spent time in Florida before, and Wylie practically lives there now. It sounds like the key is finding Wylie. I believe in some strange way; there was a connection between Joanne, Mark, Frank, and Wylie years ago. And Sam was a naïve and innocent victim in this mess."

"I agree, and Wylie is the key, and we need to get the sketch in the newspaper and on your website. Hopefully, we get something we can use. How best can we do that without causing panic?"

"I have an idea, let's get Todd and see what he suggests."

Carla nodded, and Walt dialed his number, said a few words and hung up. A few minutes later, Todd appeared and entered the office closing the door. Taking a seat in one of the chairs across from the sofa, Carla handed Todd a copy of the sketch. "What's up, who's this?"

She replied, "It's a sketch of Wylie Adkins, aka Rocky, and we need to locate him. He is the key to busting this investigation wide open. Publishing a story with the sketch hopefully will help find him; any ideas?"

Todd replied, "How about we go with a follow-up story on Sam's disappearance. The public doesn't know much about it yet. I'll have Marsh write it and include the sketch. The story will indicate the police has a possible person of interest in her disappearance. We can reference he may also be a person of interest in the murder of Frank Ramsey, Jr as well. We will need several quotes from you to give the story credibility. Then create an anonymous tip line, maybe we get a hit. What do you think?" Simultaneously, Carla and Walt nodded. "Great,

I'll get Marsh right on it. I'll brief him on what we are doing, and he will meet you in the break room in fifteen minutes, that work for you?" Carla nodded. "Carla, I want to get the son of a bitch as much as you do. We will assist you in any we can, but remember when this all breaks, we get it first before anyone else."

"You both have my word on it."

Todd left and explained to Marsh the plan to hopefully find Wylie Adkins. Marsh gathered all his notes and headed for the break room to wait for Detective McBride.

She said to Walt, "Thanks, hopefully, we get something. Oh, were you able to contact Debbie's parents?"

"Yeah, all I could get out of them was that she worked for a big politician about nine years ago in Florida. I think they're still distraught of losing their only daughter. I didn't press the issue."

"Well, maybe it is nothing and not connected to our jigsaw puzzle. But if you find out anything else, please let me know. Until then, we both need to continue to look for something we can use to solve this tangled web of mystery and murder."

"Did I just hear we, are we a team now?"

Carla left without answering. On the way to the break room, she whispered under her breath. "Wylie Adkins, game on, asshole!"

Published immediately on the *Daily Reporter* website, the local television station picked up the story. Getting ready for work, Daisy had her television on to the mid-day news. The big story was about the *Daily Reporter* story covering the disappearance of Samantha Lewis and that Wylie Adkins, aka Rocky, was a person of interest in the disappearance. She stopped everything she was doing. Thinking to herself that if Rocky had something to do with Spike's death and now, he is a person of interest in the disappearance of a college student, Daisy was wondering who might be next. Not wanting to take any chances with her life, she packed her big suitcase with enough clothes to last for several weeks and left her apartment.

Meeting with her boss, Gabe Whisman, she explained she couldn't work for several weeks because of a personal family issue. Being an understanding boss and friend, he wished her well and to stay in touch with him. At this point, Daisy didn't care whether or not she had a job or if she ever returned, the only thing that mattered was that she needed a safe-haven until they apprehended Rocky.

CHAPTER 43

Landing a big job on high-rise condo development on the Emerald Coast of Florida was something Rocky had been waiting for all his life. Through his longtime friend Casanova, he was finally getting a chance to put his stamp on a significant development. The Emerald Dunes was the first of many buildings in the Emerald Dunes complex. Having worked in the area from time to time over the past twenty years, he loved living there. Several years ago, he had remodeled a beach cottage several blocks from the ocean and had just purchased another one to remodel.

The construction business on the Emerald Coast was very good to him; however, he was waiting on his payment for services rendered before he could invest in the new property. Although he didn't carry out the assassinations of Mark and Joanne Alison himself, he coordinated it while Spike was the triggerman. As a member of Alpha Tango, Rocky had carried out many missions that resulted in deaths, and in a sense, he was also a trained assassin in a military uniform. All members of Alpha

Tango had taken someone's life but saved many in the process.

Today he was meeting with Casanova to receive his big payday for the assassinations. With Spike out of the way, all thirty thousand dollars would be his and enough to remodel his second beach cottage. A successful real estate developer on the Emerald Coast of Florida, Casanova also had a sordid array of risky business ventures with some nasty people but managed to fly under the government's radar and evade prosecution. Casanova always covered all his tracks and let nothing get in his way.

A local beach restaurant and bar near the new high rise was the setting for their meeting. Rocky was already sipping on a beer when Casanova entered the restaurant and bar. Seeing him, he motioned the server to bring a Corona with lime for Casanova. The server sat it in front of Casanova and left. After a ceremonial toast, Casanova quickly took a long draw. Although muted meaningless chatter filled the bar area, silence captured their table. Casanova no longer had any threats to worry about, the fact that one of his Alpha Tango bros was an unnecessary casualty upset him to no end. He knew Spike was a little strange and if he didn't take his meds as prescribed, his PTSD could surface. Rocky, on the other hand, was more impatient and took actions without considering the consequences.

Muted chatter continued throughout the restaurant; however, silence surrounded their table as Spike's death continued to eat at Casanova. "Why kill Spike, that's all I want to know?"

Evading the question, Rocky replied, "Did you bring the money?"

"You didn't answer my question, need I repeat it?"

"Okay, don't get all bent out of shape. Spike was panicking like he sometimes did on our missions and that always concerned me. He had the run-in with Detective McBride and Walt Blevins. I felt she was close to cracking him that would have led back to me and eventually to you. He also had a thing for a waitress called Daisy, spent a night with her. Then, there's the missing college student he had eyes for. He said he had nothing to do with her disappearance; I'm not sure whether I believe him. Anyway, you hired me to do a job, and I did it, all of your dirty secrets are safe with me, you know that, right?" Casanova nodded and drained his beer. Rocky, who had already finished his, signaled the server for another round. After the beers were delivered, Rocky continued. "The money, did you bring it?"

"Not here, what about this lady he shacked up with, is she a threat?"

"I don't think so, it was a one-night fling, and he knew to keep his mouth shut which I believe he did."

Casanova nodded and took a long draw on the Corona. "What time does your crew leave?"

"Five, why?"

"I'll come to the site around six, have a few more beers, talk about old times, Tater, Frog, and Peanuts, work for you?"

Rocky nodded and finished his beer as he needed to get back to the construction site. Casanova's phone chimed, he picked it up and stared at the screen momentarily. The expression on Casanova's face grew tense.

"Hey, is everything okay?" Rocky asked.

"Yeah, it's nothing to be concerned about. See you at six, I'll bring the hard stuff, you bring the beer. I'll call

Tater now and see if he can join us. We'll talk about old times, we'll have a good time and celebrate, we haven't done that for a long time, it's long overdue." Casanova pretended to dial Tater's number. After a short pause, he began talking. "Tater, Casanova here. How about joining Rocky and me at my new condominium complex, say around 6:00 PM?" After a short pause, he continued. "Great, see you then." The call ended. "See, nothing to be concerned about, Rocky, Tater will join us."

"Great, looking forward to seeing him."

Casanova nodded and smiled. Beers finished; they left the beach bar together. They had been in business together for quite some time, they had had each other's back as Alpha Tango buddies, saved each other's lives on several occasions. Reaching their respective cars, they shook hands and then hugged each other like long lost brothers.

CHAPTER 44

Seated on a lounge chair in his office, Mayor Lester James stared at the window wondering what in the hell was happening to his city. A lifelong native, he couldn't quite fathom the atrocities that had occurred over the past several months rocking his town like a major earthquake. As he watched cars traveled down Main Street and citizens wandering about, he rubbed his temples in bewilderment. Oakmont was supposed to be one of the safest places in Kentucky, but not any longer. Violence had taken over this sleepy little slice of heaven. At his wits' end, he wanted answers, but more importantly, he needed the cases solved, and the heinous individuals responsible brought to justice. His city needed to return to the quiet, welcoming town it had always been until an April Fool's day murder of a newspaper publisher stole that from the city.

Although Police Chief Brock Evans had been keeping him abreast on their ongoing investigations, he always felt that critical evidence was being withheld from him.

An afternoon meeting was scheduled to clear the air between them. Chief Evans thought he couldn't trust the mayor because, in the past, leaks from the mayor's office were made public and reach the media. The stakes were too high to let that happen with these cases. Panic in the community would not happen on his watch.

Mayor James arrived a few minutes early and barged into Chief Evans's office where Detective McBride was already meeting with the chief on how to proceed. Chief Evans motioned the mayor to take a seat beside Detective McBride. Mayor James had not been officially introduced to her, he only knew of her, and that was the extent of their relationship. The chief explained to him she is lead detective on these cases and asked her to join their meeting.

Mayor James had exhausted all his patience and took control of the meeting immediately directing his anger at Chief Evans. "Tell me everything, and I want all these cases solved, and now. If you can't do that, I'll find someone who can?"

"Mayor, calm down. We have a lot of fine people working on these cases. Why don't I have Detective McBride, the lead detective, bring you up to date on everything?"

"That's fine, but first, tell me why you think Wylie Adkins is involved with any of this as stated in the story in the paper? I've known Wylie ever since he returned from the service. He did some renovations on my home and worked with me on some house-flips. As far as I know, he's never been in any trouble. He's a good man."

"Mayor, we hear what you are saying; however, we found two sets of fingerprints at the crime scene where

Frank Ramsey, Jr. was murdered. One pair belonged to Frank while the other belonged to Wylie. He and Frank were in Special Forces together. I received an anonymous letter where to find Frank. I received another one that stated that Frank killed Mark and Joanne Alison and where to find the murder weapon. We believe Wylie wrote those letters and is key to solving these murders and the disappearance of Samantha Lewis."

Lashing out at them, Mayor James asked, "What the hell, what else have you not told me?"

"Let me finish, please," Carla replied. The mayor nodded. "We're not saying he is involved, just that he might have information that can help us solve the cases. I've seen him and Frank at McGruder's together. They were also seen together at Whisman's on two different occasions. We've contacted Wylie's cell number several times, but it just goes to voicemail every time. We understand he is currently working in Florida. Do you know any other way we can reach him?"

Shaking his head back and forth, Mayor James asked, "Is there anything else I need to know?" Silence grabbed hold of the room. He was growing impatient as Detective McBride, and the chief glanced at each other. "Well, by the look on your faces, there is something else, let's hear it."

Detective McBride reluctantly responded, "At each murder, a blue golf ball marker with a gold fedora embossed on it was found at every crime scene." Mayor James' face grew tense. "We found a plastic bag at Franks' house that contained the weapon used to kill Mark and Joanne Alison and at least two more of the same golf ball markers. We know where they came from, and so do you." The silence continued in the room, the mayor didn't know how to respond, or if he should. "Mayor, that's everything, do you have any further questions?"

Before the mayor could respond, Detective McBride's smartphone suddenly chimed interrupting the conversation. Both the mayor and the chief noticed anxiety in her eyes and the color on her face began to fade. She said, "I'm sorry, but I must excuse myself for a moment, I need to make an important call related to the case. It won't take long, then I will be right back to finish our discussion and answer any other questions you may have."

Reluctantly, Chief Evans and the mayor nodded. Stepping outside the office, she called Walt. The call lasted only three minutes, and she returned to the office where the mayor and chief were engaged in a casual conversation about city government. Chief Evans immediately recognized the expression on her face. He'd seen it many times before, the face of bad news. She cleared her throat and sighed, "Sorry, I had to step out, I apologize. Walt Blevins, the publisher at the *Daily Reporter*, texted me he had information on Wylie Adkins." Sighing and some deep breathing didn't erase the disappointment mirrored on her face. Mayor James and Chief Evans on the edge of their chair felt her disappointment. "Wylie Adkins was found dead at the construction site where he was currently working." Mayor James's expression represented what he felt inside, Chief Evans's eyes exploded open at the news. "Preliminary investigation indicates it was an unfortunate accident. Apparently, he was drinking beer on the fifth floor after everyone had gone home for the day. Reports indicate he may have slipped from the fifth floor and fell to his death. OSHA was now in charge of the investigation."

Stunned and speechless, Chief Evans and Mayor James sat in silence and disbelief. Mayor James had just lost a friend and golfing buddy; his face was stone gray. The best chance in solving the murders and finding Samantha Lewis died as Rocky hit the ground in Florida. Breaking the silence smothering the room, she continued, "Until the coroner completes the autopsy, they cannot absolutely rule it as an accident, but it looks that way since no one else was present at the time of death. The *Daily Reporter*'s sister newspaper in Florida will monitor the investigation and relay that information to Walt. End of story, and our investigation just died with him."

As Mayor James got up to leave, he turned around and said, "If you hear anything else, let me know. I still can't believe Wylie is dead and that he was involved in this whole mess. Guess that shows that when you think you know someone really well, you don't."

After the mayor left, Carla and Chief Evans stared at each other in disbelief. Outside, howling wind and rain pelted against the windows matching the gloominess inside his office. "Chief, I guess my investigation is dead now. Never thought it would end this way. I believe we were so close to finding the answers to all our questions. Wylie was the key to crack this mystery, and now he's conveniently dead. Why?"

"Call it dumb luck for whoever is behind all of this, they just got a 'get out of jail free card,' and we can't change that. However, if we keep trying and digging, then maybe we will catch some dumb luck of our own.

Take the rest of the day off and tomorrow, then come back refreshed, we'll solve this mystery."

"Thanks, I have a date with Jameson, my liquid lover and I'm sure he will ease my disappointment and stress." Chief Evans nodded, and a crinkled smile crossed his lips as she left.

CHAPTER 45

Surprised by the news, Todd and Walt felt like they were at a best friend's funeral service. Both looked pale and mentally drained. The death of Wylie Adkins put a symbolic nail in the coffin. All the evidence in all the unsolved cases was circumstantial and filled with assumptions, his death, for the most part, ended any current hopes of solving the murder of three individuals and the disappearance of Sam. The air was stifling, and the silence was deafening. Todd, feeling helpless, quietly broke the silence holding them hostage. "I can't believe our best chance of solving the cases died as Wylie crashed into the ground. Where do we go from here?"

Although there was nothing good about the news they received today, remaining positive, Walt replied, "I guess we keep looking for something that will provide us answers, and closure for all of us, and the community. You know, we need to keep a positive attitude; maybe, we will get lucky, discover something that ties everything together or points us in the right direction. You never know, what might fall in our lap." Todd nodded. "There's one thing that bothered me about Wylie the first time I met him. I didn't understand how a construction consultant fit in with the movers and shakers of Oakmont. I'm not sure he was smart enough to pull all this off and not get caught. Call it intuition but somebody big is behind these murders, and maybe that is why Wylie is conveniently dead. Someone is tying up every loose end, and it must be someone powerful."

Shrugging his shoulders, Todd replied, "Well, I hope you are right, guess I should get back to my office and get to work on this new revelation. If you need anything or hear anything, let me know?"

Walt nodded as Todd left. Staring at the office walls hoping something worthwhile would surface, he massaged his temples to ease the tension in his body. Wylie was dead, so was the investigation for now. They had a lot of information, but now it was meaningless. Hopefully, a cup of Foglifter would ease the frustration and tension inside him, clear his mind. After he pushed the brew button, the coffee began to fill a Styrofoam cup. Walking to the door leading out to the deck, he stepped out to breathe in some fresh air and cleared his mind. A couple of minutes later, he returned to his office walking over to the Keurig where coffee was running down the outside of the Styrofoam cup. After a silent expression of utter disgust, he glanced at the lighted brew button and laughed. He realized he pushed the wrong brew button for his small Styrofoam cup. Having a mess to clean up, he removed the full cup of coffee and set it on a paper towel beside the Keurig. Removing the overflow reservoir containing the excess coffee, he took it to his bathroom to clean it. After running water over the top portion of it, he turned it over. His face lit up with both amazement and disbelief. In his mind, he exclaimed, "My, oh my, what do we have here?"

Staring up at him was a laminated wallet-sized photo of a beautiful lady and a young child. Mark Alison wanted to keep it secret, and taped it to the bottom of the overflow reservoir. Removing the picture, he studied it for a moment. Remembering the wallpaper on the mini-laptop, the child looked very similar. His mind was running everywhere as he turned it over. Landon - 8 years old was written on the reverse side. Turning it back over, he wondered who Landon and the beautiful woman were? Todd knew Mark had an affair; could his mistress have ended up pregnant? Walt remembered in the letter from the 'G,' she stated Mark gave her a special gift that she loved more than everything in the world.

A wild and crazy thought entered his mind. KT Stopski, human resources manager, might validate his assumption. A gentle knock on her door, she glanced his way. "You have a minute?" She motioned him in. "I have a strange question to ask you, and don't ask me why I want to know, but do you know Mark Alison's middle name?"

"That is strange, I'll say. Let me pull his personnel file, and we'll see what we can find out."

Unlocking a file cabinet containing anything related to employees, past, and present, she retrieved Mark's file. Opening it up, she reviewed its contents, then handed it to Walt. Opening the folder, Walt examined, gave it back to her and returned to his office. Hitting the second number on his speed dial list, he waited for an answer. After two rings, it went straight to voicemail. He left an urgent message; however, he knew that Carla was probably off duty and didn't want to be bothered. On his way to Laura's townhome, he kept thinking about the photo of a young boy and woman hoping that it was the break they needed to revive their cases.

CHAPTER 46

Early the next morning, Detective McBride entered the *Daily Reporter* and checked in with the receptionist, then headed straight for Walt's office. He was expecting her since they had talked briefly that morning. Entering his office, she sat in one of the winged-back chairs across from him. Walt was staring at a photo in his hand. His eyes met hers, and he handed the picture to her. "Look at this photo and then we will talk."

Immediately, the photo of the young boy and a woman grabbed her attention. Turning it over, she read what was on the back. "Who is this?"

"I'm fairly sure it's Mark's mistress and his child. Mark's middle name is Landon. I believe someone took the photo about the time Mark created the spreadsheet. I think he was blackmailing the lady who wrote the letter. Still, don't know why or who she is but I will find out."

"Okay, why blackmail the mother of his child and how are you going to find out?"

"You remember Todd told us that Mark and Joanne had affairs with people in the newspaper business. I'll start there. Maybe if we can find out her identity, we can get some answers. That's all I have to go on."

"Answers to what; everyone is dead, and the dead aren't talking."

"True; however, the person being blackmailed has the answers. Are you giving up, the great Detective Carla McBride?"

"Hell, no. Any other theories you have?"

"Let's review your information. Frank and Wylie used aliases. They apparently were in Special Forces together, and they had the same tattoo as well. Frank worked in the newspaper business until his father needed his help. He returned home and reconnected with Wylie. Now, they're both dead. I don't think that is a coincidence, do you?"

She nodded and said, "I think I need to pay Frank's parents another visit."

On the way to see Frank's parents, her mind wandered, and she thought about how to get more information from them. She felt they weren't telling her everything, maybe because of the sudden shock of their son's death. After pulling into the driveway, she approached the door and knocked. Footsteps move across the hardwood floor, the door opened. "Detective McBride, what brings you back here so soon?"

"There have been some new developments in your son's death. May I come in, I need to ask you and your husband a few more questions?"

"Of course, but Frank's been sick ever since our son died. So, I'll do my best to answer your questions. What else do you need to know that we haven't already told you?"

"Our investigation showed that your son was in Army

Special Forces with a Wylie Adkins of Oakmont. Wylie died of a suspicious nature the other day in Florida, and the investigation is ongoing. Did your son ever talk about his time in the service or have any pictures? Anything will help us bring your son's murderer to justice."

"He never talked about his time in the Army, and I see why now. Frank, Jr. kept all his stuff hidden in a box in the garage, and he didn't know I knew where it was. You know a son can't keep stuff hidden from his mother forever. Anyway, I found it, but never looked in it. It was his private business, and if he wanted us to know, he would have shared it with us."

"I know this might not be the time, but I would like to look through it if you don't mind? There may be something that can help us."

"I suppose it won't hurt now, and if it helps you, then follow me."

Once in the garage, Elaine retrieved a cardboard box hidden behind several other larger boxes. She sat the cardboard box secured with tape on the workbench. Seeing a box cutter on the pegboard, Carla used it to cut away the tape and opened the box. Inside were pictures and other papers from his Army days. After glancing at several, a photo of Spike with a beautiful lady held her gaze. On a beach somewhere, maybe in Florida, the two of them were sharing an intimate embrace. They were smiling as though they didn't have a care in the world. She wondered who might have taken this picture, but that was not important. Turning it over, it was blank, she uttered in disgust. Turning her gaze to Elaine, she showed her the picture. "Do you know who she is?"

"No, I don't, pretty, isn't she?" Carla acknowledged her. "Frank never talked about his friends, especially his women friends. He was very private as we told you the other day."

Continuing to look through the pictures, Carla was taking them out one by one and putting them in a pile on the workbench. Only a few remained, and thus far, the one of Spike and the lady was the only one that might help her. On the bottom of the box, the last picture became imprinted in her brain. Six guys in uniform, showing off the same tattoos, stared up at her. Smiles on their faces, they looked happy. Showing it to Elaine, she shrugged her shoulders and shook her head back-and-forth. Turning the picture over; an inscription on the back provided her the answer.

Tater, Spike, Frog, Rocky, Peanuts, Casanova—Special Forces Alpha Tango.

Elaine read the inscription, and she shook her head back-and-forth, once more. Grabbing both pictures, Carla said, "I need to take these photos if you don't mind?" Elaine nodded, and Carla left with a glimmer of hope.

CHAPTER 47

While waiting to hear back from Carla, Walt was trying to put all his information into perspective. The identity of Mark's mistress was foremost on his mind. Mark had been a publisher at one of the company's newspapers in Florida before coming to Oakmont. Maybe his mistress worked there as well. From that affair, he had a son which he didn't know about until he received a photo of him. Needing a break from all the new information, Walt reflected on what had happened since Chad named him permanent publisher of the *Daily Reporter*. He had met Laura and was madly in love with her. The newspaper was doing exceptionally well building their audience and making lots of money. He remembered the day when Chad offered him the job, handing him the official job offer in writing. He remembered Chad telling him he believed he was the right fit for Oakmont, and discussing it with COO, Gina Dickerson.

A proverbial light went off somewhere in his brain. It was a shot in the dark, but could Gina Dickerson be

Mark's mystery lady he thought? His phone ringing interrupted his thoughts, Carla McBride lit up his screen. He answered, listened, and responded, "Yes, I'm still at the office, and I've got some..."

Carla interrupted him, and before he could complete his sentence, the call ended. He scowled and waited for her to arrive. Employees were leaving for the day when she arrived at the paper. She made a B-Line to his office, entered and closed the door. Handing him the photos, he studied them and said, "Holy shit, Carla! That could be Joanne Alison, sure resembles her."

"Yeah, that's just what I thought, too. The other photo is Frank and his Special Forces, comrades. Turn it over and read the back of it?" Turning it over, *Tater, Spike, Frog, Rocky, Peanuts, Casanova. Special Forces Alpha Tango* glared back at him. Carla continued. "We know who Spike and Rocky are, we now need to find out who the other people are and where they live?"

Walt immediately taped pieces of information they had up on the wall he used for his brainstorming sessions. Within minutes everything that might be pertinent to the case covered the wall. As they studied the wall trying to make sense of everything their thoughts wandered everywhere trying to make a connection. It was almost too much for them to digest all at once. Staring at each other for a moment, Walt wondered if he had missed anything. "Listen, I have one more item we need to look at."

"What's that?"

Standing behind his desk, he pulled up the website of the *Daily Reporter*'s parent company and clicked on the link to bring up the corporate employees. Listed under the COO was Gina Dickerson. A short bio and a recent photo piqued their interest. After printing the page, he placed it on the wall beside the picture of Mark's mystery lady and her son. "Carla, meet "G." Back at his laptop, he searched for more information to support his assumption. The usual bio information popped up; mostly Gina's professional details beginning with the most recent position and working backward. He continued reviewing older information; however, none of it was helpful. However, on the next web page, a newspaper wedding announcement about Gina Alderson marrying newly elected United States senator, John Dickerson. He printed two copies. He gave one to Carla, and they read it silently. After they finished reading it, big smiles covered their faces.

"Bingo, this is what we have been looking for. Walt, can you believe, the best man was none other than Wylie Adkins, and he is dead? Frank Ramsey, Jr., aka Spike, was a groomsman. Not sure who Charles Brown, Al Bocconi, and Hank Fisher are, but we need to find them." Walt nodded and taped the wedding announcement on the wall next to the photo of Alpha Tango.

Exhausted and needing a break, Walt fired up the Keurig to brew them a cup of coffee. Foglifter for him while she preferred decaf. Walt would have to go to the main common area for that. He picked up the only decaf K-cup there and thought that would have to do. Todd noticed Walt there and stepped out of his office to see what he was doing. "What are you still doing here, boss?"

"Come back to my office, we need your insight. We are close to finding all the pieces to our jigsaw puzzle. We just need another set of eyes." He gave Walt a funny look but followed him back to his office. As they entered, Todd noticed Carla staring at all kinds of information taped on the wall. Walt explained what all of it was. As Todd was reviewing the information, Walt placed the decaf pod in the Keurig and hit the brew button. While it was brewing, he picked up his coffee and took a sip. Within a minute, Walt handed Carla her coffee. Carla and Walt were enjoying their coffee while Todd continued to analyze the items on the wall until Walt broke the uneasy silence in the room. "We have a theory and keep an open mind as you listen."

Todd acknowledged him. "Mark had an affair with a woman who calls herself "G." We're certain that is Gina Dickerson, COO of our parent company." Todd's eyes light up. "She ended up pregnant and named her child Landon after him. Her husband, John Dickerson, a powerful United States Senator knows the baby isn't his, but never confronts her. Hurt by Mark's affair, Joanne gets revenge by having an affair with Frank Ramsey, Jr., who was the business manager at the newspaper where Mark was the publisher. Follow me so far?"

Todd gave him a quizzical look and Walt continued. "Remorseful, Gina let Mark know about his child and sends him several photos with the letter. He saved them both and kept them secret from Joanne. You said Mark loved the horses and probably owed a lot of money to a bookie, whom we have not found yet. The bookie was putting pressure on him and that caused him to blackmail John or Gina. It makes more sense that it was Gina because she said in the letter that her husband was the gubernatorial frontrunner, she also stated she hoped he would let the skeletons remain in the closet. She started paying Mark the blackmail money. In the meantime, Mark is getting more pressure from the bookie and asked her for even more money. She refused, so Mark threatened to expose this little secret which could ruin her husband's political career. Somehow John finds out and tells her he will take care of it. He contacts Wylie who hired Frank to carry out the plan to assassinate Mark. And to be on the safe side, Joanne's murder was collateral damage."

"Whoa, Walt. All of this sounds crazy. I think you and Carla have been watching too much Bones or CSI." Carla sent her best 'shut-up-look' his way. Todd, though, showing some skepticism continued, "I'm still not sold but continue the rest of this bizarre puzzle, and we'll see if it makes sense."

"Frank killed Mark and two months later takes out Joanne. There was not much evidence to go on other than the blue ball marker with the gold fedora found at each scene including at Frank's house. We believe the ball markers were a diversionary tactic to plant the seed of a serial killer scenario. The anonymous letter Carla received referred to a game, and we believe that was the game. That same letter told her where to find Frank's body and that whoever sent the letter, probably Wylie, killed Frank because he got sloppy and couldn't trust him. Frank had a one-nighter with a waitress name Daisy that worked at Whisman's. Frank and Wylie met there on two different occasions. John Dickerson probably ordered the hit. Daisy came to see Carla when she found out about Spike. Daisy helped create a sketch of Rocky which turned out to be Wylie Adkins. The sketch ran in the paper and on our website. And finally, Wylie conveniently ends up dead in a construction accident in Florida where John and Gina live. There you have it, end of story. John Dickerson is our man without a doubt."

"Wow. If that is all true, how do you two plan to

prove it since everyone that knows something is dead or not talking?"

Carla interjected, "We are working on it. Hopefully, something will surface that connects everything and everyone in this jigsaw puzzle. I feel it in my bones, were so close to blowing this wide open."

CHAPTER 48

Chief Evans, like Todd, was very skeptical of their theory behind all the murders. Carla didn't think there wasn't a reason to go after Gina because she likely wasn't involved in the crimes. Even if she were, ratting on her husband would destroy his political aspirations and her chance of being the First Lady of Florida. However, Carla made a call anyway. Gina Dickerson was unavailable, and she left a message. Hoping to get a return call; her focus shifted back to John, who was their only shot at seeking justice? They needed a miracle or John was going to get away with it all.

Carla and Laura were having lunch at Apollo Café since they had not been to lunch in several weeks. Some girl time was long overdue, and she wanted all the details on Laura and Walt's relationship. Carla didn't even know they had moved in together and not surprised at all when Laura told her. In the middle of lunch, she received a text from Walt to come to his office at 2:00 PM. Carla enjoyed her time with Laura and headed to the newspaper. As in the past, she just bypassed the receptionist and proceeded to Walt's office. The door opened, and Carla entered. In one of the wing-backs, Todd sat while Walt was across from him on the sofa. She sat in the other wing-back chair and anxiously looked at both of them. "What's going on, guys. Do you have some good news?"

Todd nodded and replied, "Sort of, we may have just got lucky. I received a call from the editor of one of our sister papers in Florida. During the autopsy, they discovered DNA from an unidentified male at the crime scene. After running it through all databases, they got a hit. It belongs to John Dickerson, and he is now a person of interest in the death of Wylie Adkins. Authorities are questioning him and his legal team about that."

Carla responded emphatically, "Imagine that, unless he confesses or they have other incriminating information, he may still get off free. We need something else to crucify the SOB."

"Carla, remember, he is innocent until proven guilty. They will let me know of any further developments. That's all I have for now." Todd left, and they just sat in silence. Although it was good news, depending on how that investigation goes, they knew it still might not lead to any justice for Mark and Joanne Alison.

"Walt, that investigation could take forever, there has to be a smoking gun somewhere."

"You said in your investigation of Mark and Joanne, only one bank account, a joint account with Chase existed. He's had to have another one somewhere to receive the blackmail money and then pay the bookie unless it involved cash transactions, which is possible, but doubtful. We need to find the bookie and follow the money. Also, we need to look at Wylie Adkins affairs as well. There might be something that definitely links him to John Dickerson."

"First, we tried to identify the bookie from the email account found on the mini-laptop, but as suspected, it was on a public server and since deleted. Now, Wylie's home is not a crime scene, so we can't just burst in there without a warrant. And we will need probable cause, and that may not be easy. Plus, we only have a PO box for an address. We'll need a physical address to get a warrant."

"I can give Keith Edwards a try again, and maybe he knows where he lives."

"Worth a shot, he knew Wylie's phone number, so, he might just know where he lived."

"I'll call him."

"No, I will go see him and put a little pressure on him. If he knows something, I'll get it out of him, trust me."

"Okay, keep me informed."

Carla had to go through the same hoops as before at the Industrial Park. Finally, she was at Alcom Industries and entered through the main doors. She smiled, it must be her lucky day she thought as Keith was visiting Kimberly, the vivacious young receptionist. Seeing Carla out of the corner of his eye, he quickly removed his hands from her shoulders and walked toward Carla.

"Hi, Mr. Edwards, I didn't know you were a massage therapist, too."

"Kimberly complained of a stiff neck, and I was just trying to help, it's not what you think."

"Yeah, right? Why don't we go back to your office, I have a few more questions for you?"

"Okay, what's this about."

"In your office, now."

Quietly he agreed, and they walked to his office in silence. Once inside his office, Carla exploded on him as he became flushed. "Keith, I don't know what was going on out there, but I'm sure your wife wouldn't approve of it, would she? I need answers, and if I get the answers I want, I saw nothing going on out there, you got it?" He nodded. "Are you aware that your buddy Wylie Adkins died in Florida allegedly from a construction accident; however, his death has been classified as suspicious in nature, and authorities are talking to a person of interest." Shocked and acting nervously, he shook his back and forth. "Wylie is somehow connected to the murders of Mark and Joanne Alison and Frank Ramsey, Jr. Do you know where he lived in Oakmont?"

Still, in shock, he let out a deep sigh. "All I know is that it is near the university in a small apartment complex."

"Name or your wife will get a call from me."

"University Terrace Apartments. But I don't know which apartment, I'm telling you the truth. He also owns a small cottage in the Pensacola Beach area as well. I think it's on Santa Rosa Island. My wife and I used it several times on vacation."

"More information than I need but thanks, and by the way, keep your dirty hands-off young Kimberly, she's not your type. And one other piece of advice; quit undressing the ladies with your roaming eyes like you are doing right now, if you know what's good for your marriage, got it?" Keith nodded and sat behind his desk trying to compose himself as Carla left.

CHAPTER 49

Back at the police station, she called Walt to inform him of her next move. Before meeting with Chief Evans, a call to Rick, the manager at the University Terrace Apartments, to get Wylie's apartment number was next on her list. As with the last time that Carla called him, it took several rings before he answered. "Rick, this Detective Carla McBride. Remember me?" After a response she didn't like, she replied, "Listen here, you frigging dickhead; I need to know which apartment Wylie Adkins rented? Whether you know it; he is dead. So, don't jerk me around, got it?" Saving face and attempting to cool her Irish temper, he quickly responded with the information. "Thanks, I'll be back with a search warrant as soon as possible. If I were you, I would contact the owners and explain what the hell is going on and why we need a search warrant. And one last thing, erase your vision of me in your mind forever, got it?"

The call ended, and she barged into the chief's office. Luckily for her, Chief Evans was not on the phone or meeting with someone. After refreshing his memory about their theory of Wylie's involvement, and his death was suspicious in nature now, and that John Dickerson was a person of interest in that death. Initially, he scoffed at her theory, but she kept pressing him with her Irish personality. After about a ten-minute discussion, he finally approved her request for a search warrant.

Two hours later, with a forensic team waiting, she handed Rick the warrant. Within minutes The forensics team entered and combed through everything. They opened drawers, looking in cabinets, and every nook and cranny for anything that might be evidence. So far, they had struck out. All this time, Carla was examining everything in the living room including pictures on a bookshelf. Nothing caught her eye, and she wondered whether a search warrant was a waste of time.

Suddenly, a forensics investigator yelled from the bedroom. Rushing to the bedroom, she found Sherry taking an old typewriter out of the closet. The IBM Selectric typewriter looked to be in good shape, and since it had a new ribbon spool in it, someone used it recently. Forensics also found a ream of white printer paper and a box of number-ten white envelopes in the closet. "Sherry, the typewriter, paper, and envelopes is a start, keep looking, we need more."

The search went on for another hour, and nothing valuable had surfaced yet. Old bank statements found didn't show any kind of unusual activity but would still be logged in as evidence. An ancient flip phone discovered in a nightstand by the bed was dead, the battery was gone. A trash basket under the sink hadn't been emptied for quite some time because it wreaked of the smell of rotten tomatoes, lettuce, and who knows what else.

Removing the white trash and holding it up, something thin and black was visible in the bottom.

Sherry exclaimed, "Carla, you need to come in here and look at this? We may have something."

As she entered the kitchen, Sherry was holding a white trash bag with something black in the bottom resembling a typewriter ribbon. Carla asked, "Is that a typewriter ribbon in the bottom?"

"Certainly, looks like one, but we don't want to disturb anything by dumping it out here. We'll take it back and sort through it carefully. If it is a typewriter ribbon, we want to be able to read what is stamped on it. Rocky's typewriter uses ribbons that can only be used once and whatever is on it, we should be able to decipher it. Be patient and keep your fingers crossed, okay?" Carla knew the drill and nodded; it would be a waiting game. "I know, but we are just about done here, so we'll get all this stuff back and sort through it tonight. Go home and have a drink, I'll call you once we analyzed everything; hopefully, that will be tonight."

Relaxing in a lounger inside her apartment, she was enjoying her second drink of the evening. A quick peek at her phone, 10:00 PM had rolled over, nothing from Sherry yet. Even though Jameson was easing her anxiety and tension, she was still on pins and needles waiting for that call. As she put Jameson to her lips, her phone lit up. Caller ID read Oakmont Police Station. Answering it, she quickly hung up. Her affair with Jameson, her liquid lover, would have to wait for another night. When she arrived at the police station, Sherry was standing at her desk with a sheet of paper. Bypassing professional courtesy and pleasantries, she asked, "Sherry, let's get right to it, what did you find?"

"As I suspected, it was a typewriter ribbon, and only used one time as I thought. We are still analyzing everything stamped on it, but we found something you will be interested in and wanted you to see it. Old typewriter ribbon spools advance as each key strikes the ribbon making it easier to recover the typed impressions. Then you…"

"Sherry, I'm sure that's fascinating as hell to you, but just tell me what you found."

"Right. First, the paper and envelopes likely match the anonymous letters you received. Wylie's fingerprints were on the typewriter. Now, what you are waiting to hear. We have been able to pull at least a few sentences."

"You are killing me, what the hell did you find?"

Handing Carla, the sheet of paper with what they were able to decipher, she read it, and let out a big sigh. A smile beamed across her face. "Thank god, we have something that ties Wylie to Casanova, who we believe is John Dickerson. Keep working to see what else you can find."

Sherry nodded. Carla had the smoking gun she needed, but it still wouldn't be enough to arrest him. Proving that Casanova was John Dickerson was paramount. Excited about the evidence, she dialed Walt's cell number. As it rang, Carla noticed the time and hung up. What she had to tell him could wait until morning. Calling it a night, she headed back home, where Jameson called her name. Jameson greeted her with bits of caramel and vanilla. After several sips, her thoughts focused on the bizarre mystery she was trying to unravel. The photo of Alpha Tango was front and center in her mind. Grabbing her iPad, she opened the photo icon and found the picture of six Army Special Forces young men defending and risking their lives for their country. *Tater, Spike, Frog, Rocky, Peanuts, Casanova—Special Forces Alpha Tango.* How could some of these brave men do something so horrible she thought?

She focused on the man known as Casanova. Enlarging it her eyes pierced his. Although the photo lost its clarity, she thought it resembled the picture on the internet. That's it; she thought, facial recognition from this photo. Crop his face and hoped it would work. Nothing to lose she thought. Hopefully, the program could identify all members of Alpha Tango. Her iPad read 11:17 PM. Without hesitation, the last drop of Jameson touched her lips. Dialing Sherry's cell number, she waited for her to answer. It rang and rang, Sherry answered ranting and raving for a few seconds as Carla flipped her the bird through the phone. "Sorry to bother you, can you take a current photo of John Dickerson and use facial recognition or reconstruction to show what he looked like as a young man?"

"The program we have helps us identify who someone might look like from a current photo, some programs take skeletal remains and predicts what they look like today. The FBI might have something much more advanced, but I'm not sure. What's on your mind?"

"You know the photo we have of Alpha Tango; can you enlarge that photo and use facial recognition to compare the face of Casanova to the picture of John Dickerson on the internet?"

"We can try, but when you enlarge an old photo like that, it gets grainy and pixilated making it harder to use and stand up in a court of law should you ever need it."

"Who cares, it's worth a shot, make it a priority first thing tomorrow morning, okay?"

Silenced buzzed from her iPhone as she flipped her another bird. Sleep was not coming quickly, and her cocktail glass had sad eyes. A trip to the bar, Jameson swirled around the bottom of the cocktail glass smiling. After sitting him on the nightstand, her pillow looked hard to resist. As her head snuggled into the soft pillow, Jameson would have to wait till tomorrow evening as shades of darkness surrounded her.

CHAPTER 50

Walt's strategic planning session went as he predicted. Thrilled with all facets of it; Chad gave it his blessing. Based on his strategic plan, building the budget was next and due in about a month. Chad left that afternoon, and Walt needed some diversion from managing a newspaper. Researching Alpha Tango would fill that need. His goal was to find as much information about them as was out there and match a real name to a nickname. He knew that would not be easy. Plus, Army Special Forces kept their identities secret. After hours and hours of searching, his fears came true. There was nothing useful on the web. It was a dead end. Needing some help, he hoped Todd was the answer. As usual, Todd's door was partially open, and Walt knocked. Todd acknowledged him, motioning him to have a seat. Walt explained what he needed, and Todd informed he would contact his college buddy in the Pentagon.

Walt returned to his office and fixed himself another Foglifter. While he walked outside to the deck, his cell phone rang. Recognizing the caller ID, he quickly put it on speaker and greeted her.

"I went to see Keith Edwards again since he had Wylie's phone number and hoped he had an address for him. I caught him massaging the shoulders of the attractive young receptionist and used it to harass him to tell me where Wylie lived. It turns out he lived in the same apartment building as Samantha Lewis, what a coincidence. Anyway, we got a search warrant and found an old IBM Selectric typewriter Rocky used to type the anonymous letters I received. We found the typewriter ribbon he used in the trash and our forensic team is still analyzing the ribbon for any other evidence. At least we can tie Wylie to John Dickerson. Hopefully, something else will turn up. I also have forensics using facial recognition software to identify who's who in the photo."

"That's interesting because I've been researching Alpha Tango on the internet, but nothing useful is surfacing. I spoke with Todd to see if he knew anyone in the Army that could help us put a real name to a nickname. He's working on it."

"Hopefully something will turn up so we can get that SOB. Walt, can you hold, I've got another call. It appears to be Elaine Ramsey. Tell you what, I call you back after I'm through talking with her." Ending the call to Walt, she picked-up the call and listened for a moment or two and ended the call. Twenty minutes later, Carla pulled into the driveway at the home of Elaine and Frank Ramsey. Elaine was waiting for her and opened the door as she approached the house. Once inside, Elaine handed Carla a letter to read. After finishing it, she thanked Elaine and giving her an emotional hug.

Thirty minutes later, Carla pulled into the parking lot

for the *Daily Reporter*. She had a habit of just barging in without notice or warning. The employees of the newspaper had seen her a lot lately, and Carla waved at a few on her way to his office. Once inside Walt's office, she handed him the letter. A few minutes later, he put his phone on speaker and dialed Tater's number and waited for an answer. After several rings, they heard Tater's voicemail greeting. Walt left an urgent message about Spike to grab his attention.

Five minutes later, Walt's phone rang, he answered and listened as Tater greeted Walt.

"Thank you for calling me back. Please don't hang up, I'm putting you on speaker so that Detective Carla McBride of the Oakmont Police Department can join the call if you don't mind."

"Well, I guess that's okay, what's this all about? Your message says you have information about Spike. Is he okay?"

"We will get to that in a moment. We know Tater is a nickname for you, what is your given name?"

"Allen Michael Bocconi, but I go by Al. Now, what's going on with Spike?"

"Mr. Bocconi, this Detective Carla McBride. We are sorry to inform you; Spike was found dead in his home last week."

"Oh, my goodness, sorry to hear that. What the hell happened?"

"I'll get to that in a minute. Spike's mother, Elaine, called me and told me she received a letter addressed to Spike several days ago. It was the letter you sent him that's how we got your number. We need your help?"

"First, what happened to Spike, and then I'll see if I can and will help you, okay?"

"Got it, here we go, this will take a few minutes."

"I'm retired, got all day."

Walt said, "Are you alone?"

"Strange question, but yes, just me and my dog, Rocket?"

Hearing Rocket barked in the background, Walt explained their entire theory to Al. He listened intently but couldn't help interjecting a few comments during the five-minute explanation. After Walt finished, nothing but silence exuded from the speaker. Finally, Rocket let out a few barks and the sound of water running filled the speaker.

Walt asked, "Tater, you there?"

"Yeah, old Rocket wanted a dog biscuit and a drink of water. So, I took care of him. I had you on speaker the whole time and heard it all. That's some crazy-ass theory you got there. I've known Casanova since we were kids growing up as cousins, and I have a hard time believing he had those people killed to keep that secret hidden."

Carla interjected, "But you know…"

"Let me finish detective, okay? And involved in Rocky's death, I don't know, Rocky worked for him a lot. Plus, we always had each other's back for a long time, if you know what I mean? We all hung around together all the time and would do anything for each other, and I mean anything. But murder, I don't know about that, it just makes little sense. We were all like blood brothers. Special forces do that to you."

Carla responded, "We get that, but people change. Politics changes people. Power leads to corruption, and people with power feel they're invincible, being an FBI agent, you know that."

"Yeah, I know, but Casanova, I don't know. Why kill

and risk everything? He had a promising political career and was a successful real estate developer as well. I believe if it got out that Landon wasn't his son, he had enough power and money to overcome it besides John had a far worse skeleton in his closet that would certainly destroy his political ambitions."

"Like what?" asked Carla.

"Look, he doesn't know I know about it, we're family, so, I plan to keep it that way, can we move on?"

Carla continued, "Yeah, will you help us?"

"How?"

"I have a photo of Alpha Tango Special Forces from Spike's mother. It has six men in army fatigues showing off their tattoos. Written on the back is…Tater, Spike, Frog, Rocky, Peanuts, Casanova—Alpha Tango Special Forces. You remember that photo?"

"Yeah, our base photojournalist, made sure we all had one before we left the service. Picman we called him, I remember the time he and John had a verbal altercation over some photo, it was sort of funny because Picman got the better of him. Sorry for the reminiscing, anyway, it's on the fridge, that's what prompted me to write the letter to Spike once I heard Rocky had passed away."

She replied, "Okay, we need you to put names to each person, and if you don't mind, I will record the rest of this conversation."

"Yeah, that's fine. I'm first, then Frank Ramsey, Jr.; Hank Fisher; Wylie Adkins; Charles Brown; John Dickerson. How's that going to help?"

She asked, "Okay, Casanova is John Dickerson, correct?"

"Yeah, that's what I said."

"Okay, we are waiting for other evidence secured

from Rocky's apartment to be analyzed to prove a direct connection to John. We have a typewriter ribbon from an old IBM Selectric typewriter that forensics is still deciphering."

"I can't believe Rocky is still using that old typewriter instead of a computer, but he was such an old-school guy, now what were you saying?"

"We need positive proof that Casanova is John Dickerson before we tie him to everything."

"Detective, if you are going after him, you better have an airtight case, and I mean really airtight. John's a powerful man with a lot of money and resources down here if you know what I mean? Other people have gone after him and failed. Even the FBI has been monitoring his activity for years but never had enough to arrest him. It better be airtight with credible evidence to haul him in, or it will all backfire in your face."

"Got it. In the letter, you mention that Frog and Peanuts died in a boating accident."

"Yeah, the Coast Guard ruled it an accident. It happened after dark while returning from a fishing trip in the gulf. Something happened to the boat, and it exploded; no witnesses and the wreckage was found the next morning scattered everywhere. Their bodies never surfaced. Although the Coast Guard thought the accident looked a little suspicious, they couldn't find any evidence of foul play or anything else. With no bodies, the investigation went nowhere. End of story."

"Um...does John like to fish or own a boat?"

"Come on now, detective, that's stretching it a little; you think John had something to do with that, too? He was really tight with them, and I doubt he had anything to do with it."

"You never know, your years as an agent should tell you that sometimes you think you really know someone when in reality, you don't. I'd watch your back if I were you." Silence blared from the speaker, as Tater ended the call.

"Walt, we've got everyone's real identity, but we still have one huge problem, and that is connecting Wylie and John in this murder for hire theory."

"Yeah, I know, but I'm hoping something else will turn up."

"I hope so because I've been saying that all along and every time we get a break, someone ends up dead. There is no doubt in my mind that John Dickerson, aka Casanova, hired Wylie who hired Frank to do Mark and Joanne Alison. No doubt about it and we are…" Carla's phone rang interrupting her conversation. She answered immediately. "Sherry, please tell me you got something that can fry John Dickerson with." Listening intently, she abruptly ended the call. A big smile covered her face as she gave Walt the thumbs-up gesture and headed for the police station.

CHAPTER 51

Once inside the station, she went to forensics where Sherry was standing in the doorway holding a sheet of paper. Impatient as usual, Carla said, "Sherry, please let it be what we've been looking for?" Sherry handed her a piece of paper. After reading what is on the paper, she hugged her. The stamped letters from the ribbon was a letter from Rocky to Spike detailing that Casanova wanted to hire them to kill Mark and Joanne Alison for $30,000.

The excitement that Carla felt went away as she remembered what Al Bocconi, aka, Tater said. She knew they didn't have an airtight case because it still didn't prove without a doubt that John Dickerson, aka Casanova, ordered the assassinations of Mark, Joanne, and Spike, only that Rocky wrote the letter stating it and he was now conveniently dead. They needed something else for the airtight case, a money trail. Meeting with Chief Evans, she explained every bit of evidence there was. Chief Evans started to answer her when his phone rang. "Yes, show them back." He hung up, and his face tensed up.

A surprised look painted Carla's face, beads of sweat dotted her forehead as she blurted out. "Show who back, chief?" At that moment, the door swung open, and two well-dressed gentlemen entered. Chief Evans introduced her to Special Agents Tom Stewart and Donnie Slack of the FBI attachment in Louisville. Stunned and dumbfounded for a moment, she stood up and lit into Chief Evans with all her red-headed Irish temper she could muster. Chief Evans clearly embarrassed lashed out at her. "Sit your ass down, now! And please listen to what Agent Slack has to tell us, got it." Carla all red-faced and whimpering sat back down. "Agent Slack, you may begin."

Being empathetic he said, "Detective McBride, I know how you feel, I've been there before."

She interrupted Agent Slack, "Yeah, right, you ass…"

Red-faced and rubbing his temples, Chief Evans stood up and glared at her. "Carla, watch…your… mouth…just listen…do not say another damn word, got it?"

With her head hung low, Agent Slack continued. "Our regional office in Pensacola has been watching John Dickerson for several years now for illegal activity but didn't have enough evidence to build an airtight case. The office down there received a tip from a very credible source about John's alleged involvement in your cases in Oakmont. The story was quite interesting, and from a credible source."

"That son of a bitch, Al Bocconi tipped you off, didn't he?"

Grimacing with anger, Chief Evans lost his cool.

"Carla, one more outburst like that and I'll kick your ass out of here for good, and I don't mean just my office today. Agent Slack, please continue."

Experiencing the lowest low, she'd ever felt, she sat helpless, and her ego deflated. Her hopes of finding justice were slipping away quickly. Feeling the bile rise from her stomach, she wanted to scream; however, knowing it wouldn't do any good, she swallowed her pride and stared stoically at Chief Evans. She knew there was nothing she could do or say to prevent her case from being turned over to the FBI.

"Detective McBride, with what we have now which is unrelated to your case and all your evidence; we feel we can finally build an airtight case and put this bastard away for a long time. That is what we all want, right?"

Fighting back all the emotions and anger she felt and not wanting to give up, she was getting ready to open her mouth, but noticed Chief Evans put two fingers to his lips. She knew what that meant. He said, "We are turning everything we have over to the FBI and putting our confidence in them to nail this asshole finally. I know you don't like how this turned out, and neither do I, but if we want to win the war, we need them to use their resources and crucify the bastard. The decision is final, and there is no further discussion on this matter, got it?"

Without saying a word, she stormed out of his office cussing a blue streak all the way out of the police station headed to the *Daily Reporter*. Arriving at the newspaper, she entered and went straight to Walt's office losing her cool. "That son of a bitch Al Bocconi tipped off the FBI in Pensacola. They are taking over our case when we were so close. They said they have been watching John Dickerson for years, but never had an airtight case to go after him. Remember, Al said we needed to have an airtight case to go after him. They believe with our evidence; they now can do that. Al will pay for this someday, trust me."

"Calm down, before you blow a gasket. We won a lot of battles, but the FBI gets to win the war. It's not the outcome we wanted, but if he is behind bars for a long time, we all win. And you know Carla, you are one hell of a detective, and I think we make a pretty good team."

Silence filled his office for a moment or two. Calmed down somewhat, she sarcastically replied, "Well, Mr. Publisher, I wouldn't go that far. I'm out of here and done for the day."

"Where are you going?"

Before leaving his office, she turned around and smiled. "Got a date with Jameson, my liquid lover, and by the way, say hello to my girl Laura, will ya?"

CHAPTER 52

As days turned into weeks and weeks into months, Detective Carla McBride had somewhat gotten over her disappointment of not being the one to take down John Dickerson, aka Casanova of Alpha Tango. Meeting with Chief Evans, Carla apologized for her behavior of late. However, she would never forgive him for handing her case over to the FBI. When she was a rookie police officer fifteen years ago, Chief Evans removed her from the Penny Miracle case. That awful feeling in her soul that day reared its ugly head all over again, and she hated it.

Walt's relationship with Laura had grown stronger and stronger. Even though their relationship quickly blossomed, he knew Laura Watson was his soulmate. Tonight, they were having a party to ring in the holiday season. Needing some fun time, Carla arrived early and a Jameson on the rocks, her liquid lover, greeted her. Laura's brother, Chris came shortly after her, and within several minutes, the festive celebration was in full swing. Drinks were flowing while the appetizers were zesty. The jovial and lively conversation echoed throughout the great room and kitchen. Although the national news with David Maxwell was playing in the background, most were oblivious to it except Carla.

Finally, Walt's big moment had arrived, and he clicked his glass several times to get everyone's attention. "I have a toast to make, so raise your glasses high. Thank you for coming and being part of our lives. To great friends, may tonight be the start of something wonderful, cheers to all!" After the sound of applause and clinking glasses subsided, Walt reached inside his sports coat and took out a small box. Down on one knee, he opened the box and gazed into Laura's eyes, her face beamed with excitement.

Before Walt could utter a single word, Carla, who had noticed a breaking news flash on the screen, suddenly blurted out. "Hush, Walt! Chris, will you turn up the sound on the television?" Shocked and surprised by Carla's unexpected interruption, all the guests knew Carla didn't care. Everyone turned their focus toward the television as the news anchor, David Maxwell, explained the breaking news.

"Just in from Pensacola, Florida. Moments ago, FBI and ATF agents swarmed the home of United States Senator John Dickerson of Florida and gubernatorial front-runner seizing computers, printers, cell phones, bank records, and other documents found in his safe. Details are sketchy, but sources tell us authorities took him into custody on federal charges of money-laundering, fraud, and sex and human trafficking to name a few. Also, included was the conspiracy to commit murder, specifically the unsolved homicides in

Oakmont, Kentucky. A spokesman for the FBI said they have been watching the activity of John Dickerson for several years but didn't have enough evidence for an airtight case until now. Recently, the FBI had received a credible tip from a former FBI agent Al Bocconi, a second cousin to John Dickerson. Hold on; we now have a live feed outside his home." The live feed shows John Dickerson in handcuffs escorted out of his home. In the background, you could hear him yelling his innocence and threats of revenge. David Maxwell continued on with the breaking news segment. "Well, there you have it. As more details become available, we will bring them to you. You can also check our website for further details. Now on a lighter note, we have a heartwarming story about..."

As the sound faded away, the focus drifted back to Carla where she stood silent, but not embarrassed. The eerie silence captivating the room ended. "Walt, that SOB Al Bocconi, never liked him when we first talked with him, and now I like him even less, a matter of fact I hate his ass. He will pay dearly one of these days, I promise you. We were so close to nailing John Dickerson, you know?"

"Yeah, does it really matter who gets the credit?"

"It matters to me, but yeah, I guess we did it. Now, what were you going to ask Laura?"

Laura, who had been waiting anxiously, ecstatically chimed in, "Yes, Yes, Yes! I will marry you!"

Carla exclaimed, "Walt, what are you waiting on, just put the damn ring on her finger and remember, she is my Bestie. So, you better treat her right, or you know what, I might just have to kill you!"

With the focus back on Laura and Walt as they shared a passionate kiss, laughter and applause bellowed throughout the room as the festive celebration continued. Walt could not let Carla have the last word and responded; however, she hushed him as she answered her phone. Once again, silence filled the room as she listened and ended the call without saying a word.

"Sorry, guys, I've got to go. I've got a possible carjacking and abduction on my hands." After downing Jameson, she walked to the door. Before opening it, she turned around and yelled. "Sláinte na bhfear Agus go Maire na mná go deo!"

As strange looks hurled at her, everyone looked at each other in amazement. Laura, surprised by Carla's ability to speak the Irish language, rolled her eyes at her. "Carla, what does that really mean, I hope it was not something off-color or vulgar?"

After a big hearty laugh, she responded, "Of course not, you know me better than that. Translated, it means, health to the men, and may the women live forever." As Carla opened the door, the cold dark winds of crime smacked her in the face. Walking to her car, the boisterous laughter and loud chanting emanating from inside Laura's townhome warmed her soul putting a smile on her face.

A LOOK AT BOOK TWO:
THE BLACK ROSE

Detective Carla McBride's experience, patience, and emotional psyche are being put to the test. Risking her life investigating dangerous situations, her nemesis, John Dickerson, is still out there—lurking in the background—and, with a psychotic game of revenge on his mind, Carla begins to worry who he will target next.

But how and when John strikes depends on which person will satisfy his psychotic thirst. And after life-altering events, Carla is prone to his clutches.

Constantly questioning her life and the changes that have had a profound effect on her destiny, she joins forces with Walt Blevins to put the pieces of this ever-changing mystery in place—once and for all.

On the hunt for justice, will Carla's fate finally be revealed… or will it remain a mystery? More importantly—will she and Walt be able to catch a psychotic antagonist who enjoys playing brutal games?

AVAILABLE JANUARY 2023

ABOUT THE AUTHOR

Author Nick Lewis lives in Richmond, Kentucky, with his wife, Bonnie. He graduated from Marshall University in the fall of 1970. Upon graduating, he taught school and coached football for one year at Eidson Elementary. He then switched directions and began a forty-year newspaper career. He held circulation and marketing positions at four different newspapers in Ohio, West Virginia, and Kentucky. In 2004, he was appointed publisher of *The Richmond Register* in Richmond, Kentucky. He retired from that position in June 2013 and began his quest to become a full-time author.

In January 2014, Nick created The Detective Carla McBride Chronicles. The first book in the series, *The Gold Fedora*, debuted in October 2019. *The Black Rose, Chasing Truth and Redemption,* and *Quandary* completes the series to date. Book five in the series, *Enigma*, is forthcoming. He has another published novel, *When Eagles Soared.*

When Nick is not writing and revising manuscripts, he enjoys golf, gardening, and creating new adventures with his wife of fifty years. Bonnie plays an essential role in his journey of writing novels. He is an avid Marshall University football fan with three grown children, three grandchildren, and two cats named Zorro and Ziva.